PROPHETS
&
DREAMERS

Also by Miriam Weinstein

Yiddish: A Nation of Words

PROPHETS & DREAMERS

A Selection of Great Yiddish Literature

Edited by

MIRIAM WEINSTEIN

STEERFORTH PRESS
SOUTH ROYALTON, VERMONT

For information about permission to reproduce
selections from this book, write to:
Steerforth Press L.C., P.O. Box 70,
South Royalton, Vermont 05068

Excerpt from "Fiske the Lame" from *The Selected Works of Mendele Moykher-Sforim,* vol.1 of *The Three Great Classic Writers of Modern Yiddish Literature,* edited by Marvin Zuckerman, Gerald Stillman, and Marion Herbst. Used by permission of Gerald Stillman.

"A Yom Kippur Scandal" and "Eternal Life" from *Favorite Tales of Sholom Aleichem* by Sholom Aleichem, translated by Frances and Julius Butwin, copyright © 1983 by Crown Publishers, a division of Random House, Inc. Used by permission of Crown Publishers, a division of Random House, Inc.

"Three Gifts," by Y. L. Peretz, from *The Great Tales of Jewish Fantasy and the Occult,* compiled, translated, and introduced by Joachim Neugroschel. Copyright © 1976 by Joachim Neugroschel. Reprinted with the permission of The Overlook Press.

"Bontshe Shvayg" and "And Maybe Even Higher" are used by permission of Eli Katz.

"Mendl Turk," by S. An-ski, from *The Dybbuk and Other Writings,* edited by David G. Roskies and translated by Golda Werman, is used by permission of the Fund for the Translation of Jewish Literature.

"The Bus," from *The Collected Stories of Isaac Bashevis Singer.* Copyright © 1982 by Isaac Bashevis Singer. Reprinted by permission of Farrar, Straus and Giroux, LLC. Published in the United Kingdom by Jonathan Cape. Reprinted by permission of The Random House Group Limited.

"Bread and Tea," "To My Beloved," and "Autumn Leaves," from *Poet of the Ghetto: Morris Rosenfeld,* are used by permission of Edgar J. Goldenthal.

"A Toast to Life" is used by permission of Jerry Silverman.

"Seventeen Moons," "From Nakhman of Bratslav to His Scribe," Like a Mouse Trap," and "My Tent" are used by permission of the Jewish Publication Society.

"War," "Poems from My Diary 1974–1985," "Deer at the Red Sea," and "To My Wife, Narocz Forest, September 30, 1944," from *A. Sutzkever: Selected Poetry and Prose,* translated and edited by Barbara and Benjamin Harshav, copyright © 1991 Regents, published by University of California Press, is used by permission of the University of California Press.

"I Am Lying in This Coffin, Vilna, August 30, 1941" and "On the Death of Yanova Bartoszewicz Who Rescued Me," are used by permission of Mosaic Press Valley Editions.

Library of Congress Cataloging-in-Publication Data

Prophets and dreamers : a selection of great Yiddish literature / edited
by Miriam Weinstein. — 1st ed.
    p. cm.
Includes bibliographical references.
  ISBN 1-58642-047-X
  1. Short stories, Yiddish — Translations into English. I. Weinstein,
Miriam, 1946–
  PJ5191.E8 P76 2002
  839'.130108—dc21
                            2002007238

FIRST EDITION

*To a new generation of prophets,
dreamers, and lovers of Yiddish*

"I say: every good heart and honest eye sees the purpose of mankind, as well as of the individual, as the
general integration of all peoples and languages and
the end of disputes, wars, and conflicts — the dream
of the prophets, the dream of every pure heart. . . .
We see now a depraved chauvinism, an anti-
Semitism that captures the hearts of the educated
and enlightened and seduces its audience with its
teachings. People stand at the head of their generation, and on real mountains, raise up the banner of
divisiveness and hate. Now it is evening. Night will
yet come. And after that, when our hair will have
turned white, tomorrow will also come. . . ."

Letter from Yitzhak Leib Peretz
to Sholom Aleichem, 1888

ACKNOWLEDGMENTS

I would like to thank Steerforth Press for making this book happen. Chip Fleischer came up with the idea. Kristin Camp, Robin Dutcher, Helga Schmidt, and Nicola Smith also worked hard to produce a wonderful product.

In addition, Mirka Feinstein provided excellent research assistance. Sally Brady played the agent role with grace. Rabbi Myron Geller was a helpful linguistic resource.

I would also like to thank my husband, Peter Feinstein, for leading the cheering squad at home.

CONTENTS

The World That Told the Tales

Anyone who has choked back a tear at the finale of *Fiddler on the Roof*, when Tevye says good-bye to his beloved, decrepit village to wander adrift, knows something about Yiddish literature. Anyone who has agonized over the fate of Tevye's adored children knows in his bones the urgent hopes and fearsome anxieties that prompted the outpouring of stories of all sorts from which we take our selections here.

Because Tevye was Yiddish, down to his imaginary core. It was his situation, his outlook, his fate, that propelled the phenomenal growth and rapid flowering of Yiddish literature, as well as its precipitous decline. The dairyman's words were Yiddish; his response to his world could only have issued from what, in Yiddish, is called a *yidishe kop*, literally a Jewish head; a Yiddish worldview.

His character emerged through a series of short stories written over the course of two decades, beginning in 1894, by the great storyteller Sholom Aleichem. But Tevye is only one of Aleichem's memorable characters, and Aleichem is only one of many great Yiddish writers.

If you are not familiar with this toothsome slice of literary history, be prepared for a treat. This morsel will conjure up an entire world. Yiddish literature counts tens of thousands of different book titles, a onetime audience of millions who argued and ranted over and *kvelled* — found prideful joy in — an international outpouring of journals, newspapers, and books about every subject, in every style, and from every conceivable point of view.

Now most of them are silent — the journals, the newspapers, and the readers as well. But the literature remains. And that is our business, and our pleasure, here. You will meet rapscallions and wise men, market scolds and pious innocents; the rich panoply of human existence as presented by a people who delighted in the full range of human character and characters. And you will understand the mission of Yiddish literature. Because, by and large, this body of work had a purpose: Yiddish speakers, by which we mean more or less Eastern European Jews, as they found themselves liberated, released, or expelled from their insular, timeless *shtetl* existence, had to invent their place in the modern, anonymous world. Finding their voice in their beloved Yiddish, these people wrote to forge answers to their most pressing question: how to construct a place for themselves in a period of wrenching change. They were writing furiously, and under great time constraints, with a very clear mandate: They had to invent a future.

The Yiddish past had been long and warm. Knit between poles of exile and belonging, it strengthened the heart and protected the spirit against the onslaughts of a world that had no secure place for Jews. Language was the strong binding fiber.

Yiddish was born between 900 and 1100 in what is now Germany. Jews had arrived in Europe almost a thousand years before, having walked from Jerusalem after the destruction of the Temple. As they spread out across Europe, they continued to recite their daily and festival prayers in Hebrew, the language they had spoken in their homeland. But they also learned European languages. And they created Jewish versions of a dozen European tongues.

So, around the end of the first millennium, when Jews from what are now Italy, France, and Germany found themselves living together in German-speaking lands, they had many words in their linguistic packs. It was from this full grab bag that Yiddish was formed. The new language coalesced over a Hebrew base. The majority of the vocabulary came from German; a smattering of words from the Romance languages that some of the endlessly wandering Jews had picked up along their way.

Yiddish was immediately useful; it bound Jews together while separating them from their Christian neighbors. And because of its intimate links with Hebrew, it connected Jews to their glorious past. The name itself means "Jewish." The language was written in the Hebrew alphabet, from right to left.

Almost as soon as Yiddish became a separate language, many of its speakers moved east, to what is now Poland, Russia, and Ukraine. A new layer of Slavisms was added to the tongue. The stage was set for this ghetto upstart to become one of the great languages of the world.

Yiddish quickly became the lingua franca of European Jews, the everyday tongue of millions. But even while they spoke Yiddish, they never lost their Hebrew. The ancient language, which had taken on an aura of sanctity, was used primarily for commentary and prayer. Almost all of the Jewish men, as well as some women, read it. This was an extraordinary achievement. Even during the Dark Ages when, for Christians, reading and writing were the province only of monks who lived in isolation, Jewish men by and large knew how to read at least a minimum of the holy language. By default, they could also read Yiddish.

Yiddish was largely defined by what it was not. It was not Hebrew, so it was not held in high regard. Begun as a folk language, its lowly status was its curse and its strength. It was called, derisively, the language of the uneducated, the language of women. Early books printed in Yiddish often began with an apology for not being Hebrew. But the language's lack of status kept it vibrant and alive, sensitive to the real needs of daily life. That intimacy gave Yiddish a straight path to the Jewish heart. Because it was the language of home and of family, its speakers called it *mame loshn,* mother tongue.

In medieval Europe, Yiddish troubadours roamed the countryside, reciting Yiddish stories and singing Yiddish songs, telling romantic and fantastical tales. By the fifteenth century, stories of an outsized character named Bove had become commonplace, and *Bove meyses,* Bove stories, were told aloud and written down. Today, because the word for grandmother, *bube,* sounds much like Bove, that early piece of literature is recalled in the expression *bube meyses,* grandmothers' stories, or outrageous tales.

Yiddish has always had a female association. In the women's sections of the synagogues, women called *firzogerins,* interpreters, translated the Hebrew prayers into Yiddish, often explaining or embellishing as they went. Women also composed personal prayers in Yiddish called *tkhines.* Here is Sarah Bat Tovim, who lived in the early seventeenth century, in what is now Ukraine, asking for God's help: "God should have great compassion for me and for all Israel. I should not be homeless for long. . . . The fact that I am homeless should be a sacrifice for my sins. God Almighty, blessed be He, should forgive me for talking in the synagogue during services in my youth."

One Yiddish book of Bible commentary and tales for women was so popular that it has been in print since the early seventeenth century — more than 350 editions. The *Tsenerene,* named for its opening line, "Come out and see," is still used by ultra-Orthodox Jews today. If a Yiddish speaker wants to describe a rare occurrence, he can say, *vi a yidene on a tsenerene;* like a Jewish woman without a tsenerene.

Cultural references such as this made Yiddish not just a language but a universe. For a thousand years, Yiddish-speaking Jews created their own alternate reality. The Yiddish stories we will read here will introduce not only the works of particular authors, but to that vibrant world as well.

Yiddish speakers lived in shtetls. The word means simply "town," but these hamlets or neighborhoods were the manifestations of a floating, extraterritorial community both removed from and part of their Christian "host" countries. Some of these towns were composed primarily of Jews. In others, Jews and Christians lived side by side. But Yiddish-speaking Jews defined themselves not as living in the Europe of such-and-such a century, but as inhabiting a timeless world that looked back to the Creation and forward to the coming of the messiah. They identified more with fellow Jews who lived hundreds of miles away than with their Christian neighbors.

Shtetls were tightly organized around ritual observance, religious education, and social welfare. In them, the spiritual was interwoven with the practical. Judaism was not so much a religion as a total life system marked by an emphasis on family, community, and right behavior. Here is how Yiddish literary critic and theorist Shmuel Niger described the life of the traditional Jew: "He did not believe in Judaism because he lived it, in fact he was it. It was the air he breathed, the bread he ate, the water he drank, along with the appropriate blessing in each instance."

Although the shtetl community could be as corrupt as any other, it was remarkably inclusive and cohesive, taking responsibility for all its members. This was necessary because, even though the Jews had a glorious heritage, in Diaspora Europe all they had was each other. European Jews could not own land, they were severely limited in their vocations, and they could expect to be the objects of continual violence, both government sanctioned and ad hoc. The antennae of shtetl-dwelling Jews were attuned to the varieties of human character and characters. Because their life possibilities were so limited, they focused on their community.

In one Sholom Aleichem story, "If I Were Rothschild," the narrator, imagining himself magically rich, first provides for his family and then quickly turns his attention outward, conjuring a new roof for the synagogue, an improved community bathhouse and poorhouse, a loan society open to all, even a Society for Outfitting Brides. Shtetl Jews were less likely to appreciate a beautiful object or person than to extol a beautiful deed.

Language linked it all. Most pervasive was the Hebrew–Yiddish braid. Boys as young as three or four learned to read and write Hebrew, but they discussed their lessons in Yiddish, so it was easy for the ancient language, with its key concepts and cultural references, to leak through. Biblical stories suffused people's imaginations. When Isaac Bashevis Singer wanted to conjure up his close boyhood friendship he wrote, "We were like David and Jonathan." Shtetl dwellers lived in their collective Hebraic past.

The writer known as Mendele said that knowing only Yiddish or only Hebrew was like breathing through only one nostril. Folklore described it this way: Yiddish is the handmaiden of Hebrew. Hebrew one learns; Yiddish one knows. God speaks Yiddish during the week and Hebrew on the Sabbath. As we read, we will notice words and phrases that are borrowed or quoted from Hebrew. There are allusions to scripture, commentary, and prayer. The always-living past produced a bank of powerful images and a frame of reference. Hebrew was the backstory that informed the way people lived every day.

In the eighteenth century, the first breeze of modernity blew through the Yiddish world. The Enlightenment arrived first in Germany, where many Yiddish speakers still lived. The door to German society opened slightly, and many Jews were eager to enter. Some converted outright, while others reduced their Jewishness to a contained religion, becoming "Germans of the Mosaic persuasion." They abandoned Yiddish, the language that reminded them of the medieval ghetto they hoped to leave behind.

Meanwhile, in Eastern Europe, the opposite impulse took hold, as an ecstatic, participatory movement called Hasidism, pietism, swept through the Jewish world. It encouraged direct, joyous communication with God, a conversation that took place in Yiddish. The eighteenth-century Hasidic leader Nakhman of Bratslav wrote about his typical follower, "In the sacred tongue [Hebrew] it will be difficult for him to say everything that he wishes and he will not be able to be as sincere since we do not speak the sacred tongue. . . . In Yiddish, it is possible to pour out your words, speaking everything that is in your heart before the Lord."

From this time forward, European Jews became more conscious of whether, or when, they were speaking Yiddish. The language became a badge of belonging or of shame, a statement of where one stood on the assimilation scale.

More sweeping change arrived in the middle of the nineteenth century, when the industrial revolution hit Eastern Europe. The advent of first the telegraph and, later, mass-produced newspapers put local storytellers out of business and gave even the rabbis real competition. Now, if a Jew wanted to make sense of a puzzling question — say, how to project himself into a Jewish *and* a European future — he could read the new Yiddish newspapers, which, thanks to the Jewish Telegraphic Agency, gave him a more worldly, cosmopolitan slant on the day's news. He could see traveling productions of Yiddish plays, such as Sholem Asch's *God of Vengeance* or a translation of *King Lear,* listen on the new phonograph to Yiddish songs, such as the frankly sentimental "Belz" or "Oyfn pripetshik," or dance to klezmer music influenced by musicians thousands of miles away.

Railroad cars replaced wagons, transforming business and personal boundaries. Sewing machines made old crafts redundant, and new, urban factories lured Jews from their small towns. As the weekly markets and seasonal fairs lost their critical role in the regional economy, the shtetls went into free fall.

This dislocation spawned both uncertainty and opportunity, and the Yiddish world responded with an immense outpouring of creative energy. Yiddish-speaking theoreticians invented a dazzling rainbow of "-isms," from Anarchism and Assimilationism to Yiddishism and Zionism. Yiddish writers created new genres, which in turn encouraged new markets for their books. What had been largely a folk language was transformed into an instrument of politics, science, literature, music, theater, and art. This multibloomed flowering in turn transformed a people.

As Eastern European Jews became aware of their place in historical time, many took the next step — actively working to promote historical change. It was here, at the crossroads of political, technological, and cultural upheaval, that the literature thrived.

It is possible to mark just when modern Yiddish literature began. In 1862, one year after the relatively liberal Russian czar freed the serfs, a weekly Hebrew newspaper in Odessa published a Yiddish supplement called *Kol mevaser* (Voice of the People). In an empire with five million Yiddish-speaking Jews, it was the first mass-market Yiddish publication. A vast, literate audience was starved for tales about itself. One of its first contributions was "The Little Man," a story by Mendele Moykher-Sforim. The story and the newspaper were immediate successes.

Within a generation, Jews were writing Yiddish novels, stories, poems, and polemics on all subjects. They were reading Yiddish translations of everything — Shakespeare, Ibsen, Dickens, and Whitman. And they were responding in their own language, through their own lens. For chroniclers, artists, and politicians, Yiddish became the place to be, the creative address. The audience was waiting and educated. People of all stations read short stories, novels, and poems in newspapers and cheap pamphlets. They rented or borrowed books. Everyone, it seemed, was reading everything.

One writer described the scene outside his house in early-twentieth-century Ukraine. As his father read a Yiddish newspaper, a "number of bearded Jews in long shabby gabardines and weather-beaten headgear, their hands clasped behind them, were strolling leisurely down the street. They were returning from the House of Study. . . . The plain, unassuming townsmen clustered about us, eager for worldly news: 'What's going on in the outside world?' they asked. And then followed the inevitable query: 'Anything new by Peretz or Sholom Aleichem?' "

The writers responded with great creativity. They called on their shared frame of reference, using typical shtetl characters and situations to make their points. It was a heady time, except for one unavoidable truth: Just as the literature gained momentum, the forces that would bring about its demise were moving at an even faster rate. It was the tragedy of Yiddish literature that it came of age just in time to describe a world that was dying. Shtetl dwellers, their heads full of tales, were leaving for nearby cities or faraway lands.

The lives of many Yiddish writers followed the transitional arc their literature described. Born in shtetls, they attended *heders,* traditional schools. Then, typically, the writers moved to cosmopolitan cities in Europe, the United States, or Israel. They learned other languages; they read contemporary literature, either the original or in translation. They responded to the currents of modernism.

But they also peered backward. Yiddish writers reached into their collective, traditional past to make sense of an uncharted, rapidly changing world. They revisited Hasidism; they constantly drew from the biblical world. Even as they went on international lecture tours or freelanced for publications an ocean away, Yiddish writers continued to extract meaning from their collective memory to address their splintering situations.

It should come as no surprise that, for a people confronting late-nineteenth- and early-twentieth-century issues of national, religious, and ethnic identity, modern Yiddish culture was intensely political. Most often, the politics leaned toward the left. Even the decision to write in Yiddish, rather than in, say, Russian, German, or Polish, was a political one. Yiddish was the language of the Jewish masses, and Jewish intellectuals who decided to use it were advertising their allegiance. Over and over again, we hear of the cosmopolitan Jew who, in order to reach an audience, deigned to speak and write Yiddish, only to fall in love with its clarity, directness, and warmth.

By the early twentieth century, the language even became an end in itself. The theoretician Chaim Zhitlowski described how he came to his decision to write in Yiddish: "My father, greatly learned in rabbinic literature, a sharp mind and a thorough one, was just as ignorant as the shoemaker or tailor of Western culture. . . . One had to use the language that everyone understood. That was Yiddish, the vernacular of every Jew."

In the first third of the twentieth century, many cultural leaders took on Yiddish as a cause, creating an international movement. Yiddishists thought that, as religion declined, the language would replace ritual and become a moral force.

But this was not the only Yiddish voice that was heard. By this time, Yiddish speakers and writers had spread across several continents. The drama of the language and its literature was playing itself out simultaneously on several stages.

Beginning in the 1880s, the settlers who moved from Europe to resettle Israel linked their reclamation of the ancient ancestral land with a renewal of the ancient language, Hebrew. Over the course of a thousand years, Yiddish, with its close links to Hebrew, had kept the biblical language in what one scholar called a kind of "warm storage." Hebrew was accessible through study and prayer, but since Yiddish was used for everyday speech, the Hebrew of the Bible remained unchanged. The new settlers, however, did allow themselves to acknowledge their debt to Yiddish. Like teenagers asserting their shaky adulthood, they made a great show of casting away the old language of intimacy, of home. In Israel, Yiddish became the enemy. In 1914, when Zhitlowski traveled to Israel, mobs prevented him from lecturing in Yiddish.

On the other side of the world, in the United States, Yiddish speakers were welcomed, but with one caveat: In the land of the melting pot, the old language would have to become part of the broth. Early immigrants established a vibrant Yiddish culture, with Yiddish theaters, films, radio broadcasts, newspapers, and publishing houses, but, because of the cultural imperative to fit in, the language quickly faded. Yiddish speakers turned to English.

In Russia and the Soviet Union, Yiddish suffered a very different fate. In the early years after the Russian Revolution, the new Communist government supported Yiddish literature and culture. There were state-supported Yiddish newspapers, publishing houses, theaters, even a Yiddish educational system. Many leading Yiddish poets who had left Russia before the Revolution returned to what looked like a utopia for Yiddish literature.

Unfortunately, as time went on, Yiddish became an easy target for the anti-Semitism that never faded from the Russian and then Soviet scene. Because the language was international, its writers were always suspect. This dark chapter ended in 1952, with an event that has come to be called the Night of the Murdered Yiddish Poets. A dozen of the top Yiddish cultural leaders were killed. After that, Yiddish was effectively silenced in the Soviet Union.

The Holocaust saw the destruction of the Eastern European centers of Yiddish culture, as well as the murder of two-thirds of the world's Yiddish speakers. Most survivors made their way either to Israel or to the United States where, for two very different reasons, nation-building and assimilation, Yiddish was in steep decline.

In the post–World War II years, a much-diminished number of Yiddish writers in the United States and Israel continued to produce work of great power and sophistication. But, its readership dying and its cultural institutions faltering, it would have taken a miracle to breathe life into the language and its literature again.

These days, a potential miracle comes from a strange corner. There is an upsurge in the use of spoken and written Yiddish among the ultra-Orthodox in Europe, the United States, and Israel. However, literature does not fit into their theocratic, separatist culture and for now, only a small number of children's and women's books are finding their way into print.

Today's ultra-Orthodox speak Yiddish for the same reasons their ancestors did centuries ago: The language is a comfort to the community within, and a way to keep the outside world at bay. The difference is that, this time, much of that outside world is made up of fellow Jews. And, in a new twist, the ultra-Orthodox see the Yiddish language as having gained a kind of sanctity. It was, after all, the language of the six million martyrs.

However, we must be clear that the Yiddish language and its literature are in sharp decline. A thousand-year tradition may be coming to an end. At this time, the writer to read might be Shimon An-ski, who journeyed through devastated sections of Eastern Europe at the end of World War I.

> As we crossed over the mountain we saw a terrible scene — a dead town in the valley. It was a big town, with many streets and houses; but all the houses were burned and demolished.

Remarkably, in a store, he found a Jewish family.

> "Do you have something to eat?" we asked. At first the shop owner said that he had only rolls, but when he found out that we were Jewish he invited us into the other room. It was Friday evening and his wife was about to light the Sabbath candles.
> "We have a pot of sour cream," she said, "and we'll give you half. You have to eat, too."

An-ski put his story into context this way:

> While one is in the midst of a misfortune, the elements of pettiness and wailing numb the senses and veil the essential mystery of the tragedy. Only with time, when all the trivia and inessentials, all that is ephemeral and unimportant are forgotten, does the tragedy crystallize into the splendid, unalloyed truth that is used by artists to create the immortal epics of the world.

Yiddish writers have always been expert at transforming tragedy into something crystalline. They have also managed to do this without losing their pleasure in the ordinary joys of daily life.

Isaac Bashevis Singer, who won the Nobel Prize in literature, and whose short story "Growing Old" we are priveleged to present for the first time in English, spent a lifetime writing about a people, and a culture, poised between life and death. He said:

While I hope and pray for the redemption and the resurrection, I dare to say that, for me, these people are all living right now. In literature, as in our dreams, death does not exist.

Whatever the future of Yiddish literature, we have a body of writing that does exist, and that we can enjoy. Life and death, tragedy, comedy, and farce tumble round and round in human history. Yiddish literature goes directly to its beating heart.

A reader could search high and low for the author named Mendele Moykher-Sforim, Mendele the Book Peddler, only to find that this person never lived. Yet this fictitious character played a critical role in allowing European Jews to take their place on the modern stage.

The author of the Mendele tales, Sholem Abramovitsch, became forever identified with his fictional alter ego. Mendele is known, with affection and gratitude, as the grandfather of Yiddish literature.

He was the first writer to depict the pre-modern European Jewish world as a recognizable whole, portraying the characteristic Eastern European Jewish shtetl community. He also regularized and enlivened the

Yiddish language, showing that it was fully capable of supporting a serious literature. Both his choice of subject and his decision to render it in full and expressive Yiddish burst a centuries-old literary logjam. Abramovitsch presented a vision and opened a path. His influence on later Yiddish writers cannot be overemphasized.

In addition, he continued to write in Hebrew throughout his long life, working to bring the ancient, biblical tongue into the nineteenth century. By all standards, Abramovitsch was a remarkable man.

He was born in 1836 in Kapulye, a small town in Russia. When he was thirteen his father, a community leader and biblical scholar, died, forcing the boy to leave home and become an itinerant scholar, dependant on charity. He even traveled for a year with an old beggar.

When he settled down, he fell under the influence of a local *maskil,* a follower of the Jewish Enlightenment. He studied science and mathematics as well as European languages and literature. A natural teacher and proselytizer, Abramovitsch decided that if his fellow Jews expanded their learning to include these secular disciplines they could free themselves from their hidebound parochialism.

He began writing for secular Hebrew journals. These publications were forward looking, but they used stilted vocabulary culled from ancient religious texts. And the audience they reached was minuscule. Abramovitsch faced a dilemma.

As he later explained, "[Yiddish] in my time was an empty vessel, filled only with ridicule, nonsense, and the twaddle of fools. . . . The women and the commonest people read this stuff without understanding what it was they read. Other people, though they knew no other language, were ashamed to read Yiddish, not wanting to show their backwardness. . . . The Hebrew writers . . . despised Yiddish and mocked it." But Abramovitsch was torn. "If I started writing in this 'unworthy' language my honor would be besmirched. . . . But my concern for utility conquered my vanity and I decided, come what may, I would have pity for Yiddish, that rejected daughter, for it was time to do something for our people." What began as duty soon became something more. "I fell in love with Yiddish and wedded her forever."

The turning point came in 1864, when Abramovitsch published a short story, "The Little Man," as a serial in the first Yiddish newspaper in Russia. (The paper had debuted the year before.) The work was an immediate success. It was the first time that Yiddish-speaking Jews recognized themselves in print.

He published his story under the name of Mendele Moykher-Sforim, as if the book peddler were telling the tale. Abramovitsch wrote under that name from then on, and was always referred to simply as Mendele.

Abramovitsch/Mendele painted a portrait of Jews that was often unflattering, veering toward caricature. But he was writing for an internal audience; his goal to awaken, to teach, and to goad to action.

He also took on the charge of regularizing and expanding the Yiddish language. Up until this point, if people wanted to make Yiddish sound more "respectable" they would slant their vocabulary toward Russian or German. Because Mendele had been born in the northern part of the Yiddish-speaking world but later lived in the south, he made a special point of using a Yiddish that minimized regional differences.

He worked to expand Yiddish vocabulary, finding exactly the right word, as he said, "for the gestures and gesticulations of the *shnorer* [beggar], for the scholar's thumb-turn, for the ecstasy of the Hasid, the sigh and groan of the artisan, and the wink and nod and shrug of a garrulous woman." He described how he would work: "Searching for an expression, for a word, I suddenly see a shame-faced little word, shy and humble, retiring, modest, gentle, all-a-tremble. It feels an intruder, out of place, finger in mouth in the company of so many giants. Tears in its eyes. Come here, little one! I need you! Just you!"

For all his popularity, however, Mendele was unable to make a living as a writer. In 1881 he was offered a job as head of a new Jewish school in Odessa, a sophisticated modern city. It proved a very good fit.

In his later years, Mendele was honored by the Yiddish-speaking public, who understood that he had given them the gift of themselves. He toured the Jewish areas of Russia, where he was met by thousands of fans.

But the non-Jewish world did not hold him in the same regard. In 1905, anti-Semitic pogroms swept through Odessa, and Mendele was forced to hide in a pigsty. He wrote: "Like a pig I lay hidden! Instead of taking hold of an axe and splitting their heads — , I crawled away and hid for days — like a pig! I cannot write about that! If I should sit down to write I would not be able to keep from writing something that would become my 'act of accusation' to send me to exile."

He chose self-exile instead, eventually escaping to Geneva, where he lived for three years. By that time he had shifted his focus from producing new work to revising his oeuvre, and translating his stories back and forth between Yiddish and Hebrew.

When he returned to Russia in 1908, he was honored by the Yiddish-speaking community. He died in 1917 and was mourned throughout the Yiddish world. Generations of writers who came after him acknowledged their debt to his work. Even today, when Yiddish enthusiasts create communities in cyberspace, they often invoke the name and image of Mendele.

Fishke the Lame

TRANSLATED BY GERALD STILLMAN

To my dear, beloved friend, Menashe Margolius*
I dedicate this book from the depths of my heart.

Dear friend,
Sad is my melody in the symphony of Yiddish literature. My
works express the very core of a Jew who, even when he
does sing a merry tune, sounds from afar as if he were sobbing and weeping. Why, even his festive *shabes* hymns sound
as if they were taken out of the Book of Lamentations.
When he laughs, there are tears in his eyes. When he tries to
make merry, bitter sighs escape from the depths of his heart
— it's always *oy vey,* woe is me, *vey!*

I am not, God forbid, trying to give myself airs by saying
that I am a nightingale in Yiddish literature, although, in one
respect, there is a great deal of similarity between me and him.
This melancholy poet of the birds pours out his sad heart and
sings his avian melodies precisely in springtime when all the
world is newborn, when the buds burst into bloom, when
delicious aromas tickle the nostrils, when everything looks
bright and rosy and one's heart skips a beat for joy.

You and I, my dear friend, both began our work in
Yiddish literature in the springtime of Jewish life here in our
land. From 1860 onward, a new life seemed to have begun
for Jews — a more relaxed life, a life full of hope for the
future. At that time, we were both still very young. Each of

---

*A Jewish-Russian writer who was a good friend of Mendele's. He wrote a number of
reviews of Mendele's works in the Russian Jewish press in the period around 1890.

us seized his pen with zeal and began to work away lustily, each according to his own bent. The people licked their fingers from your writing. They were thoroughly delighted to read the sweet words you wrote about many important matters in Jewish life. You were an advocate of righteousness among Jews and lectured them gently, in friendly fashion, on how to know themselves, to learn how to live and become the equals of other peoples. Pearls fell from your lips, lustrous pearls which shine and will always be an ornament for Yiddish literature.

I, too, hummed a tune in my own way during those happy spring days, but there was always one note which repeated gloomily and cast a spell of melancholy over the listeners. Some of them listened readily, although with heavy hearts; others made faces, scratched themselves unhappily, and were annoyed because I reminded them of unpleasant things and made their ears tingle. Be that as it may, I sang my song the only way I could.

That promising spring has long since passed. Woe, oh woe is to the life of a Jew! Trouble has made me lose my desire to write.* It has been a good while since I have lost my tongue.

And if I now take my gaunt and shriveled pen in hand and again attempt to use my voice, it is only thanks to you, you whose company has restored my balance and renewed my strength. Your clever words, your unrelenting labors in behalf of our people have refreshed me and inspired me with the desire to undertake some useful labor also. A spark has risen from the holy fire which ever burns in your Jewish heart and has alighted in my breast where it burst into flame and is now burning with the vigor of my youthful years.

Yes, we both commenced our literary labors at the same time, but our fortunes have not been the same. You scale the great heights. There you deal with the gems and jewels of

---

* Mendele refers here to the period from 1877 to 1884, which he described as a time when writing "has become impossible for me. My brain is filled with lead . . ."

Jewish history. You put our best foot forward by exhibiting our most sparkling antique diamonds, the best and dearest in the life of our people. You deal with Rabbi Hillel, Rabbi Meir, Rabbi Akiba and other greats — men of the highest renown.

On the other hand, it has been my lot to descend to the depths, to the cellars of our Jewish life. My stock in trade is rags and moldy wares. My dealings are with paupers and beggars, the poor wretches of life; with degenerates, cripples, charlatans, and other unfortunates, the dregs of humanity. I always dream of beggars. Before my eyes, I always see a sack soaring — the old, familiar Jewish beggar sack. No matter which way I turn my eyes, the sack is before me. No matter what I say or do, the sack comes soaring up to me! Oy, it's always the sack, the Jewish beggar sack! Yes, dear friend, through you the fire for the writing has revived in me and has again produced a punishment for our numerous iniquities, a sack! A *Fishke der Krumer* [Fishke the Lame] with which I am appearing before the public after such a long period of silence. I know that my *Fishke der Krumer* is not the most suitable gift with which to express my gratitude for your friendship, but knowing your warm heart and your understanding of people, I dare to hope that you will accept my poor Fishke with a "Welcome!" Possibly, you will invite him into your home and introduce him to your family and friends. Fishke will gladly rest with you for a while, put his basket aside and tell you tales which you will enjoy. With this picture before my eyes, I smile with pleasure and thank you from the depths of my heart,

THE AUTHOR

Chapter I

Just when the bright sun begins to shine proclaiming another summer to the land, when people feel newly born and their hearts fill with joy at the sight of God's glorious world — just then the time for wailing and weeping arrives among Jews. This time of sorrow brings with it a host of mournful days: days of fasting, days of self-torment, days of grief and tears — starting at the end of Passover and lasting well into the damp cold and deep mud of autumn.

This is the very time when I, Mendele the Book Peddler, am busiest. I travel from fair to fair and from town to town to provide the children of Israel with all the wares needed for shedding tears: Books of Lamentations, Penitential Prayer Books, women's Books of Supplication, ram's horns for the Day of Atonement, and prayer books for festivals. In short, while Jews weep and wail all summer long, my business thrives. But that's not the point . . .

Early one morning on the road, it was the seventeenth day in the month of Tammuz, I sat on my wagon in my prayer shawl and *tfiln,* my whip in my hand, in an altogether Jewish manner. My eyes were shut to keep the distracting light of day from interfering with my prayers. Satan would tempt me, though. Nature, or whatever it is called, was wondrously beautiful, a sight to behold. I was strongly driven, as though by witchcraft, to steal a glimpse. I wrestled with myself for quite a while.

My Good Mentor said, "For shame! You mustn't!"

"It's all right! Enjoy yourself, silly!" prodded my Evil Genius and at the same time forced open one of my eyes.

As if for spite, I was overwhelmed by the exquisite panorama which greeted my eye.

Fields peppered with blooming buckwheat as white as snow were embroidered with stripes of golden-yellow wheat and pale green stalks of corn; a pleasant valley, the sides of which were covered with groves of nut trees; and below, a brook — clean and clear as crystal — into which the rays of the sun ducked and leaped out again in a shower of blinding golden sparks. In the distance, the cows and sheep at pasture looked like gray and red specks.

"*Fe, fe!* For shame!" my Evil Genius mocked and flung the well-known precept at me: "Should a Jew, while traveling, interrupt his prayers and say, 'How pretty is the tree, how beautiful the field,' he commits a grievous sin." But, at the same moment, he blew into my nostrils the delicious fragrance of the stacks of newly cut hay, of herbs and roots — fragrances which trickled into my very extremities; the tricky melodies of the myriad songbirds drifted into my ears and tickled my soul. He sent a soft warm breeze across my face; it rippled through my prayer curls and whispered: "Look, enjoy yourself and be a man, silly Jew that you are!"

I babbled and gabbled, and truth to tell, I myself did not know about what. My thoughts ran away with themselves; curses and sneers pecked at my brain:

"Cadaverous creatures! Neither substance nor soul! Creatures with their souls absorbed in eating! Creatures without taste or smell. Dried out, useless rubbish!"

I began to rock back and forth with forced devotion so as to keep my mind from wandering. But I suddenly heard my mouth twist the prayer to say, ". . . he who returns to the dead carrion their souls."

Why? To whom did this refer? I almost jumped, so ashamed did I feel of my ugly thoughts. To smooth over my error against the One Above, I acted as if I had meant something entirely different: it was this horse of mine. I flicked the good-for-nothing with the whip and growled, "A-a-a-h! You carrion, you!"

This was indeed a clever act, but today it was of little use. Somehow I was deeply concerned that such thoughts should occur to me today of all days — on this day, when we bewail and lament the great misfortune that once befell of children of Israel: the army of Nebuchadnezzar, King of Babylonia had entered Jerusalem and razed it to the ground. Forcing myself to feel contrite, I said the penitential prayer for this day in a tearful voice which mounted in pitch until it reached a climax of sorrow at those bitter words of the refrain:

"And the horned monster, the Tatar from the North, swept me from my feet like a jet of water and carried me far, far away . . ."

Once a Jew has shouted a psalm to his heart's content or talked himself hoarse repeating penitential prayers, he feels greatly relieved and, like a child who has had a good cry after a whipping, is quite happy again. So I felt now, half reclining in my wagon, smoothing my beard, with a beaming countenance as if to say: "Well, my share is done, I've done my duty. And now, *Gotenyu,* the rest is up to You; show Yourself, O Father, Merciful and Just One!"

"Come now, come! Forgive me!" I looked at my horse with good will, apologizing in my heart for having called him "carrion" before. My *shli-mazl* was kneeling on his forelegs, his head bowed to the ground, and groaning as if to say:

"Your lordship! How about something to eat?"

"True! You're as bright as the light of day," I said, signaling that he might rise now, that is, get up on his feet. Not in vain is it stated in the Book of Lamentations: "Zion, even your cattle and poultry are clever ..." But that's not my point.

This profound thought led to others concerning the children of Israel; I mused about their wisdom, their mode of living, their communal leaders, and their sorry condition. My thoughts strayed hither and thither. Before me I saw the horned monster, Nebuchadnezzar and his army, bloody battles, confusion and commotion. The army tore down walls, smashed out doors and windows. Jews, many with packages of wares and old clothes, cried for help and, mustering their courage, fled. I seized a stick and was about to — when boom! I found myself stretched out flat on my back on the ground.

Apparently, let it not be repeated to others, I had been napping in the midst of my prayers. My wagon, I saw, had run into a puddle, of the type known in the coachmen's jargon as "an inkwell." The axle hub of another wagon was caught in my rear wheel. My poor horse stood in agony with one leg over the shaft, all twisted in the harness and puffing like a goose. From the other side of the wagon flowed a stream of deadly curses, in Yiddish, interrupted only by a spell of coughing and choking.

"A Jew," I thought, "then there is no danger." And I strode in anger to the other side of the wagon. There, underneath, lay a Jew smothered in his prayer shawl and *tfiln,* his whip entangled in the leather thongs of his *tfiln,* struggling for all he was worth to free himself.

I shouted, "What do you call this?"

And he: "What do you mean, 'What do you call this'?"

"How does a Jew dare to fall asleep while praying?" I exclaimed.

"How can a Jew snore away like that?" he retorted.

I cursed his father and his entire generation and his mother and hers. I whipped his horse and he, freeing himself, ran in a fury to whip mine. Both horses reared on their hind legs. In a frenzy, we flew at each other like two raging cocks and were about to seize each other's prayer curls, when we stopped and stared at each other for a silent moment. It must have looked strange indeed: two Jewish champions in their prayer shawls and *tfiln,* facing each other in a rage, ready to exhibit their prowess and slap each other, right in the middle of this open field, as though they'd been arguing in a House of Study, forgive the comparison! It would really be worth going to some trouble to witness a charming scene like this one. We stood there, ready to slap each other in a moment, when suddenly we both jumped back several paces and, in great surprise, shouted in one voice:

"*Oy,* Reb Alter!"

"*Oy, oy!* Reb Mendele!"

Alter Yaknehoz was a powerful little man with a big belly. His face was overgrown with a thick mat of dirty yellow hair of which there was enough to provide for prayer curls, beard, and mustaches not only for himself but for several more Jews as well. In the midst of this sea of hair lay an island — a broad, fleshy nose which, being stuffed almost all year, defeated its own purpose. But occasionally a change in its condition would occur, say, in the spring just before Passover, when everything else was in thaw, when the ice floes on the river crashed with thunderous blasts, like those of the *shoyfer* on Yom Kippur. The whole town of Tuneyadevke* reverberated to its clarion calls which, together with gobbling of the tom turkeys, made for a real spring concert. Everybody in the town stood gaping, and offerings of snuff and good wishes for health poured in from all sides.

In Jewish towns especially, noses break into song at this time of year. Perhaps the odors and aromas of the season have something to do with it. Or, maybe it is the order of things, for does it not say in the Scriptures . . . But that's not my point.

---

*Mendele uses the humorous device of playing on place names. *Tuneyadets,* in Russian, is a sluggard or parasite. *Tuneyadevke* might be translated as "Sluggardtown."

Alter Yaknehoz was a book peddler from Tuneyadevke, an acquaintance of mine of many years standing. He was a man unto himself, not too sharp, a man of few words, always gruff as if angry with the world, although he was not at all a bad sort.

After a round of warm greetings, we began to inquire after each other's business. Among us Jews this investigation usually involves a peek into the other fellow's wagon, possibly accompanied by a searching hand or a nose sniffing for a clue — a revealing odor.

"And where is a Jew going!" I tried to feel Alter out.

"Where a Jew is going? *Ett . . .*" Alter answered with a question since it is the custom among Jews not to answer such a question directly but rather to put the inquirer off with an *"Ett,"* which could signify a lot or a little depending on how adept one is at taking a hint.

"A Jew is going! He's going to the dogs, that's where! And where is Reb Mendele headed?" Alter was trying to feel me out in return.

"Yonder! Where I'm usually headed this time of year."

"I'm afraid I can guess where 'yonder' is: Glupsk!* Just where I'm headed myself," Alter said, his face expressing worry about the possible effect of competition on his earnings. "But why, Reb Mendele, by way of a side road? Why not with the main highway?"

"It happened to be more convenient this time. I'm glad. I haven't been this way for a long time. And you, Reb Alter? Why the back road!" I tried to feel him out again. "Where have you been?"

"Where I've been? On the road to ruin, that's where! I've been to the fair at Yarmelinets — may it sink into the earth!"

While my Alter was fuming and cursing Yarmelinets and its fair, some peasants in wagons approached. They shouted and demanded why the road was blocked. When they came closer and saw Alter and me in our prayer shawls, with the big leather *tfiln* boxes held on our foreheads with broad leather thongs, the shouts became coarse and mocking:

"Hey, there! Look at that pair! What a sight! Hey, the devil take your mothers' mothers! Clear the road! Snappy there, little Jews, lazy bones!"

Alter and I began to work on the wagons quickly and with vigor.

---

*Again, a play on place names. *Glupsk* stems from the Russian *glupi,* meaning stupid or foolish. *Glupsk* can be taken as "Foolstown."

Several of the peasants, although not children of Israel, but the truth must be told, had the goodness of heart to come and help us in this, our time of need. By dint of their pushing, my wagon was soon out of the "inkwell." Were it not for them, we would have puttered around for God knows how long and would probably have torn our prayer shawls to tatters. But together with the peasants it was an entirely different story: they pushed in real earnest, for the hands were the hands of Esau; but with us it was only the voice, and the voice was the voice of Jacob. We grunted and groaned and struggled as if we were really pushing. . . . But that's not my point.

As soon as the road was cleared, these vulgar louts went their way, turning only to mock and jeer at us for being dressed like orthodox priests, forgive the comparison, and for walking alongside the horses, serving the Creator with whip in hand. Some of them, grasping the lower corner of their coats to form the shape of a "sow's ear," pointed them at us, shouting: "Jewish swine!" Alter was hardly bothered. "Remember whence it comes," he shrugged. "Who is there to get insulted at?" But I was deeply hurt by their mocking. *Gvald,* Father in Heaven, why? Why?

"Almighty God!" I began in the plaintive style of the women's *tkhines.* "Open Thine eyes and do mark, from Thy retreat which is the Heaven above, how Thy dear Name is holden by them, for in awe do they stand of Thy might, and Thy word do they cherish most reverently. Do Thou then cause to descend upon us Thy compassion that we may find Favor and Grace in Thine eyes and in the eyes of all people. Do Thou then shield Thy most surely beloved sheep and let Thy Mercy dwell among Thy constant worshipers. Do Thou also improve my fortune for having this day praised and glorified Thy Name in deep reverence. Cause to descend upon me, Thy slave Mendl, son of Thy maid Gnendl, and upon all of Israel, some good bit of business that our spirits may be at ease, Amen!"

Chapter II

Without further ado, we climbed up on our wagons and off we went. My wagon was in front. Behind me rode Alter in a van with tattered matting, four crooked wheels with wedges between the spokes, and rims tied together with rope. The greased wheel blocks tossed from side to side on their axles, creaking and groaning, unable to find themselves a comfortable position. A tall, strikingly lean beast put itself to the trouble of drawing this van — a scrofulous mare with a flea-bitten back full of blisters, with long ears, a twisted and tangled mane matted with wisps of hay and wads of cotton padding, which were coming out of her collar.

All that remained to be said of my morning prayers were the last few verses, about which, even under ordinary circumstances, little fuss is made. Having done with my prayers, an entirely new contest developed with my Evil Genius.

"Go ahead," he urged. "Take a sip of brandy! It will refresh your heart."

"*Ai, Ai!*" I wrinkled my nose in refusal. "On the seventeenth of Tammuz! On such a day of fasting!"

"*Ett!*" came back a reply. "There's a bit of difference between a Jew today and one in the times of Nebuchadnezzar! There are bigger troubles today and yet . . . nothing. Don't be silly. You're old and weak, poor man. There's no harm in it!"

I swept my hand across my face as if to brush away a troublesome fly and in the meanwhile stole a wee glance at the little satchel back in the wagon — the little satchel where I always kept a good bit of brandy, buckwheat cookies, rye cakes, garlic, onion, and other greens. My mouth watered, my heart grew faint, my stomach growled:

"*Gvald,* help! A drop of brandy! *Gvald,* something to eat!"

I turned my head away swiftly and fixed my attention on the fields about me in an effort to drive away these evil thoughts.

The sky was blue and clear without a trace of cloud. The sun baked and broiled. There was not the slightest breeze, not even a breath of air, for relief. The stalks of grain in the fields, the trees in the woods stood stock still — as though petrified. The cows at pasture lay fatigued, their necks outstretched, wiggling their ears from time to time and chewing their cud. Some dug up the earth with their horns and pushed it underneath them with their hoofs while bellowing from heat. The bull lifted his head and went galloping madly, tossing his head from side to side, stopped suddenly and lowered his brow almost to the ground. He sniffed, blew hard through his nostrils, let out a great bellow, and stamped his feet. Near an old, gnarled, half dried-up willow, split in half by a thunderbolt long ago, stood a herd of horses, their heads thrown over each other's rumps to create some shade; they whisked their tails to and fro to get rid of the troublesome flies. High up in a tree, a magpie swayed back and forth on a branch. It looked, for all the world, as if she wore a little white prayer shawl with the blue stripes in front and was praying with a rocking motion. She bowed her little head in supplication, hopped and chirped a few times . . . then remained still again, without a sound, extending her little neck and staring into the world with sleepy little eyes.

Along the road there was only silence, not the slightest sound, not a peep; there was not even a bird in flight; only mosquitoes and midges carried on like demons, flying by with a hum and a hiss, whispering a secret into one's ear and then — gone again. Only in the haystacks, among the stalks, crickets chirped incessantly; they were in full cry.

It was hot. It was quiet, and wondrously beautiful. Hush! God's creatures were resting. . . .

On account of the heat, I sprawled in my wagon in my shirt sleeves, pardon my appearance, and prayer shawl. I had pushed my stitched felt cap to the back of my head and rolled my heavy woolen stockings, from Breslau, down to my ankle stockings, which, in expiation of our manifold sins I wore even during the summer, and perspired profusely. Because I love to perspire, I would have enjoyed the heat if the sun were not beating directly into my eyes; I could lie for hours on the upper bench in the steam bath in the very greatest heat. My father, his memory be praised, had accustomed me to it even as a child. He was a hot, smoldering, burning, fiery Jew. He loved to steam himself through and through and thereby made a name for himself. He was greatly beloved among the people, for the very gist of Jewishness is to be found in this fiery nature. Therefore they regarded him as a respectable Jew who was close to God. They spoke of him with reverence:

"Oh, yes, as far as whipping goes, he is a deep scholar. He's a past master on the subject 'steam bath.' He knows . . . he knows all there is to know about sweating!"

Sweating is a Jewish thing. Not a Sabbath goes by, not a holiday, when a Jew does not find himself in a good sweat. Who, among all the seventy nations of the world, has sweated more than the Jew? But that's not my point.

And while I lay there sweating, how I did need refreshment! My throat was dry, my lips were parched and crying for a drink, I was dying for some food. My Evil Genius seized upon me again, stronger than ever, and enumerated the whole list of Jewish delicacies:

"Broiled *ledvetsa* with porridge; sweet-and-sour meat; a *lokshn* pudding with a 'thief' — a stuffed neck of chicken hidden within; boiled *farfl,* fried with bits of chicken skin." I became faint; my limbs turned limp. My appetite was ferocious. But he went right on:

"Thin dough stuffed with meat, jellied calves' feet with liver slices, radish and onion, the crop of a tom turkey in a candied parsnip sauce . . ."

And suddenly, I don't know how it happened, the little satchel appeared before me, as if it had sprung out of the earth.

"*Lekhayim,* to your health, silly!" the demon spoke through me. "You've been foolish enough for one day, you dolt!"

My hand stretched forth, by itself somehow, opened the satchel and swiftly snatched the bottle. I looked about like a thief when suddenly my horse's eye brought me to a dead halt. In the process of scratching his neck on the shaft, he had turned his head toward the wagon and scowled at me with resentment, as if to say:

"Here, look! My hind leg is all swollen and bandaged with rags; one of my eyes keeps on watering; my neck is chafed; my mouth, a useless organ, has forgotten the taste of oats. Still and all, what can I do? I just drag along, hungry, sick, and wretched — not even thinking of throwing off the yoke, God forbid."

The bottle slid out of my hand, back into its resting place. I pushed the little satchel away from me in great shame, groaning from the depths of my heart:

"So this is what has come to pass! This is who must serve me as an example; from him must I learn wisdom! *Milpani mibheymes hoerets* — he teaches us by means of the cattle of the earth. . . . No, horse o'mine! I will not throw off the yoke either. We'll live somehow, Reb Horse, the devil won't take either of us! *Adam ubheyme* — man and beast — *toyshiah adonai* — are both saved by the Lord!"

Once a Jew has broken himself of the vile passion of eating, food ceases to be a matter of importance to him and he can spend the rest of his life requiring almost nothing. To this very day, in these modern times, many a Jew can be found who has only the vestige of a stomach, truly the size of an olive pit. And there are great hopes that with the passing of time — if only the kosher meat tax is retained and the activities of the charity workers and their brethren go unhampered — Jews will drift further and further away from eating until among future generations there will be no trace left of the digestive tract at all, except for piles. Jews will then present a pretty picture to the eyes of the rest of the world. . . .

The point of this discourse is that, having pushed the little satchel away, I somehow felt much stronger. I lay back thinking about business and hummed a sad little tune. Everything appeared to be in order. But the devil had to bring into being a peasant lass, ugly as they come, with a pot of mushrooms, my favorite dish. Any pious man in my position would have taken it for granted that this was the Evil Genius himself, disguised in the form of a female in order to . . . But not I! I had to take a good look. It really was only a simple peasant lass! And asking me to buy the mushrooms together with the pot for only ten groschen, she pushed it right under my nose. I was almost overcome by the aroma. It went to my heart. My mouth watered and I felt faint. Oh God, how I wanted it! Fearing that I would lose control of myself, I jumped off the wagon as if I were running from a fire. It was a sheer miracle that I did not break nape and neck. I shouted with a voice that was not mine: "Reb Alter!" My purpose was that Alter should be my chaperon.

There, in his wagon, my Reb Alter lay flat on his back, both hands under his head, red as a beet: his shirt was open, forgive his appearance, and his woolly red-haired chest exposed, burnt, roasted, and so covered in sweat, oh enemies of Zion, that my heart almost broke to see him thus.

"Wh-a-a-at?" called Alter without stirring when he heard my cry. "What's the matter?"

A quick glance told me that she of the mushrooms was gone. It was as though she had evaporated. Since I had to say something, I asked Alter: "Tell me, what time do you think it might be now?"

"What time do I think it might be now?" repeated Alter in a hollow voice. "How should I know? Our eyes will probably pop from their sockets waiting for the first stars to appear. That's certain. My, it's awfully hot!"

"A delicious heat, eh? Are you sweating, Reb Alter?" I asked, walking alongside his wagon. "I think it's time to rest. Our lions are weary, they are barely dragging along. It is still many *versts* to Glupsk; and then maybe a couple more. Down yonder where the woods start, I see a good spot on the left for the horses to feed. It's not far."

A few minutes later, we turned off the road to the spot where the woods started, among pretty fields and a good green meadow. We unharnessed our lions and let them feed in freedom at the edge of the woods. We lay down under a tree.

Chapter III

Alter Yaknehoz breathed heavily because of the heat. His moans and groans affected me so that my heart melted with pity. To cheer him up a bit and partly to make the time pass more quickly, I engaged him in the following conversation:

"Well, Reb Alter, is it hot enough for you?"

"Beh!" Alter answered briefly and somewhat vexed, as he slid further under the tree in an effort to hide himself from the rays of the sun which cut through the branches.

"Feh! This day of fasting is making me sick! Is that you groaning like that?" I probed Alter again, having firmly resolved that though I should die in the attempt I would get him to speak.

"Beh!" Alter answered, and slid still further under the tree.

I was not disposed to be happy with only a *"Beh!"* for an answer. "Aha!" I thought. "You hide-bound old mule! I'll fix you! I'll make you talk. If heat and sweat won't do it then the subject will have to be business — the best, in fact the only topic to make a silent Jew talkative. A Jew, even if he be on his deathbed, will come alive as soon as he hears something about business; he comes alive and even the Angel of Death cannot come near him at that moment. God help the man who must cross the path of a rich merchant when he is occupied with business: he will demolish anyone, even his best friend, his own brother, with his glance. . . . But that's not my point.

I turned to Alter and said: "You and I, Reb Alter, are going to do some trading, I think! I'm glad that we met each other today. Oh, I have some stuff with me today that is worth its weight in gold!"

My new tactic had its effect. Alter was a changed man. He raised his head, turned toward me, and pricked up his ears. I continued to feed the fire:

"This time, Reb Alter, all our trading will be on a cash basis. You say you're coming from the fair at Yarmelinets, so your pockets must be bulging with money, may the Evil Eye not harm them."

"Bulging pockets, yes! A heart bulging with trouble is all I have," said Alter testily. "I tell you Reb Mendl . . . but — nothing . . . an unlucky man would be better off if he hadn't been born. I was looking for deals, special deals! Had it been someone else, heh-heh-heh! But with me, it all came to nothing. Everything goes downhill with me. Only misfortune comes my way! It hurts to talk about it. Cut your nose to spite your face. . . . it's no more than nothing."

It was clear that things were not going smoothly with my Reb Alter. He had troubles. But as long as his tongue had loosened, a wee little push was all that was needed to keep it wagging. I was of no mind to prevent this. I gave him a good push, and my Alter was on the move, telling about his misfortune in his unique way:

"Anyway, I go to the fair in Yarmelinets. When I arrive at the market place, I unhitch my wagon in the square, you understand, and unpack my bit of goods. Well, to make a long story short — nothing! I stand there waiting for customers. What brought me to this fair, God only knows. I, it shouldn't happen to you, am in a tight spot right now. The printer wants his money. Well, that's a small matter — so he wants it. But he wants, you understand, to stop giving me goods! My older daughter is not getting any younger. A girl of her age, you understand, should be getting married. So I have to find her a husband. There are plenty of bachelors, but a husband, you understand, a husband is not so easy to find! And then, with all this going on, my wife decides to have a baby boy, and when? Just before Passover! You understand me? A boy! You know what that means? But — nothing!"

"Don't be offended with me," I said to Alter, "for interrupting you. But why, at your age, did you marry a young wife who has children so easily?"

"God protect you!" cried Alter in amazement. "I had to have a house-wife to take care of the household. What does a Jew want to get married for at all? All the poor man wants is a good housewife."

"Tell me then, Reb Alter," I asked, "why did you divorce your first wife and ruin her life? She was a good housewife."

"*Beh!*" Alter winced, looking wretched.

"Nor was she a sterile woman, glory to His Holy Name, this first wife of yours," I persisted in the same vein. "What happened to your poor children by your first marriage? Do you know?"

"*Beh!*" Alter scratched under his prayer curl uncomfortably, waved his hand helplessly, and sighed from the depths of his heart.

"*Beh!*" is a priceless word for us Jews. It has so many meanings and serves to answer so many difficult questions.

"*Beh!*" can be used at any time during a conversation and will always be in place. A Jew in a difficult situation, with his back to the wall, can always wriggle out of it with one word: "*Beh!*" A swindler or a bank-rupt will use "*beh*" as a payment to his creditors when they press him too hard. "*Beh!*" stands by a man in time of need, as, for example, when the poor fellow is caught telling a lie. "*Beh!*" is a fitting comment to one who has been drumming in your ears for hours on end and you haven't lis-tened to or heard a word of what he said. "*Beh*" is the apology of a bigwig who has hoodwinked the public; of a man of reputed virtue whose true character has finally been uncovered. In a word, "*beh*" has a variety of tastes and all sorts of interpretations, such as, for example: come, if you dare! the goose is cooked! I'm on your side! do your worst! a plague upon you! A Jewish mind will always divine the proper meaning of "*beh*" under the given circumstances. The direction in which the barb is aimed will always be clear.

Alter's last "*beh*" was a bitter one. Contrition, repentance, and self-accusation seemed to be wrapped up in it. Surely, his mean treatment of his first wife and their children must have left a wound in his heart. He must have seen in the many misfortunes that had befallen him a pun-ishment for his sins. This was clearly expressed by the bitter, heartfelt sigh, by the helpless way he waved his hand, and also by the sheepish scratching under his prayer curl, as if to say: "Bite your lip and keep your mouth shut! The devil take you!"

I was angry with myself for having scratched Alter's old wounds. That is the trouble with a Jew who must needs butt into someone's personal affairs and get under his skin with all sorts of questions, while all the time the poor man is choking down his troubles in silence. In addition, I was angry with myself because I would have to start all over again. After loosening Alter's tongue so that it was merrily wagging away like clockwork, I had to touch a little wheel and make the pendulum grind to a halt! I fell back on my former tactic. Once more I fed him hints about the possibility of our trading. I was not stingy; I gave him a full measure of tongue loosener. I found the little key that fitted him, wound him up so gently that he did not even notice, and soon the pendulum was swinging merrily again.

Chapter IV

"Well, I was waiting for customers near my wagon," Alter began again where he had left off. "In short, I stood there, looking around and watching the fair. Well, a fair is a fair — it's noisy. The crowds are big. Jews are busy, carried away; they're really living. A Jew at a fair is like a fish in water — it's lively, if you know what I mean. Our Father Jacob's blessing: 'And ye shall multiply like fish in the waters of the earth!' That's the way it goes, doesn't it Reb Mendele? And don't we always say: 'There's a fair in the air way up there'? That means that for a Jew Paradise is a fair. Anyway, whatever it means, people were hard at it. They ran around. They bargained. No one stood still for a minute. Among the storekeepers, I saw Ber Teletse.* He used to be a flunky once, then an errand boy, but today he's Reb Ber with a big store in the market place. He stood in front of it and argued so loud you could hear him all over the square. In short — nothing! It was all hustle and bustle. A man ran by, then another, and a third — all in a sweat, their caps pushed back on their heads. They tapped something here, felt something there. They talked with their hands and all at the same time. Then they suddenly stopped to think. They chewed the tips of their

---

*Teletza (from the Russian *telionok*) means a calf.

beards quietly — a sign that they'd soon agree. Then, uproar again. Brokers flew by gasping for breath, matchmakers, traveling repairmen, commission men, women with little baskets, Jews with big baskets, young gentlemen with canes, older gentlemen with bellies, all of them with flaming faces. Nobody had time! Time was a ruble a minute.

"Well, in short, nothing! It looked as if any one of them would strike it rich in a minute. *Ai, ai,* how their luck filled me with envy! There they were, earning money, raking in gold, and I, *shlimazl* that I am, what was I doing? Standing with folded arms like a clay statue near my tattered van! *Oy,* my van with the prayer shawl tassels and little charms dangling on the outside, and inside, the packs of books and other junk. The whole thing is a joke, I tell you. Go ahead, try to make a living and marry off a daughter when a whole pack of *tkhines* brings in no more than three rubles! In my heart, I cursed the whole lot of them — my daughter, the van, that dried-out mare of mine! I wished that I'd never seen them. Enough, I had to get down to work, and try my luck too! Maybe the One Above, blessed be His Name, would have mercy. Why not?

"In short, my cap flew to the back of my head, my sleeves rolled themselves up, my feet carried me to my van by themselves, a straw found its way from the wagon right into my mouth. My mouth began to chew on the straw and my mind began to work: it took only a few wrinkles and furrows before I slapped my forehead. I had it! A good idea — a match between two merchants, both of them with big stores here on the market place. Respectable men, both of them. Do you know whom I mean? Reb Elyokum, Reb Elyokum Sharograder was one of them! The other one — Reb Getzl Graydinger! I decided to get down to business. To hell with the wagon, the mare, and the printer! I went to work in real earnest. Luck was on my side and it looked like something might come of it. To make a long story short, I cracked the whip and things started moving. I ran from Reb Elyokum to Reb Getzl and from Reb Getzl to Reb Elyokum. I was now running around, blessed be His Name, like the best of them. I sweated and strained. The match had to go through, and right here, at the fair. Why not? Is there a better place than a fair?

"To make it short, the two merchants were in a big hurry: they looked each other over in passing, liked each other, wanted each other —

wanted each other badly! *Nu*, who could ask for anything better? The two of them were straining at the leash.

"I tell you, I could have hugged myself! My commission was as good as in my pocket. I had decided how much dowry to settle on my daughter. I was already bargaining with a ragpicker for an old satin coat for myself. Shirts were my last worry. They could wait until later. The good Lord would provide. . . . Well, to make a long story short — nothing! Just listen to what had to happen to me! I tell you, a man with no luck is better off not being born. Just as we were ready to break the pots in celebration, we happened to remember the bride and groom, and what do you think? Believe me, it hurts to even talk about it. The whole thing was a flop! No, it was ten times worse than a flop! It just blew up in my face! Listen to my misfortune and how the wrath of God descended on me: the two merchants each had — what do you think they had? They each had a son!"

"What do you mean, Reb Alter?" I shot out in a peal of laughter. "How can that be? You would never do anything as foolish as that! How could you arrange a match before finding out which of the two parties has a son and which a daughter?"

"Of course, it's simple enough!" Alter winced in vexation. "I still have as much sense as anyone else and nobody has to teach me how to live! Who ever heard of a Jew who doesn't know how matches are made? Reb Mendele, you know what our customs concerning matchmaking and marriages are like. Then why are you so surprised at my misfortune? It could have happened to anybody.

"I knew that Reb Elyokum was supposed to have a marriageable daughter — and what a daughter! May I have such a jewel myself! I saw her last year with my own eyes, may I see Paradise just as surely! But when a man has no luck, everything he knows is worth nothing! How was I supposed to know that this beautiful girl was in a hurry, that she had rushed off, and got herself married! She must have been seized by some fever. I didn't know a thing about it, may I know as much about my poverty! Now, let me ask you, whom could I have meant when I started working on this match between Reb Elyokum and Reb Getzl? Reb Elyokum's daughter, of course! His daughter and Reb Getzl's son! It was so clear that people would have laughed at me if I'd said anything about it. Everybody knows that two males don't get married! A male marries a female — that's our custom! How else could it be? All I know is that I did what was right. No one else, as I am a Jew, could have done any better.

"To make a long story short, I had worked fast: the important things — the dowry and living quarters for the couple — were all settled. Don't forget, at a fair with two busy merchants, there's no time for empty talk or nonsense. Each word counts. You have to come right to the point without wasting time. That's my story. Now, let's take Reb Elyokum. When I first brought up the match, he must have been sure that the talk was about his son. How else? He himself wasn't going to marry Reb Getzl! And he'd never imagine that his daughter was meant when he knew very well that he had a son and not a daughter to marry off. So that's his story and you can see that both sides are right. But — nothing! Now, do you understand?"

"*Beh!*" I said, barely able to contain my laughter and straining to keep a straight face.

"*Nu,* thank God for making you understand!" Alter pointed his thumb at me and, with raised eyebrows, drawled a knowing "Aha!" as if my beh had hit the nail on the head.

To tell the truth, Alter's explanation did make certain amount of sense. Why not? Considering the way we Jews arrange our matches, why shouldn't such a thing occur? Unconsciously, I again said, "*Beh!*" and looked at Alter in a most friendly way.

"Aha!" said Alter, pointing his thumb at me again. "Aha, so now you understand! But nothing . . . I'm not finished yet. I still had hopes about patching things up. Once I start something, I don't give up so easily, if you know what I mean."

"Reb Alter, God have mercy on you! What are you talking about?" I actually sat up in amazement, feeling certain that the terrible heat had made Alter lose his mind. "What kind of hope could you have had when both fathers had only sons?"

"Don't get excited," Alter soothed me. "It wasn't as bad as that, Reb Mendele. I had another idea. When God visits a plague on us, He also provides the remedy. You see, I still had Reb Ber Teletse to fall back on. He had plenty of eligible daughters. As a matter of fact, right from the start, those three names danced around in my head — Elyokum, Getzl, Teletse. It was just my luck to pick the wrong pair and leave Teletse out. The best way to patch things up was to bring Teletse into the picture, the honorable Reb Berishl! To make a long story short, I tried to smooth over my blunder with both merchants. Wasn't it everybody's fault — mine a little, theirs a little, and also our luck a little? It was probably not ordained by heaven, not in the cards, you understand! Then I started on the list of praises for Reb Berishl: he was, may the Evil Eye not harm him, wealthy, good-natured, generous to charities, an honored member in many societies. After all, this was Reb Berishl, no less! I didn't have to say anything about what a sage he was: you never have to say anything about a rich man's wisdom — it's understood. But, nothing! My hopes rose like dough with yeast. 'It will all turn out for the best yet,' I said to myself. 'Elyokum's and Getzl's sons have to get married and Teletse's daughters are like made to order! God willing, Reb Berishl is the answer to all my troubles.'

"To make a long story short, I had the runs again back and forth at full steam. The arrangements were going along well enough. Things were looking up. But, nothing! Suddenly, the fair was over. The stores closed, the wagons drove off, the people disappeared, and I was left alone in the empty market square! All my hard work, all my aggravation, was thrown out!

"Now do you understand?" Alter appealed to me in a plaintive beseeching voice, extending both hands. "Do you see what I mean? When you have no luck, then all the wisdom in the world won't help! *Oy,* the wrath of God has been upon me for a long time. It's a punishment for my sins. And you talk to me about doing business on a cash basis? I don't even have a groschen to my name, woe is me!"

"*Ai,* just like in the bathhouse!" I said, and moved away.

Alter glared at me with eyes wide open, shaking his head. Highly incensed, he turned and spoke, as though to the world at large:

"What a crooked, false-hearted man! Oh, enemies of Zion, here I am in agony, my troubles are breaking my heart, and he? Nothing! He's just thinking about himself, that's all! I can see right through the whole act! I know the Jewish tricks. I can tell pretty well when a man wants to back out of an offer as soon as he finds out that he doesn't have a cash customer! I can tell when a man doesn't want to do business."

"Really . . ." I exclaimed and tugged at Alter's beard playfully. "How can such thoughts even occur to you, Reb Alter? I meant something entirely different. The way your story ended with the disbanding of the fair reminded me of a very interesting tale which I can't forget to this very day. It's a story about a bathhouse and it ends just like yours. There's not even a hair's breadth difference between them, except the other story is short. It's worth hearing. Oho, you're sweating, Reb Alter! Move over a little, if you please, and we'll be able to lie here with our backs to the sun and talk."

Alter wiped the perspiration from his face with the back of his sleeve. From his bosom pocket, he brought out a meerschaum pipe with a female figure painted on the bowl. He cleaned the mouthpiece and the beaded stem with a short piece of wire which hung from a chain attached to the bowl cover. He lit the pipe, took a peek at the female figure, and settled back in all his glory under the tree. I cleared my throat and began my tale.

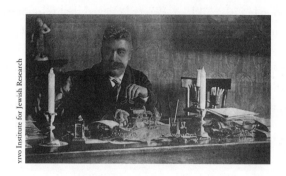

YIVO Institute for Jewish Research

Yitzhak Leib Peretz, also known as Isaac Leib or I. L., was a hero to his people and the father of Yiddish literature. This thoroughly modern writer mined the Yiddish folk past. He helped Jews who were moving from the medieval world to the modern by giving them images of themselves along the way.

Peretz was born in the small but cosmopolitan Polish city of Zamosc in 1852. Control of the area shifted among Russia, Austria, and Poland; it was, at the time, Russian. His family was comfortable and, although they provided him with a traditional religious education, they had no objection to his indulging his wide-ranging curiosity. He studied the literature of the Hebrew Enlightenment and learned Polish, German, and Russian. He had a reputation as a prodigy and a lively and mischievous boy.

Peretz's young adulthood was a succession of false starts: an introduction to the Warsaw literary world, a job as a bookkeeper, a foray into writing in Polish and Hebrew, an arranged marriage that ended in divorce. In time, he became a successful lawyer in his hometown, embarked on a second marriage, and involved himself in the Jewish community. His growing political consciousness expressed itself in helping to establish evening classes for Jewish workers as well as secular classes for poor Jewish children. Peretz believed that religious influence would diminish, and that a worldly education was the key to Jewish future.

But his personal and communal aspirations were soon frustrated. Russian authorities, fearing left-wing influences, shut his classes down. In 1888, without warning, Peretz was disbarred, apparently having been denounced as a socialist. At age thirty-six he found himself without a livelihood. He was thrown back into the arms of the Jewish world.

Peretz wrote to Sholom Aleichem, who at the time was publishing a Yiddish magazine aimed at the common folk.

> I don't look upon "Jargon" [Yiddish] as an object of hatred, nor as a means whose usefulness will one day pass. I want it to become a language, and, therefore, we must broaden and multiply its treasures and add, at each opportunity, brand-new expressions.

He also had more practical concerns.

> If you can send me the honorarium for the poem immediately, and maybe also an advance for the stories, you will do me a great favor, because I need it now.
> And if not — send me half.

Peretz was reborn as a Yiddish writer. He moved to Warsaw. But he still had to find a reliable income. Evenutally, the Warsaw Jewish Community Council gave him an administrative job running the cemetery department. He continued at that post, which gave him time to write, until the end of his life.

Peretz also created a new, de facto post: father figure and salon-keeper for Yiddish writers. A generation of intellectuals passed through his apartment. Hersh Nomberg remembered: "We used to sing folk songs at Peretz's every Saturday. [Judah Leib Cahan] scooped them up firsthand, in the Warsaw barrooms and in all the places where fellows and their girls used to dance and sing. . . . On Peretz and on his circle these songs acted like prophecy, revelation. We all felt that a fresh spring had been tapped, lively and bubbling."

Peretz wrote poems, short stories, plays, and nonfiction. He also published compilations; writings that were alive with the political, educational, and artistic ferment of the time.

One publication designed to bypass the censors was called *Yontef bletlekh* (Holiday Pages), a series of monthly booklets nominally issued to commemorate Jewish holidays. But the authorities were not fooled. In 1899, Peretz was arrested for his political activities and served three months in prison.

While there he turned backward, mining the parables and allegories told by the Hasidim, the mystic, anti-intellectual separatist Jews. Sometimes he retold the old stories with little change; more often he recast them through modern eyes, tweaking them so they could be read as calls to action.

His stories were tremendously popular among Jews of every persuasion. As the writer Shimon An-ski described it: "Peretz was an argument, a banner. In his works young people studied the Jewish people and Judaism, and because of him assimilated boys and girls learned Yiddish. There was seldom a Jewish soiree, whether Zionist or Bundist (both parties considered Peretz 'theirs'), that passed without a reading from Peretz's works."

In 1901, to mark Peretz's fiftieth birthday and the twenty-fifth anniversary of his first Yiddish publication, celebrations were held throughout the Yiddish-speaking world. The gift he most valued was a well-worn copy of the magazine he published that had comforted political prisoners, passed from hand to hand.

In later life Peretz enjoyed his position in the Yiddish literary community. Just as Mendele was the acknowledged grandfather, Peretz was known as the father. A fastidious dresser (he received guests wearing a smoking jacket) with a well-tended walrus mustache, he went on lecture tours to Odessa, St. Petersburg, Vilna, and Vienna. He lent his considerable prestige to the cause of Yiddish, pressing for its enrichment and acceptance among European languages.

The Yiddish writer Hersh D. Nomberg wrote,

> He was not a founder of a literary school, for until the last day of his life he was a seeker and a striver, always springing from style to style. The literary generation around him, his disciples, did not walk in his steps. Nearly everyone had his own trodden path, his domain, and his style. Peretz was a father of a literary family. His living interest for literature, his urge to create, his deep love for everything beautiful and sublime which ruled all the passions of his stormy nature — these acted magnetically upon all that was alive and creative in our world.

During World War I, Peretz worked to help the Jewish war refugees who streamed into Warsaw. He was involved in establishing a modern Yiddish children's school, and set to work writing children's poems, completing more than a hundred.

When he died in 1915, one hundred thousand supporters followed his coffin to the cemetery. Yiddish speakers around the world mourned. For decades after, schools for children and adults would be named in his honor. In 1925, a grateful people erected a majestic stone monument, with steps leading up to a sheltering half-dome and ornate columns. Amazingly, after all the destruction of World War II, the memorial still stands.

And Maybe Even Higher

TRANSLATED BY ELI KATZ

And every morning at the time for the penitential prayers, the Nemirover rebbe would disappear; vanish!

He was nowhere to be seen; not in the synagogue, not in either of the study-houses, not at a prayer gathering, and surely not at home. The house stood open. Anyone who wanted to could go in or out; *nobody* stole from the rebbe. But not a living soul was to be found in the house.

Where can the rebbe be?

Where *could* he be? In heaven, of course. Do you think a rebbe doesn't have a lot of affairs to attend to during the Days of Awe? Jews, God save them, need to earn a living; need peace, health, good marriages for their children; want to be good and God-fearing. But their sins are great, and Satan with his thousand eyes watches, and accuses, and informs . . . and — who is to help if not the rebbe?

That is what the people thought.

Once, though, a Litvak arrived in town, and he scoffed! You know the Litvaks: they don't have a high opinion of the books of ethics; instead they cram themselves full of Talmud and commentaries. And the Litvak quotes an explicit text and leaves you with your mouth open: Even Moses wasn't allowed to ascend to heaven during his lifetime, but had to stop ten handbreadths below! Try to argue with a Litvak!

— Where else does the rebbe go, then?

— How should I know? — he answers with a shrug. And before the words are out of his mouth (what a Litvak is capable of!) he resolves to get to the bottom of it.

The very same evening, just after the evening prayers, the Litvak steals into the rebbe's bedroom, creeps under his bed, and lies there. He intends to wait all night and see where the rebbe goes; what he does during the time of the penitential prayers.

Someone else might have dozed off and missed the occasion, but a Litvak finds a way: he repeats from memory an entire tractate of the Talmud! I can't remember whether it was "Profane Things" or "Vows."

Before sunrise he hears the call to prayers.

The rebbe had already been awake for a time. He had heard him groaning for almost a whole hour.

Anyone who has ever heard the Nemirover groaning knows how much sorrow for the Jewish People, how much suffering there was in each groan . . . Hearing the rebbe groan would dissolve you in pity. But a Litvak's heart is made of iron. He hears it and just keeps lying there. The rebbe lies there too: the rebbe, God bless him, on the bed; the Litvak under the bed.

The Litvak hears the beds in the house begin to creak; hears the inhabitants leave their beds, hears the murmur of a blessing, hands being washed, doors opening and closing. The people leave the house, and once again it is quiet and dark. Through the shutter a small gleam of moonlight barely penetrates . . .

The Litvak confessed that when he was left all alone with the rebbe he was seized with terror. His skin prickled with fear and the roots of his earlocks pierced his temples like needles.

It's nothing to laugh about: alone in a room with the rebbe, before daylight in the Days of Awe! . . .

But a Litvak is stubborn, so he shivers like a fish in the water, but he continues to lie there.

Finally the rebbe, God bless him, gets out of bed . . .

First he does all the things a Jew is obliged to do, then he goes to the clothes chest and removes a bundle . . . Peasant garments appear: linen trousers, great boots, a coat, a big fur hat, and a large leather belt studded with brass nails.

The rebbe puts them on. From the pocket of the coat a thick rope sticks out; the kind of rope peasants use!

The rebbe leaves; the Litvak follows.

On his way out the rebbe goes into the kitchen, stoops, removes an ax from under a bed, thrusts it through his belt, and leaves the house.

The Litvak trembles, but he doesn't falter.

A quiet autumnal sense of awe hovers over the dark streets. Often a cry can be heard from one of the prayer groups reciting the penitential prayers, or a sickly groan through a window . . . The rebbe keeps to the edges of the street, in the shadow of the houses . . . He glides from one house to the next with the Litvak behind him . . .

And the Litvak hears his own heartbeats mingle with the heavy footfalls of the rebbe: but he continues nevertheless, and together with the rebbe he arrives outside of the town.

Beyond the town there's a wood.

The rebbe, God bless him, enters the wood. He walks thirty or forty paces and stops beside a young tree. And the Litvak is amazed to see the rebbe take the ax from his belt and begin to hack at the tree.

He watches the rebbe chop and hears the tree groan and snap. And the tree falls, and the rebbe splits it into logs and the logs into chunks of wood; and he makes a bundle of these chunks and ties it with the rope in his pocket. He throws the bundle over his shoulder, sticks the ax back in his belt, and walks out of the wood and back to town.

In a back street he stops before a half-collapsed house and knocks at a window.

— Who is it? — a frightened voice calls from within. The Litvak recognizes a woman's voice; the voice of a sick woman.

— Me! — the rebbe answers in a peasant dialect.

— Who "me"? — the voice from inside asks again.

And the rebbe answers again in Ukrainian: "Vasil!"

— Vasil who? And what do you want, Vasil?

— Wood — says the supposed Vasil — I have firewood for sale. Very cheap. I'm practically giving it away!

And without waiting for an answer, he walks into the house.

The Litvak steals in behind him and by the gray light of dawn he sees a bare room with rickety furniture . . . A sick woman lies in bed, covered with rags, and she says bitterly:

— Buy wood? With what should I buy it? I'm a poor widow; what money do I have?

— You can have it on credit! — answers the supposed Vasil, — it comes to six groschen altogether!

— How will I pay it? — the poor woman groans.

— Foolish woman, — the rebbe lectures her, — here you are, a poor sick woman, and I trust you for this bit of wood; I have faith that you'll pay me. And you have such a great and powerful God, and you don't trust Him, and you don't have faith in Him even for a silly six groschens' worth of wood!

— But who will lay the fire for me — the widow groans — Do I have strength to get out of bed? My son had to stay away at his job.

— I'll lay the fire for you, too — says the rebbe.

And having put the wood in the oven, the rebbe, with a groan, recited the first verse of the penitential prayers . . .

And when he had lit the fire and it was burning merrily, he recited the second verse, somewhat more cheerfully . . .

And he recited the third verse when the fire had subsided into a steady glow and he closed the oven door . . .

The Litvak who saw it all stayed and became a Nemirover *khosid*.

And later, whenever a *khosid* said that the Nemirover gets up every morning during the Days of Awe and flies up to heaven, the Litvak would not laugh at all, but would add quietly:

— And maybe even higher!

Bontshe Shvayg

TRANSLATED BY ELI KATZ

Here, in *this* world, Bontshe Shvayg's death made no impression whatsoever. Ask anyone for the life of him who Bontshe was, how he lived, or what he died from! Did his heart simply burst? Did his strength finally give out? Was his backbone shattered under a heavy load? Who knows? Perhaps he even starved to death.

If a horse had collapsed while pulling a streetcar, more notice would have been taken. There would have been write-ups in the newspapers, hundreds of people would have gathered to examine the carcass, or even just the spot where the accident had happened . . .

But even the horse wouldn't have enjoyed such notoriety, if there were as many horses in the world as there are people — a thousand million!

Bontshe lived quietly and died quietly; he passed through the world like a shadow — through *our* world, that is!

At Bontshe's circumcision no wine was drunk; no glasses klinked! At his bar mitzvah he delivered no resounding speech. He lived like a small gray grain of sand on the beach, surrounded by millions like him. And when the wind lifted him and transported him across the ocean to the opposite shore, no one noticed.

During his lifetime his footprints were lost in the soggy mud. After his death the wind blew down his wooden gravemarker; the gravedigger's wife found it far from his grave and used it to boil a pot of potatoes. Three days after Bontshe's death the gravedigger couldn't have told you where he was buried!

If Bontshe had had a tombstone, then perhaps a hundred years from now an antiquarian might have found it, and the name Bontshe Shvayg might have been heard again in our sphere.

A shadow? There was no one who retained an image of him in mind or heart. Not a trace of him remained. He left nothing behind, neither heirs nor possessions. Alone he lived and alone he died.

If not for all the noise of human activity, someone might have heard Bontshe's spine cracking under his load. If the world had had more time, someone might have noticed that Bontshe (a human being, after all), while still alive, had eyes that were already extinguished, and horribly sunken cheeks; that even when there was no burden on his shoulders his head was bowed toward the earth, as though he were already searching out his grave. If there were as few human beings in the world as there are cart horses, it might have occurred to someone to ask what had become of Bontshe.

When Bontshe was taken to the hospital his basement corner did not remain vacant. There were ten others like him waiting for the spot, and they auctioned it off amongst themselves. When he was carried from his hospital bed to the morgue, twenty sick indigents were waiting for it. And when he was taken from the morgue, a hundred corpses were brought in, victims of a building that had collapsed. Who knows for how long he will inhabit his grave in peace? Who knows how many are waiting for that little plot?

He was born in silence, he lived in silence, he died in silence, and in silence he was buried.

But not so in the *other* world. *There* Bontshe's death made a great impression, indeed.

The great ram's horn that will announce the coming of the messiah blasted throughout the seven heavens: Bontshe Shvayg has passed over! The greatest angels with the broadest wings flew about proclaiming the news: Bontshe has been summoned before the heavenly council! And Paradise was filled with joy and excitement: Bontshe Shvayg — no small matter — Bontshe Shvayg!

Bontshe was met joyfully by cherubs with sparkling eyes, gold-filigree wings, and silver slippers on their feet. The whirring of their wings, the tapping of their slippers, and the happy laughter of these rosy-lipped angel-children filled the heavens until they reached the throne of the Almighty, and God Himself learned that Bontshe was on his way!

Our father Abraham placed himself in the gates of heaven with his right hand extended in warm greeting, and with a sweet smile on his ancient face.

Why are wheels rolling in heaven? Two angels are rolling a gilded armchair into Paradise for Bontshe to sit on.

What shines so brightly? It is a golden crown, set with precious jewels. All for Bontshe!

"But even before the verdict of the heavenly court?" ask the saints with amazement and a trace of envy.

"Oh," the angels answer, "that will be a mere formality. Even the prosecutor won't find a word to say against Bontshe Shvayg. The hearing won't last five minutes. This is Bontshe Shvayg we're talking about."

When the cherubs accosted Bontshe in midair and serenaded him, when Abraham shook hands with him like an old friend, when he heard that his seat in Paradise was waiting, and that a crown was ready for his head, when he learned that the hearing would go off without a word said against him — Bontshe remained silent. He remained silent out of terror — just as in the other world. He was petrified. He was sure that it must be a dream, or an outright error!

He was used to both. More than once he had dreamed in the other world that he was gathering gold pieces from the floor, a treasure, only to awake the next morning poorer than before. More than once someone had smiled at him in a friendly way, only to turn away after discovering his mistake, spitting to avoid the evil eye . . .

"That's my luck," he thought.

He is afraid to raise his eyes, for fear that the dream will disappear, that he will awaken in a pit surrounded by serpents and scorpions. He is afraid to let a sound escape from his lips or to move a muscle, lest he be recognized and cast into purgatory.

He is trembling and doesn't hear the compliments of the angels, nor see them dancing about him. He doesn't answer Abraham's warm greeting, and, when he is presented to the heavenly court, he forgets to say "Good morning."

He is beside himself with fear.

And his fear increased when he noticed that the floor of the heavenly court was made of alabaster and precious jewels. "My feet on this floor?" he thought, terrified. "Who knows which millionaire, which rabbi, which saint they are expecting! And when he arrives, I'll get what's coming to me."

In his terror he did not even hear the presiding judge call out explicitly: "The hearing of Bontshe Shvayg!" before handing the brief to the defending angel with the words: "Proceed; but make it short!"

The entire hall was spinning around Bontshe's head. There was a roaring in his ears, but every more clearly he could discern the sweet voice of the defending angel, melodious as a violin:

"His name, Bontshe the Silent, fits him as an elegant garment adorns a slender form."

"What is he talking about?" Bontshe asks himself, and he hears an impatient voice interrupt:

"Spare us the metaphors!"

The defending angel resumes:

"He never raised his voice in complaint, either against God or against man. Never did a spark of hatred light in his eyes. Never did he come forward with claims against the justice of the universe."

Again Bontshe fails to understand a single word, but the harsh voice interrupts again:

"No rhetoric, please!"

"Job complained. *He* was more unfortunate than Job!"

"Just the facts," says the presiding judge, more impatient than ever.

"On his eighth day he was circumcised."

"Omit the graphic details!"

"The circumciser botched it and couldn't stanch the flow of blood."

"Go on."

"He remained silent," the angel continued, "even when he lost his mother at the age of thirteen and acquired a stepmother who was a vicious snake."

"Do they really mean me, after all?" thought Bontshe.

"No reflections on third parties!" says the judge with annoyance.

"She begrudged him every bite of food; she gave him moldy bread and gristle while she drank coffee with cream."

"Stick to the point!" shouts the judge.

"But on the other hand, she wasn't stingy with blows, and black-and-blue marks showed through every hole in his tattered, moldy clothing. On the coldest winter day he would chop wood for her in the courtyard, his arms not yet strong enough, the logs too thick for him, and the ax too dull. More than once his arm was wrenched from its socket; more than once his feet were frostbitten. But he remained silent. Not even to his father . . ."

"That drunkard," interjected the prosecutor, and Bontshe felt a chill run through his body.

". . . did he complain," the angel continued. "Always lonely, no friends, no school, not a single article of clothing that was whole, never a free moment . . ."

"Just facts!" the judge reminds him.

"He remained silent even later when his drunken father grabbed him by the hair one freezing winter night and threw him out of the house. He quietly picked himself up from the snow and fled wherever his legs would carry him . . .

"And all along the way, he remained silent. When he was suffering the sharpest pangs of hunger, he would beg only with his eyes.

"On a dizzying rainy spring night he arrived in a large city. He entered it as a drop of water enters the sea. The very same night he spent in jail, but he remained silent; he didn't ask what for. When he was released he looked for the hardest work, and still he was silent.

"Harder than work itself was finding it. But he was silent!

"Bathed in cold sweat, bent under the heaviest burdens, suffering the cramps of an empty stomach, he was silent.

"Spattered with mud, spat upon, driven with his load from the sidewalks to make his way in the streets among carriages, streetcars, and cabs, facing death every minute, he was silent.

"He never calculated how many pounds he carried to earn a half-penny, nor how many times he fell under his load before earning three cents. He never figured the effort it sometimes cost to collect the meager earnings owed him. He kept accounts neither of his own nor of anyone else's fortunes. He simply remained silent.

"Not even his own earnings would he ask for aloud. He stood at the door with the look of a begging dog in his eyes. When he was told to come again later, he left quietly, like a shadow, to return later and even more timidly ask for his pay.

"And he even remained silent when he was cheated of part of his wages, or paid with counterfeit coins. He was always silent."

"They *are* talking about me," Bontshe consoled himself.

The defending angel took a drink of water and continued:

"One day his life changed. A coach with rubber tires was being dragged down the street by runaway horses. The coachman was lying on the pavement with his head split open. The frightened horses sprayed foam from their lips and sparks from their hooves. Their eyes blazed like burning torches in a dark night, and a man, more dead than alive, was sitting in the coach.

"Bontshe stopped the horses!

"The man he had saved was a philanthropist and did not forget what Bontshe had done for him. He presented him with the whip of the dead driver, and Bontshe became a coachman. And more yet: he provided Bontshe with a wife . . . and even a child. And still Bontshe remained silent."

"They really are talking about me." Bontshe was sure, now, but did not dare to look directly at the heavenly court. Again he heard the angel:

"He remained silent when his benefactor went bankrupt and failed to pay him his wages. He remained silent when his wife ran off and left him with an infant to care for. Fifteen years later he remained silent when the child had grown strong enough to throw him out of the house."

"Yes, it's me!" Bontshe rejoiced.

The angel resumed with a sadder and softer voice:

"He was silent when the same benefactor settled all his debts but paid him not a penny of his wages — and even when his new, rubber-tired coach ran him over.

"He remained silent. He never told the police who had done it.

"He was silent even in the hospital, where screaming is permitted! He was silent when the doctor refused to approach his bed without payment, and the orderly refused to change the linen. He died without saying a word against God or man.

"I have spoken."

✧ ✧ ✧

Once again Bontshe began to tremble. He knew the defending angel would be followed by the prosecutor. Who knew what he might say? Bontshe could not remember his life. In the other world he could never remember at any given moment what the previous one had been like. The defending angel had reminded him of it all. Who knew what the accuser might recall?

"Gentlemen," the prosecutor began in a sharp, stabbing voice.

"Gentlemen," he repeated somewhat more softly.

Finally, in a voice almost mild, he announced:

"Gentlemen! *He* remained silent; I, too, shall remain silent!"

All was quiet. And then there was a new, soft, quavering voice:

"Bontshe, my child! My dear child Bontshe!"

Bontshe's heart began to weep. By this time he would have opened his eyes, but they were obscured by tears. He had never experienced such tearful sweetness. "My child, my Bontshe . . ." Since his mother had died no such words had reached his ears.

"My child," continued the elder of the court, "you have suffered everything in silence. Not a single limb, not a single bone in your body remained unscathed. Nowhere, not even in the most secret recesses of your soul, is there a spot that has not bled . . . and you remained silent.

"In the other world, no one appreciated that. Perhaps you yourself did not realize that you could cry out and that your cries would cause the walls of Jericho to tremble and fall. You yourself did not know your own sleeping strength.

"In the other world your silence was not rewarded. But *that* is the world of lies. Here in the world of truth you will receive your reward! The heavenly court will not presume to judge you! For you there need be no verdict; no weighing and measuring of your share of Paradise! Take what you will; everything belongs to you!"

At last Bontshe raised his eyes. He is dazzled at the radiance that surrounds him. Everything sparkles and gleams; the walls, the furnishings, the angels and the judges.

He lowers his weary eyes. "Really?" he asks, doubtful and embarrassed. "Really," answers the elder, firmly. "I tell you truly that everything is yours. Everything in the heavens belongs to you. Choose what you wish; you will only be taking what is yours."

"Really?" Bontshe asks again, but with a more confident tone.

"Really, really, really!" the answer reaches him from all sides.

"Well, in that case," Bontshe smiles, "every morning I would like a hot roll with fresh butter!"

The angels and the judges lowered their heads in shame. The prosecutor burst out laughing.

Three Gifts

TRANSLATED BY JOACHIM NEUGROSCHEL

By the Scales

Once, generations and years ago, a Jew passed away.

Well, a Jew passed away — you can't live forever — and he was given his due, a decent Jewish burial.

The grave was closed. The bereft son spoke the prayer for the dead — the soul flew up, to judgment, the celestial court. . . .

When he arrived, the scales were already hanging before the court. To weigh the good deeds and the bad.

The dead man's defender came — his former Good Spirit — and stood with a snow-white sack in his hands to the right of the scales. . . .

The dead man's accuser came — his former Bad Spirit, his seducer, and stood with a filthy sack in his hands to the left of the scales. . . .

The snow-white sack contained the good deeds, the filthy sack — the bad deeds.

The defender poured out the good deeds on the right-hand scale. They wafted like perfumes and sparkled like the stars in the sky.

The accuser poured out the deeds on the left-hand scale. They were (may you be spared!) coal black and stank like pitch and tar.

The poor soul stood and gazed and gaped. He had never imagined there was such a difference between good and bad. Down below, he had often been unable to tell them apart, mistaking one for the other.

And the scales rose slowly, up and down. Now one pan, now the other. . . . And the pointer trembled in the air. Shifted a hair's breadth to the left, a hair's breadth to the right. . . .

Only a hair's breadth . . . and not all at once! He had been a simple

Jew, with no great crimes, or any martyrdom. And thus — tiny virtues, teensy peccadilloes. Bits and pieces, specks of dust. . . . Some barely visible to the naked eye.

But still, when the pointer shifted a hair's breadth to the right, the higher worlds resounded with joy and pride. When it shifted to the left, heaven forbid, a sigh of melancholy passed through the air, all the way up to the Throne of God.

And the angels poured slowly, with devotion, bit by bit, speck by speck. The way simple people at a charity auction bid penny by penny. . . .

But every well runs dry. The sacks were empty.

"Are you through already?" asked the court attendant, a very busy angel.

The Good Spirit and the Bad Spirit turned their sacks upside down. That was all! The attendant went over to the pointer to see where it had stopped, right or left.

He peered and peered and saw something that had never happened since the creation of the heavens and the earth. . . .

"What's taking so long?" asked the presiding judge.

The attendant stammered:

"It's even! The pointer is right in the center! . . . The good deeds and the bad deeds are perfectly balanced."

"Perfectly balanced?" they asked at the celestial bench.

The attendant peered again and replied: "On the dot!"

The celestial court deliberated and then issued the following verdict:

"Since the sins do not outweigh the virtues, the soul shall not go to hell. . . .

"On the other hand, the virtues do not outweigh the sins, and so we cannot open the gates of heaven for him.

"Hence, he shall be a vagabond. . . .

"He shall fly about in the middle, between heaven and earth, until God remembers and takes pity and summons him with His grace."

And the attendant took the soul and led him out.

The poor soul bewept and bewailed his fate.

"Why are you crying?" asked the attendant. "You won't enjoy the delights of paradise, but you won't know the pains and torments of hell. You're even!"

But the soul couldn't be comforted:

"The worst torments are better than nothing! Nothing is awful!"

The attendant felt sorry for the soul and gave him some advice:

"Fly down, little soul, and hover about the living world. Don't ever look at the sky, what will you see? Only stars! And they're bright but cold creatures, they have no sense of pity, they won't do a thing for you, they'll never remind God of you. . . .

"The only ones who can intercede for a poor homeless soul are the saints in paradise . . . And they, my little soul, they like presents . . . lovely gifts . . . That," he added bitterly, "is what saints are like nowadays!

"So fly, my little soul," he went on, "hover low around the living earth and watch life, watch what happens. And if you see anything of extraordinary beauty and goodness, grab it and fly up. It will be a gift for the saints in heaven. . . . And with that gift in your hand, knock and announce yourself in my name to the angel at the window. Tell him I said it was all right!

"And once you've brought them three presents, you can be sure that the gates of paradise will open for you. The gifts will do the trick. At the Throne of Honor, they don't like the high-born, they prefer those who make it on their own."

And with these words, he mercifully pushed the soul out of heaven.

The First Gift

The poor soul flew low. Hovering around the living earth. Seeking presents for the saints in paradise. He flew and flew, over villages and cities, wherever Jews could be found. Through burning rays in the worst heat spells. Through raindrops in wet seasons. Through silver gossamer that drifted in late summer, and snows that fell in winter. He looked and looked, and he looked his eyes out. . . .

Whenever he sighted a Jew, he hastily flew down and stared into his eyes. Was he about to sacrifice himself for God?

Wherever a light seeped through a crack in a shutter at night — the soul was there. Were God's fragrant blossoms growing in the quiet house, secret good deeds?

Alas! Usually the soul sprang away from eyes and windows, terrified and trembling. . . .

And as the seasons and years wore on, he was stricken with melancholy. Towns had already become graveyards. Graveyards had already been plowed up as fields. Forests had been cleared. Stones near water had turned into sand. Rivers had changed their courses. Thousands of stars had fallen. Millions of souls had flown upward. And the Good Lord did not remember this one soul. And the soul found nothing of extraordinary beauty and goodness. . . .

He thought to himself:

"The world is so wretched, people are so mediocre, their souls so gray and their deeds so small. . . . How can there be anything 'extraordinary' about them? I'll be a homeless outcast forever!"

But as he was thinking, a red flame caught his eye. In the middle of the dark, dense night, a red flame.

He looked around. The flame darted from a high window.

Bandits were attacking a rich Jew, bandits with masks on their faces. One was holding a burning torch to light their way. A second one was holding a shiny knife against the rich man's chest, and saying: "One more, Jew, and it'll be your last! The blade of my knife will come out your back!" The rest were opening chests and closets and looting them.

The Jew stood there with the knife at his chest and watched calmly. Not a lash twitched over his clear eyes, not a hair stirred in the white beard that reached down to his loins. Why should he care? "The Lord giveth, the Lord taketh away," he thought, "blessed be the name of the Lord! You're not born with it, and you can't take it with you," his pale lips whispered.

And he watched quietly as they opened the last drawer of the last chest and hauled out bags of gold and silver, sacks of jewelry and all kinds of valuables. And he kept silent.

Perhaps he was glad to be rid of them!

But all at once, when the robbers reached the last hiding place and yanked out a small bag, the last one, the best concealed, he forgot himself, shuddered, his eyes blazed, he reached out his right hand to stop them and tried to scream: "Don't touch that!"

But instead of a scream, a red torrent of steaming blood shot out of his mouth. The knife had done its work. It was his heart's blood, splashing on the bag!

He dropped to the floor and the bandits tore open the sack. This would be the best, the most valuable!

But they were bitterly mistaken. The blood was shed in vain. There was no silver, no gold, no jewelry in the bag. Nothing that was precious or had any value in this world! Just a little soil. From the earth of Palestine, for his grave. And that was what the rich man wanted to save from thieving hands and eyes and splashed with his blood. . . .

The soul grabbed a bloody speck of soil from Palestine and took it to the window in heaven.

The first gift was accepted.

The Second Gift

"Remember," the angel called out as he closed the window behind the soul: "Only two more gifts!"

"God will help!" thought the soul hopefully, and he cheerfully flew back down.

But in the end his optimism waned. Years and years wore on, and he saw nothing of extraordinary beauty. And again he was haunted by the dismal thought:

"The world emerged from God's will like a living source, and keeps running and running in time. And the further it runs, the more dust and earth it takes in, the muddier and murkier it becomes, the fewer presents one can find in it for heaven . . . and the smaller the people grow, the pettier the virtues, the tinier the vices, and the good deeds cannot be seen with the naked eyes! . . .

"If God," he went on to himself, "were to weigh the good and bad deeds of the world, the pointer would barely stir, barely quiver. . . .

"The world cannot go up or down either. . . . It too is a homeless vagabond between radiant heavens and dark abysses . . . and the defender and the accuser would grapple over it forever, the way light and darkness, heat and cold, life and death, grapple on and on. . . .

"The world balances, but it can't move up and it can't move down, and there will always be marriages and divorces, circumcisions and funerals, festivities and mournings . . . and love and hate . . . forever and ever. . . ."

There was sudden blare of trumpets and horns. . . .

He looked down. A German city (of long ago, naturally), slanting roofs edged the square in front of the town hall, the area was filled with people in parti-colored garb, the windows were crowded with heads, people were lying on the roofs, some of them perched astride the wooden beams that stuck out of the walls beneath the roofs, and the balconies were packed. . . .

In front of the town hall stood a table covered with green cloth and lined with golden fringe and tassels. The magistrates were sitting there in velvet garments with golden frogs, and sable hats with white feathers and diamond buttons. Above them, by himself, was the presiding magistrate. A gluttonous eagle fluttered over his head.

Off to the side, a Jewish girl stood all bound up. Not far from her, ten servants held a wild horse. The magistrate rose, turned to the marketplace, and read a verdict from a document:

"This Jewess, this child of Jews, has committed a grave sin, a sin so grave that even God in his vast mercy could not forgive it. . . .

"She stole out of the ghetto and went about our pure streets during our sacred holiday. . . .

"Her shameless eyes sullied our holy procession, our holy images, which we carried through the streets with hymns of praise and a beating of kettledrums.

"Her accursed ears took in the singing of our innocent white-robed children and the beating of our holy drums. And who can tell whether or not the devil, the filthy devil, who assumed the shape of this Jewess, this daughter of an accursed rabbi — who can tell whether or not the devil touched and soiled some purity of ours?

"What did he desire, the devil in that beauteous shape? For I cannot deny it — she *is* beautiful, beautiful as only a devil can make himself — Just look at those eyes radiating insolence under the silken lashes that she lowers so chastely. . . . Look at the alabaster face, which has only gotten paler rather than darker during her long imprisonment! Look at her fingers, her long, slender fingers, transparent in the sunshine.

"And what did he desire, the devil? To tear a soul away from its devotion in our procession. . . . And he succeeded!

"'Look at that beautiful girl!' one of our knights exclaimed, a member of one of our most illustrious families! . . .

"And that was too much! Halberdiers noticed her and seized her. He didn't even resist, that devil! And why? They were pure, absolved of any sin, and so he had no sway over them.

"And this is the judgment for the devil in the shape of the Jewess:

"Her hair, her long diabolical braids, shall be bound to the tail of the wild horse. . . .

"The horse shall gallop away and drag her through the streets like a corpse, the streets that carried her feet against our sacred law.

"Let her blood bespatter and scour the stones that her feet have defiled!"

A wild scream of joy tore from all throats, and when the wave of ferocious shouting had washed by, the condemned woman was asked whether she had any final wishes.

"I do," she replied calmly. "I would like some pins."

"She's crazy with terror!" said the magistrates.

"No," she retorted, cold and placid, "that is my last wish and desire."

They brought her some pins.

"And now," commanded the presiding judge, "tie her to the horse!"

Halberdiers strode over and with trembling hands they tied the long black braids of the rabbi's daughter to the wild horse, which they could barely restrain.

"Make way!" the magistrate shouted to the crowd in the square, and there was an uproar. The people hugged and massed along the house walls, and all of them held up their hands, some clutching a whip, some a rod, others a cloth, all of them ready to egg on the wild horse, their breath bated, their face ablaze, their eyes flashing. And in the turmoil no one noticed the condemned woman bend over quietly and fasten the hem of her dress to her legs, sticking the pins deep, deep into the flesh, so that her body would not be exposed when the horse dragged her through the streets . . .

It was noticed only by the homeless vagabond, the soul . . .

"Release the horse!" came the command of the magistrate. The servants leaped back, and the horse tore forward. And a scream whirled from all the mouths, and there was a whirling and whistling of lashes, rods, and cloths, and the terrified horse dashed across the marketplace through streets and back alleys and out of the town. . . .

And the soul, the homeless vagabond, had already pulled a bleeding pin out of the condemned woman's leg and was flying up to heaven with it.

"Just one more gift," the angel at the window comforted him.

The Third Gift

And down flew the soul again. He needed only one more gift.

And more and more seasons and years wore on, and again he was stricken with melancholy, the world seemed to be getting even smaller, tinier people and tinier actions, both good and evil. . . .

Once, the soul thought: "And if God, praised be His Name, should ever stop and judge the world as it is, all at once, and if there should be a defender on one side, pouring out the bits and specks from a white sack, and an accuser on the other side, pouring out his shreds and pieces — it would take years and years for the sacks to empty. So many trivia, so many!

"But if the sacks were ever empty, what would happen?

"The pointer would stay put in the center!

"With so many trivia, so many trivia, neither side can outbalance the other. And then what! Another tiny feather, a wisp of straw, a speck of chaff, a mote of dust?

"And what would God do? What would His judgment be?

"Back to the primal chaos? No. The sins do not outweigh the virtues.

"Redemption? No again! The virtues do not outweigh the sins.

"Then what?

" 'Keep going,' He would say. 'Keep flying between hell and heaven, love and hatred, tears of pity and smoking blood. . . . between cradles and grave . . . on and on!' "

But the soul was destined for redemption. A roll of drums aroused him from his brooding.

Where was he? When?

He couldn't tell the place or time. . . .

All he could make out was a square in front of a prison. The rays of the sun played and flashed along the iron bars and the tiny windows. They sparkled on the weapons stacked along the wall. The soldiers held — rods in their hands.

They stationed themselves in two long rows with a narrow passage between them. To run someone through the gauntlet.

Who?

A little Jew with a tattered shirt on his scrawny body, a skullcap on his partly shaven head.

Now they led him in.

Why was he being punished? Who could say! A matter of olden times. Perhaps a theft, perhaps a robbery or murder, perhaps he was the victim of a blood libel. Those were olden times!

And the soldiers smiled and thought: Why did they order so many of us out here? He won't even endure half of it!

But now they pushed him into the passageway between the two rows. He walked straight and did not stumble and did not fall. . . . He was lashed and he endured it. . . .

A fury took hold of the soldiers! He was still walking, still walking!

And the rods whistled through the air like demons and swished around his body like snakes. And the blood from the scrawny body splashed and splashed, and didn't stop splashing!

All at once, a soldier struck out too high and lashed the skullcap from the victim's head. He only noticed it after a few steps. He stopped, deliberated, made up his mind, and spun around. He would not go bareheaded. He strode back to the skullcap, bent over, straightened out, turned around, and walked on, placid, bloodstained, but with his skullcap on his head, walked until he dropped.

And when he dropped, the soul flew over and grabbed the skullcap, which had brought the victim so many unnecessary lashes, and he flew up to the window of heaven.

And the third gift was accepted!

And the saints interceded for him. The gates of paradise opened up for the soul after the three gifts!

And the oracle, the "light and truth," said:

"These are really gifts of beauty, extraordinary beauty . . . but rather useless. Not practical, but beautiful — extraordinarily so."

The Miracle on the Sea

TRANSLATED BY JOSEPH LEFTWICH

In a little cottage, half sunk in the mud of a little fishing village on the coast of Holland, there lived a dumb soul, a Jewish fisherman named Satya. He may have been named after some ancestor of his, who had been named Sadyah. But of this he knew nothing; he knew little of anything Jewish.

As far back as was known, from father to son, his family had been fishermen, had spent their days and nights upon the sea, and had lived, one isolated Jewish family, among non-Jews. What could he have known of Jewishness?

Satya caught fish; his wife repaired his nets and looked after the house; the children played in the sand and searched for shells. And when Satya went fishing, and a storm arose, and the lives of those that were on the seas were in peril, neither Satya in his boat, nor his wife and children at home, could say even *"Sh'ma Yisrael!"* Satya gazed silently up to heaven, his wife tore her hair and looked angrily at the black skies, and the children threw themselves upon the sand, and like all the other children, they cried aloud: "Sancta Maria! Sancta Maria!"

And how should they have known better? The nearest Jewish community was far away, in the town; it was impossible to go there often on foot, and the poverty-stricken family, who had hardly enough to eat, could not afford to spend money in traveling. Besides, the sea would not let them go.

Satya's father, Satya's grandfather, and Satya's great-grandfather had all died at sea; but the sea has a wonderful power of attraction. It is man's greatest enemy, very often a false enemy, and yet men love the sea, they are drawn to it as by magic. It is impossible to tear ourselves away from the sea; it fascinates us, and we are content to live upon it, we are content to die in it.

One Jewish observance this fisher family retained — Yom Kippur. On the day before, they all rose very early, and taking with them the largest fish of the previous day's catch, the whole family walked to the town. There the fish was handed to the shoykhet, in whose house they stayed over the fast. All day they sat in the synagogue, listening to the singing of the choir, to the fumbling of the organ, and to the cantor's recital of the Hebrew prayers. They did not understand one word of it; they just looked at the Ark of the Law, and they watched the cantor in his gold-embroidered cap. When the gold-embroidered cap stood up, they also stood up, and when the gold-embroidered cap sat down, they also sat down. Sometimes Satya fell asleep, and then someone sitting near him nudged him till he awoke.

And this was the whole of Satya's Yom Kippur. That it was the Great Judgment Day, the Great Day of Atonement, that even the fishes trembled in the waters, of all that took place in Heaven on this dread day, Satya knew nothing. He knew that it was a custom to go to synagogue on Yom Kippur, to listen to the choir and to the organ, without tasting food all day; and after "Ne'ilah" (he did not even know that it was called "Ne'ileh"), he knew that he had to go to the shoykhet's house for supper.

Probably the shoykhet himself knew little more. Holland! . . . Immediately after supper, Satya and his wife and the children got up, and they said good-bye to the shoykhet and his wife, and they walked all through the night, back to the sea.

Not "home"; back to the sea! They consistently refused to stay overnight. "Think," argued the shoykhet and his wife, "you have not even seen the town." Satya's face clouded. He spoke little; the sea had taught him silence. He hated the town: it was crowded, there was no air in it, and no heaven, except a little strip of it that showed between the houses. And he was accustomed to the free life of the sea, where there is a vast expanse of sky, and where it is possible for a man to breathe. "But," people argued with him, "the sea is your enemy, it is your death." "A kindly death," he replied. Satya wanted to die as his father and his grandfather had died, in full health, upon the sea; he did not want to lie on a bed, and suffer, God knows how long, and then be buried in the hard earth — Ugh! He felt cold all over, when he thought of such a burial.

So they walked all through the night, back to the sea.

And when the dawn broke, and they saw the golden shimmer of the sandheaps, and the reflection of the rising sun in the waters of the sea, they were overwhelmed with joy, and they clasped their hands. A bridegroom could not greet his bride more joyfully.

And so it went on from year to year . . . custom remained custom. And the custom is a mix-up of a fast, a choir, and an organ, together with a huge fish, and a supper after "Ne'ileh" in the shoykhet's house, the parting and the good wishes, all rolled into one. And this mix-up, all of it together, is the single thread which binds Satya to all-Israel.

And it came to pass about dawn, when the east was beginning to redden, that the sea awoke silently, breathing softly, so that one could scarcely hear its murmuring, and it stretched itself lazily, half dreamily, and then it drew back. . . . Somewhere white wings flapped in the air, a bird cried out, and again it was still. Silent shapes flew across the sea, golden shadows gilded over the yellow sands. The fishermen's huts on the shore are shut. One door opens, and Satya comes out.

It is the day before Yom Kippur. Satya's face is earnest and composed, and his eyes are gleaming. He is going to perform a holy duty, he is going out to find a fish for Yom Kippur. He takes hold of the chain by which his boat is fastened to the shore, and the chain falls and clangs. The fishermen thrust their heads through the little windows of their homes, and they warn Satya not to go. Don't! . . .

Quietly, calmly, the sea spreads far and wide, and is lost in the fresh, laughing morning skies. There is scarce a breath of air, there is not a ripple upon the surface, save near the shore; and there, even as in the face of a good, kindhearted mother, silvery dimpled smiles are dancing among the ripples. And the sea murmurs softly, and it tells a wonderful story to the scattered rocks, all overgrown with great weeds and water plants that look like hair growing upon their heads. And the sea strokes their hair, smilingly, playfully. . . . But the fishermen know the sea well, and they will not trust it. And they warn Satya not to venture out upon it. Don't! . . . The sea rocks gently, and so it will continue to rock, faster and faster, and then its playfulness will fall away, and it will change to earnest, and the soft murmurings will grow into clamorings and thunder, and the ripples will rise up as waves, and will swallow boats and ships, even as the Leviathan swallows little fishes.

Don't! . . .

A barefooted old fisherman, with a head of uncovered, shaggy gray hair, with a face wrinkled like the sea, but without its false sweet smile, approaches Satya, and taking him by the arm, he points up at the sky: "Look!" And upon the edge of the horizon, he shows him a tiny speck, which only a fisherman's eye can discern. "That grows into a cloud," he remarks quietly. "I shall be back long before then," answers Satya, "I am going to catch only one fish." The old man's face grows hard and grave. "You have a wife and children, Satya." "And a God in Heaven," Satya answers, pushing off his boat and jumping into it. Lightly as a feather Satya's boat travels across the sea, and the ripples rock it, murmuring softly, lovingly, and enfold it with their most beautiful froth pearls. And the old fisherman stands on the shore, and mutters: "Sancta Maria! Sancta Maria!"

The boat glides easily across the sea. Satya throws his net skillfully, and at once it grows heavy. Exerting all his strength, Satya slowly raises the net, and it is full of weeds and starfish . . . there is not even a single small fish entangled in the meshes. The old fisherman upon the shore has lost sight of the boat. And Satya pulls up his net for the third and the fourth time; it is not easy to pull the net up, for it is heavy, and it is filled with seaweeds, and with all manner of water plants; but there is not a single fish among it all. The sea is now rocking more violently. The sun is high in the heavens, but it is pale, moist and weeping. And the black speck upon the edge of the horizon spreads out like a long snake, and it grows darker and darker, and it moves rapidly toward the sun.

It is noon, and Satya is still on the sea, searching for his fish.

"God does not wish me to observe the custom this year," he mutters sadly, and his heart grows heavy. "I must have sinned against Him, and He will not accept my offering." He grips his oars and turns the boat toward home; but immediately the spray dashes into his face, and, looking around, he sees a huge, marvelous golden fish, sporting quite close to him, playfully throwing the water up with its tail. "There!" shouts Satya excitedly, "there is my fish!" Surely God had answered him out of his anguish of heart, out of his longing, that he might fulfill his holy duty. And he is off, after that fish! The sea grows agitated and enraged; the waves rise higher and higher. The sun is now almost hidden by clouds, but its rays force themselves through and beat down upon Satya. The fish is breasting the waves, and Satya's boat flies after it, quickly. Suddenly the fish is lost to sight; a wave has rolled up between them, and the boat is being tossed high upon the crest of a huge wave, whipped up and swollen by the storm. "I am befooled; my eyes are deceiving me," Satya mutters to himself, and he is about to turn the boat toward home when suddenly the wave subsides as if it had been sucked into the sea, the fish comes up, and looks at him imploringly with its great eyes, as if appealing to be taken . . . so that Satya might fulfill in him his holy duty. Satya turns, and immediately the fish has vanished; a huge wave rolls once more between them, and the sea begins its song again. It is no soft, pleasing melody the sea is singing; it is an angry outburst against the rash human who has dared it in its wrath. As if afraid of its anger, the sun hides behind a mass of cloud, and the wind breaks loose with a savage roar. It rages wildly, and it swirls and beats upon the sea, but the sea becomes more angry, and it shouts and thunders as if a thousand drums were being beaten within its bosom.

Satya determines to return, and he gathers his nets into the boat. He grips his oars and he rows back with all his strength. The veins swell and stand out upon his hands, as if about to burst. Huge waves, high as mountains, toss his boat up and down like an empty nutshell; the heavens are black, the sea rages tempestuously, and Satya rows back toward his home, his heart beating like the wild flood about him. Suddenly there is something drifting alongside his boat; it is a human form — the body of a woman, drowned or drowning. Her black raven hair is spread out like a net before her. His wife's hair is black like that! And her hands are white, just like the hands of his wife! And a voice calls "Help!" It is she, the mother of his children. She must have followed him, and she is drowning, she is calling for help! Satya turns his boat toward her, but the sea thrusts him back, huge waves roll over her, and the storm shouts and shrieks. And above it all, he hears her voice, "Help, Satya! Help!" Satya exerts all his strength in one mighty effort. He is near her, her hair has already gone under, and her form is sinking; with the oars he pulls her toward him, and he is reaching over to pull her into the boat when suddenly a huge wave pushes him away, and the form has disappeared.

"An illusion!" he mutters, remembering his experience with the marvelous golden fish. He looks toward the shore and he sees the lights gleaming through the windows of the little fisher huts.

"Yom Kippur!" he cries, and drops his oars.

"Do with me what you will!" he calls up into heaven, "I will not row on Yom Kippur!" The wind rages madly, the waves toss his boat up and down, and Satya is sitting quietly, his hands resting on his knees; his eyes are wide open, and he looks calmly up to the frowning heavens, then down to the boiling, seething seas. "Do with me what you will!" he repeats aloud. "Your will be done, Oh God!" He seems to hear the choir, accompanied by the organ, singing in the synagogue, and he joins in — this dumb, silent soul, who has only this solemn melody with which to communicate with his God! And as he sings, the heavens grow blacker and blacker, the waves rise higher and higher, the storm rages more fiercely, and his boat is tossed from one mountain wave to another. One wave carries away his oars, another comes up from behind and follows him with mouth gaping, ready to swallow him. The wind shrieks like a thousand wolves, and amid all this clamor, Satya calmly sings *"Mi Yenuach, Umi Yenui,"* and the choir of the synagogue, accompanied by the organ, is singing with him. The waves break against his boat, and Satya determines that he will die like this, singing.

Suddenly his boat is overturned; but Satya is not yet destined to die. Two forms, nebulous as if woven out of the mist, are walking barefoot on the sea; their hair streams behind them, and their eyes gleam like fire. And as Satya's boat is overturned, they hold him up, between them, and they walk with him across the waves, as over mountains, through storm and tumult. Satya tries to speak to them, but they stop him, saying: "Sing, Satya! Sing! Your song will calm the fury of the seas!"

✧ ✧ ✧

And turning around, Satya sees his boat following them and the golden fish in the meshes of the net. They left him on the shore, and when he came home, he found the shoykhet and his wife in his hut. There had been a fire in the town, so they had come to him, to be his guests over the fast.

And the golden fish was killed, and custom remained custom.

If Mendele gave birth to modern Yiddish literature and Peretz refined it, Sholom
Aleichem taught it to sing. The third of the
trio of *Di klasikers,* the classic Yiddish writers,
he was a virtuoso of linguistic subtlety, a
master of the comic sketch. But his warm and
breezy surface was only the top layer of a
deep, dark pool. Even as he described a world
that had nourished a people, he knew that it
was breaking apart. The narrative would
become the talisman of memory.

Like Mendele, Sholom Aleichem was a pen name. Sholom Rabinovitch, an upper-middle-class businessman who made his living on the Kiev and Odessa stock markets, did not want to be identified with the lowbrow Yiddish stories published in cheap pamphlets and newspapers. In time, however, his enormous popularity helped boost the status of his language and its literature.

Rabinovitch was born in 1859 in a small town in what is today Ukraine. His family was respected and well-to-do. Although they were traditional Jews, the boy's religious education was supplanted by learning Russian.

But his life came apart when he was thirteen: His father lost all his money and his mother died. As a youth he held a variety of jobs in a succession of towns, and continued to experience life's extremes. He married, for love, the daughter of a wealthy Jew who died soon after the wedding. The young couple inherited his fortune, but lost it in a stock-market crash.

Rabinovitch continued to manage money. He also wrote occasional stories in Hebrew. But, as his daughter Marie Waife Goldberg later described it, "He was struck by the realization that Hebrew, with its difficult vocabulary, its flowery style, and the scholarship needed for its mastery, was serving only the special few. . . . Besides, a Jewish author *thought* in Yiddish even if he wrote in Hebrew, so why not write directly in the language of his thinking?"

Rabinovitch published his first Yiddish story in 1883. He took a pseudonym (*Sholom aleichem* is a standard Yiddish greeting that comes from the Hebrew and means, literally, "Peace, friend") and began his Yiddish career to immediate acclaim. Like Mendele, the man became twined with his persona. But Sholom Aleichem was a more sophisticated writer who could deftly strike all of the notes on the human scale.

He lectured extensively, traveling as far as the United States. As his popularity grew and he came to understand the importance of Yiddish literature to the Jewish people, he championed the cause of the language itself, and underwrote a Yiddish periodical and publishing a book of Yiddish folk songs. He wrote prodigiously, creating a cast of characters and a group of fictional locations to which he returned over the decades of his prolific career.

His stories were translated into other European languages. When he was called the Jewish Mark Twain, the American author had the wit to respond that *he* was only the American Sholom Aleichem. And Aleichem/Rabinovitch was eventually able, with great effort, to support his family on his literary income.

When pogroms swept across Russia in 1905, the Rabinovitch family fled to Western Europe, but in 1908 the beloved author made a triumphal return. This period was short lived, however, as his health began to fail. Tuberculosis and diabetes drove him and his family to a succession of European spas and sanatoriums. When World War I broke out, they found themselves in Germany. As Russian citizens they were deported, and sought temporary refuge in Denmark. But Rabinovitch, now in precarious financial straits as well as in poor health, was compelled to move again. This time his American fans rallied, advancing first-class passage to the United States for the entire family. In 1915, Rabinovitch, his wife, and two of his children arrived in New York. (Unfortunately, Rabinovitch's son suffered from tuberculosis. His case was more advanced than his father's, and the family was forced to leave him in Denmark, where he later died.)

As war raged in Europe, Rabinovitch settled down in the Bronx and drove himself to write. In his stories, he returned to his fictional hometown only to find it rent by schism and despair. He revised one of his tales of Tevye the Dairyman, from a series he had worked on for two decades. An earlier version of this particular tale showed Tevye deflecting a crowd of peasants bent on violence. But now, the archetypal shtetl-dweller was cast out of his home, his refuge gone. It was the Tevye stories that formed the basis of the play and movie *Fiddler on the Roof.*

Both success and tragedy were constants in Rabinovitch's life. He was welcomed in the United States even as war destroyed the communities he had known in Europe. A new story was translated and serialized in American newspapers, reaching five million English-speaking homes. He turned out plays and an autobiography. But work and will could not save him.

Rabinovitch died in 1916, a year and a half after arriving in America. His body was prepared by fellow immigrants from Pereyeslav, his home shtetl. His will, in which he asked to be buried among the poor and common folk, was entered into the U.S. Congressional Record. He directed that these words, in Yiddish, be written on his grave:

> Here lies an ordinary Jew
> Who wrote in Yiddish, it is true;
> And for wives, and plain folk rather,
> He was a humorist, an author
> Poking fun at all and sundry;
> At the world he thumbs his nose.
> The world went on swimmingly
> While he, alas, took all the blows
> And at the time his public rose
> Laughing, clapping, and making merry
> He would suffer, only God knows,
> Secretly — so none was wary.

A Yom Kippur Scandal

TRANSLATED BY JULIUS AND FRANCES BUTWIN

"That's nothing!" called out the man with round eyes, like an ox, who had been sitting all this time in a corner by the window, smoking and listening to our stories of thefts, robberies, and expropriations. "I'll tell you a story of a theft that took place in our town, in the synagogue itself, and on Yom Kippur at that! It is worth listening to.

"Our town, Kasrilevka — that's where I'm from, you know — is a small town, and a poor one. There is no thievery there. No one steals anything for the simple reason that there is nobody to steal from and nothing worth stealing. And besides, a Jew is not a thief by nature. That is, he may be a thief, but not the sort who will climb through a window or attack you with a knife. He will divert, pervert, subvert, and contravert as a matter of course; but he won't pull anything out of your pocket. He won't be caught like a common thief and led through the streets with a yellow placard on his back. Imagine, then, a theft taking place in Kasrilevka, and such a theft at that. Eighteen hundred rubles at one crack.

"Here is how it happened. One Yom Kippur eve, just before the evening services, a stranger arrived in our town, a salesman of some sort from Lithuania. He left his bag at an inn, and went forth immediately to look for a place of worship, and he came upon the old synagogue. Coming in just before the service began, he found the trustees around the collection plates. 'Sholom aleichem,' said he. 'Aleichem sholom,' they answered. 'Where does our guest hail from?' 'From Lithuania.' 'And your name?' 'Even your grandmother wouldn't know if I told her.' 'But you have come to our synagogue!' 'Where else should I go?' 'Then you want to pray here?' 'Can I help myself? What

77

else can I do?' 'Then put something in the plate.' 'What did you think? That I was not going to pay?'

"To make a long story short, our guest took out three silver rubles and put them in the plate. Then he put a ruble in the cantor's plate, one in the rabbi's, gave one for the cheder, threw a half into the charity box, and then began to divide money among the poor who flocked to the door. And in our town we have so many poor people that if you really wanted to start giving, you could divide Rothschild's fortune among them.

"Impressed by his generosity, the men quickly found a place for him along the east wall. Where did they find room for him when all the places along the wall were occupied? Don't ask. Have you ever been at a celebration — a wedding or circumcision — when all the guests are already seated at the table, and suddenly there is a commotion outside — the rich uncle has arrived? What do you do? You push and shove and squeeze until a place is made for the rich relative. Squeezing is a Jewish custom. If no one squeezes us, we squeeze each other."

The man with the eyes that bulged like an ox's paused, looked at the crowd to see what effect his wit had on us, and went on.

"So our guest went up to his place of honor and called to the shammes to bring him a praying stand. He put on his tallith and started to pray. He prayed and he prayed, standing on his feet all the time. He never sat down or left his place all evening long or all the next day. To fast all day standing on one's feet, without ever sitting down — that only a Litvak can do!

"But when it was all over, when the final blast of the shofar had died down, the Day of Atonement had ended, and Chaim the *melamed,* who had led the evening prayers after Yom Kippur from time immemorial, had cleared his throat, and in his tremulous voice had already begun — 'Ma-a-riv a-ro-vim . . .' suddenly screams were heard. 'Help! Help! Help!' We looked around: the stranger was stretched out on the floor in a dead faint. We poured water on him, revived him, but he fainted again. What was the trouble? Plenty! This Litvak tells us that he had brought with him to Kasrilevka eighteen hundred rubles. To leave that much at the inn — think of it, eighteen hundred rubles — he had been afraid. Whom could he trust with such a sum of money in a strange town? And yet, to keep it in his pocket on Yom Kippur was not exactly proper either. So at last this plan had occurred to him: he had taken the money to the synagogue and slipped it into the praying stand. Only a Litvak could do a thing like that! . . . Now do you see why he had not stepped away from the praying stand for a single minute? And yet during one of the many prayers when we all turn our face to the wall, someone must have stolen the money. . . .

"Well, the poor man wept, tore his hair, wrung his hands. What would he do with the money gone? It was not his own money, he said. He was only a clerk. The money was his employer's. He himself was a poor man, with a houseful of children. There was nothing for him to do now but go out and drown himself, or hang himself right here in front of everybody.

"Hearing these words, the crowd stood petrified, forgetting that they had all been fasting since the night before and it was time to go home and eat. It was a disgrace before a stranger, a shame and a scandal in our own eyes. A theft like that — eighteen hundred rubles! And where? In the Holy of Holies, in the old synagogue of Kasrilevka. And on what day? On the holiest day of the year, on Yom Kippur! Such a thing had never been heard of before.

"'Shammes, lock the door!' ordered our rabbi. We have our own rabbi in Kasrilevka, Reb Yozifel, a true man of God, a holy man. Not too sharp-witted, perhaps, but a good man, a man with no bitterness in him. Sometimes he gets ideas that you would not hit upon if you had eighteen heads on your shoulders. . . . When the door was locked, Reb Yozifel turned to the congregation, his face pale as death and his hands trembling, his eyes burning with a strange fire.

"He said, 'Listen to me, my friends, this is an ugly thing, a thing unheard of since the world was created — that here in Kasrilevka there should be a sinner, a renegade to his people, who would have the audacity to take from a stranger, a poor man with a family, a fortune like this. And on what day? On the holiest day of the year, on Yom Kippur, and perhaps at the last, most solemn moment — just before the shofar was blown! Such a thing has never happened anywhere. I cannot believe it is possible. It simply cannot be. But perhaps — who knows? Man is greedy, and the temptation — especially with a sum like this, eighteen hundred rubles, God forbid — is great enough. So if one of us was tempted, if he were fated to commit this evil on a day like this, we must probe the matter thoroughly, strike at the root of this whole affair. Heaven and earth have sworn that the truth must always rise as oil upon the waters. Therefore, my friends, let us search each other now, go through each other's garments, shake out our pockets — all of us from the oldest householder to the shammes, not leaving anyone out. Start with me. Search my pockets first.'

"Thus spoke Reb Yozifel, and he was the first to unbind his gabardine and turn his pockets inside out. And following his example all of the men loosened their girdles and showed the linings of their pockets, too. They searched each other, they felt and shook one another, until they came to Lazer Yossel, who turned all colors and began to argue that, in the first place, the stranger was a swindler; that his story was the pure fabrication of a Litvak. No one had stolen any money from him. Couldn't they see that it was all a falsehood and a lie?

"The congregation began to clamor and shout. What did he mean by this? All the important men had allowed themselves to be searched, so why should Lazer Yossel escape? There are no privileged characters here. 'Search him! Search him!' the crowd roared.

"Lazer Yossel saw that it was hopeless, and began to plead for mercy with tears in his eyes. He begged them not to search him. He swore by all that was holy that he was as innocent in this as he would want to be of any wrongdoing as long as he lived. Then why didn't he want to be searched? It was a disgrace to him, he said. He begged them to have pity on his youth, not to bring this disgrace down on him. 'Do anything you wish with me,' he said, 'but don't touch my pockets.' How do you like that? Do you suppose we listened to him?

"But wait . . . I forgot to tell you who this Lazer Yossel was. He was not a Kasrilevkite himself. He came from the Devil knows where, at the time of his marriage, to live with his wife's parents. The rich man of our town had dug him up somewhere for his daughter, boasted that he had found a rare nugget, a fitting match for a daughter like his. He knew a thousand pages of Talmud by heart, and all of the Bible. He was a master of Hebrew, arithmetic, bookkeeping, algebra, penmanship — in short, everything you could think of. When he arrived in Kasrilevka — this jewel of a young man — everyone came out to gaze at him. What sort of bargain had the rich man picked out? Well, to look at him you could tell nothing. He was a young man, something in trousers. Not bad looking, but with a nose a trifle too long, eyes that burned like two coals, and a sharp tongue. Our leading citizens began to work on him: tried him out on a page of *Gemara,* a chapter from the Scriptures, a bit of *Rambam,* this, that, and the other. He was perfect in everything, the dog! Whenever you went after him, he was at home. Reb Yozifel himself said that he could have been a rabbi in any Jewish congregation. As for world affairs, there is nothing to talk about. We have an authority on such things in our town, Zaidel Reb Shaye's, but he could not hold a candle to Lazer Yossel. And when it came to chess — there was no one like him in all the world! Talk about versatile people. . . . Naturally the whole town envied the rich man his find, but some of them felt he was a little too good to be true. He was too clever (and too much of anything is bad!). For a man of his station he was too free and easy, a hail-fellow-well-met, too familiar with the young folk — boys, girls, and maybe even loose women. There were rumors. . . . At the same time he went around alone too much, deep in thought. At the synagogue he came in last, put on his tallith, and with his skullcap on askew, thumbed aimlessly through his prayerbook without ever following the services. No one ever saw him doing anything exactly wrong, and yet people murmured that he was not a God-fearing man. Apparently a man cannot be perfect . . .

"And so, when his turn came to be searched and he refused to let them do it, that was all the proof most of the men needed that he was the one who had taken the money. He begged them to let him swear any oath they wished, begged them to chop him, roast him, cut him up — do anything but shake his pockets out. At this point even our rabbi, Reb Yozifel, although he was a man we had never seen angry, lost his temper and started to shout.

"'You!' he cried. 'You thus-and-thus! Do you know what you deserve? You see what all these men have endured. They were able to forget the disgrace and allowed themselves to be searched; but you want to be the only exception! God in heaven! Either confess and hand over the money, or let us see for ourselves what is in your pockets. You are trifling now with the entire Jewish community. Do you know what they can do to you?'

"To make a long story short, the men took hold of this young upstart, and threw him down on the floor with force, and began to search him all over, shake out every one of his pockets. And finally they shook out . . . Well, guess what! A couple of well-gnawed chicken bones and a few dozen plum pits still moist from chewing. You can imagine what an impression this made — to discover food in the pockets of our prodigy on this holiest of fast days. Can you imagine the look on the young man's face, and on his father-in-law's? And on that of our poor rabbi?

"Poor Reb Yozifel! He turned away in shame. He could look no one in the face. On Yom Kippur, and in his synagogue . . . As for the rest of us, hungry as we were, we could not stop talking about it all the way home. We rolled with laughter in the streets. Only Reb Yozifel walked home alone, his head bowed, full of grief, unable to look anyone in the eyes, as though the bones had been shaken out of his own pockets."

The story was apparently over. Unconcerned, the man with the round eyes of an ox turned back to the window and resumed smoking.

"Well," we all asked in one voice, "and what about the money?"

"What money?" asked the man innocently, watching the smoke he had exhaled.

"What do you mean — what money? The eighteen hundred rubles!"

"Oh," he drawled. "The eighteen hundred. They were gone."

"Gone?"

"Gone forever."

Eternal Life

TRANSLATED BY JULIUS AND FRANCES BUTWIN

If you are willing to listen, I shall tell you the story of how I once took a burden upon myself, a burden which almost, almost ruined my life for me. And why do you think I did it? Simply because I was an inexperienced young man and none too shrewd. So far as that goes, I may be far from clever now, too, because if I were clever, I might have had a little money by now. How does the saying go? If you have money, you are not only clever, but handsome too, and can sing like a nightingale!

Well, there I was, a young man living with my father- and mother-in-law, as was the custom with young married couples in those days. And, as was also the custom in those days, I sat in the synagogue all day studying the Torah. Now and then I glanced into secular books too, but that had to be done on the sly so my father- and mother-in-law should not find out; not so much my father-in-law as my mother-in-law, a woman who was the real head of the family. You can really say she wore the pants. She managed all their affairs herself, picked out the husbands for her daughters herself, and herself arranged the entire match. It was she who had picked me out too, she who examined me in the Torah, she who brought me to Zvohil from Rademishli. I am from Rademishli, you know — that's where I was born. You must have heard of the town; it was recently in the papers.

So I lived in Zvohil with my mother-in-law, struggled over the Rambam's Guide to the Perplexed, never stepping out of the house, you might say, till the time came when I had to register for military service. Then, as the custom was, I had to bestir myself, go back to Rademishli, straighten out my papers, see what exemption I could claim, and arrange for a passport, which I would need if I ever left the district.

That, you could say, was my first venture into the outside world. All by myself, to prove that I was now a responsible person, I went forth into the marketplace and hired a sleigh. God sent me a bargain. I found a peasant who was going back to Rademishli with a freshly painted, broad-backed sleigh with wings at the sides like an eagle. But I had failed to pay attention to the fact that the horse was a white one, and a white horse, my mother-in-law said, was bad luck. "I hope I'm lying," she said, "but this trip will be an unlucky one." "Bite your tongue," burst out my father-in-law, and at once was sorry, because he had to take his punishment right on the spot. But to me he whispered, "Women's nonsense," and I began to pack up for the trip: my *tallis* and *tfiln,* some freshly baked rolls, a few rubles for expenses, and three pillows — a pillow to sit on, a pillow to lean against, and a pillow to keep my feet warm. And I was ready to go.

So I said good-bye to everybody and started on my way to Rademishli. It was late in winter; the hard-packed snow made a perfect road for the sleigh. The horse, though a white one, went as smoothly as a breeze, and my driver turned out to be one of those silent fellows who answers everything either "Uh-huh," meaning "yes," or "Uh-uh" for "no." That's all. You couldn't get another word out of him.

I had left home right after dinner and made myself as comfortable as I could, with a pillow under me, a pillow at my back, and one at my feet. The horse pranced, the driver cluck-clucked, the sleigh slid along, the wind blew, and snowflakes drifted through the air like feathers and covered the wide expanse around us. My heart felt light, my spirits free. After all, it was my first trip alone into God's world. I was all alone, a free man, my own master! I leaned back and spread myself out in the sleigh like a lord. But in winter, no matter how warmly you are dressed, when the frost goes through you, you feel like stopping somewhere to warm yourself and catch your breath before going on again. And I began to dream of a warm inn, a boiling samovar, and a fresh pot roast with hot gravy. These dreams made me crave for food. I actually became hungry. I began to ask the driver about an inn, asked if the next one was far away. He answered, "Uh-uh," meaning "no." I asked if it was close, and he answered, "Uh-huh," meaning "yes." "How close?" I asked. But that he would not answer, no matter how hard I tried to make him.

I imagined what it would have been like if this were a Jew driving the sleigh. He would have told me not only where the inn was, but who ran it, what his name was, how many children he had, how much rent he paid, and what he got out of it, how long he had been there, who had been there before him — in short, everything. We are a strange people, we Jews.

But there I was, dreaming of a warm inn, seeing a hot samovar in front of me, and other good things like that; till God took pity on me, the driver clucked to the horse, turned the sleigh a little aside, and there appeared before us a small gray hut covered with snow, a country inn standing alone in the wide, snow-covered field, like a forsaken, forgotten tombstone.

Driving up to the inn with a flourish, the driver took the horse and sleigh into the barn and I went straight toward the inn itself, opened the door, and stopped dead. Here is what I saw. On the floor in the middle of the room lay a corpse covered with black, with two copper candlesticks holding small candles at its head. All around the body sat small children in ragged clothes beating their heads with their fists and screaming and wailing, "Mo-ther! Mother!" And a tall, thin man with long, thin legs, dressed in a torn summer coat entirely out of season, marched up and down the room with long strides, wringing his hands and saying to himself, "What shall I do? What shall I do? I don't know what to do!"

I understood right away what a happy scene I had come upon. My first thought was to run away. I turned to leave, but the door was slammed shut behind me and my feet felt rooted to the ground. I could not move from the spot. Seeing a stranger, the tall man with the long legs ran up to me, stretched out both arms like a man seeking help.

"What do you think of my misfortune?" he asked, pointing to the weeping children. "Poor little things . . . their mother just died. What shall I do? What shall I do? I don't know what to do!"

"Blessed is He who gives, and He who takes," I said, and started to comfort him with the words one uses on such occasions. But he interrupted me.

"She was as good as dead for the past year, poor thing. It was consumption. She begged for death to come. And now she's dead and here we are, stuck in this forsaken spot. What can I do? Go to the village to find a wagon to take her to town? How can I leave the children here alone in the middle of this field, with night coming on? God in heaven, what shall I do? What shall I do? I don't know what to begin to do!"

With these words the man began to weep, strangely, without tears, as though he were laughing, and a queer sound came from his lips, like a cough. All my strength left me. Who could think of hunger now? Who remembered the cold?

I forgot everything and said to him, "I am driving from Zvohil to Rademishli with a very fine sleigh. If the town you speak of is not very far from here I can let you take the sleigh and I'll wait here. If it won't take too long, that is."

"Long may you live!" he cried. "For this good deed you'll earn eternal life! As I am a Jew, eternal life!" he exclaimed, and threw his arms around me. "The town is not far away, only four or five *versts*. It will take no more than an hour and I'll send the sleigh right back. You are earning eternal life, I tell you! Eternal life! Children, get up from the ground and thank this young man. Kiss his hands and his feet! He is letting me use his sleigh to take your mother to the burial ground. Eternal life! As sure as I'm a Jew, eternal life!"

This news did not exactly cheer them. When they heard their father talk about taking their mother away they threw themselves around her again and began to weep louder than ever. And yet it was good news that a man had been found to do them this kindness. God himself had sent him there. They looked at me as at a redeemer, something like Elijah, and I must tell you the plain truth: I began to see myself as an extraordinary being. Suddenly in my own eyes I grew in stature and became what the world calls a hero. I was ready to lift mountains, turn worlds upside down. There was nothing that seemed too difficult for me, and these words tore themselves out of my lips:

"I'll tell you what. I'll take her there myself, that is, my driver and I. I'll save you the trouble of going and leaving the children behind."

The more I talked the more the little children wept, wept and looked up at me as at an angel from heaven, and I grew in my own eyes taller and taller, till I almost reached the sky. For the moment I forgot I had always been afraid to touch a dead body, and with my own hands helped to carry the woman out and lift her into the sleigh. I had to promise the driver another half-ruble, and a drink of whiskey on the spot. At first he scratched the back of his neck and mumbled something in his nose. But after the third drink he softened up and we started on our way, all three of us, the driver and I and the innkeeper's wife, Chava Nechama. That was her name, Chava Nechama, daughter of Raphael Michel. I remember it as if it had been this morning, because all along the way I kept repeating to myself the name that her husband had repeated to me several times. For when the time came to bury her with the proper ceremony, her full name would have to be given. So all the way I repeated to myself, "Chava Nechama, daughter of Raphael Michel. Chava Nechama, daughter of Raphael Michel. Chava Nechama, daughter of Raphael Michel." But while I kept repeating the woman's name, the husband's name escaped me completely. He had told me his name too and assured me that when I came to the town and mentioned the name, the corpse would be taken from me at once and I would be able to go on my way. He was well known there, he said. Year after year he came there for the holidays, contributed money for the synagogue, for the bath house, and everywhere he paid well. He told me more, filled my head with instructions, where I should go, what I should say and do, and every bit of it flew out of my head. You'd think that at least a word of it would have remained. But it didn't. Not a word.

All my thoughts revolved about one thing only, here I was, carrying a dead woman. That alone was enough to make me forget everything, even my own name; for from early childhood I had been mortally afraid of dead bodies. You'd have to pay me a fortune to make me stay alone with a corpse. And now it seemed to me that the glazed, half-open eyes stared at me and the dead, sealed lips would open any minute and a strange voice would be heard as though from a sepulchre, a voice so terrible that merely thinking of it almost threw me into a faint. It is not for nothing that such stories are told of the dead, of people who have fainted out of mere fright, and lost their minds or their powers of speech.

So we rode along, the three of us. I had given the dead woman one of my pillows and had placed her crossways in the sleigh, right at my feet. In order to keep myself from thinking melancholy thoughts I turned away from the body, began to watch the sky and softly to repeat to myself, "Chava Nechama, daughter of Raphael Michel. Chava Nechama, daughter of Raphael Michel," until the name became jumbled in my mind and I found myself saying, "Chava Raphael, daughter of Nechama Michel," and, "Raphael Michel, daughter of Chava Nechama."

I had not been aware that it was getting darker and darker. The wind was blowing stronger all the time and the snow continued to fall until it was so deep that we could not find the road. The sleigh went hither and yon, without direction, and the driver began to grumble at first softly, then louder and more insistently, and I could swear that he was blessing me with a threefold blessing. I asked him, "What is the matter with you?" He spat into the snow and turned upon me with such murderous anger that I shrank back. "Look what you've done!" he cried. "You've been the ruination of me and my horse!" Because of this, because we had taken a dead woman into the sleigh, the horse had strayed from the road, and here we were wandering, and God alone knew how long we would keep on wandering. For night was almost here, and then we would really be lost.

At this good news I was ready to go back to the inn, unload our baggage, forget eternal life. But it was too late, said the driver. We could neither go ahead nor turn back. We were wandering in the middle of the field, the devil alone knew where. The road was snowed under, the sky was black. It was late. The horse was dead tired. May a bad end come to that innkeeper and all the innkeepers of the world! Why hadn't he broken a leg before he had stopped at the inn? Why hadn't he choked on the first glass of whiskey before he had let himself be talked into this folly, and for a miserable half-ruble perish here in the wilderness, together with his poor little horse. As for himself, it didn't matter so much. Maybe it was fated that he should come to a bad end, and at this spot. But the poor little horse, what had he done? An innocent animal, to be sacrificed like that?

I could swear that there were tears in his voice. And to make him feel better I told him that I would give him another half-ruble and two more glasses of whiskey. At this he became furious and told me plainly that if I didn't keep my mouth shut he would throw our cargo out of the sleigh altogether. And I thought to myself: what would I do if he threw the corpse and me out into the snow? Who knew what a man like that could do when he lost his temper? I had better be quiet, sit in the sleigh buried in pillows and try to keep from falling asleep, because in the first place, how could a person fall asleep with a dead body in front of him? And in the second place, I had heard that in wintertime you mustn't fall asleep outside, because if you did you might fall asleep forever.

But in spite of myself my eyes kept shutting. I would have given anything at that moment for a short nap. And I kept rubbing at my eyes but my eyes would not obey. They kept shutting slowly and opening and shutting again. And the sleigh slid over the soft deep white snow and a strange sweet numbness poured through my limbs and I felt an extraordinary calm descend on me. And I wished that this sweet numbness and calm would last and last. I wished it would last forever. But an unknown force, I don't know where it came from, stood by and prodded me. "Do not sleep. Do not fall asleep." With a great effort I tore my eyes open and the numbness resolved itself into a chill that went through my bones and the calm turned to fear and shrinking and melancholy — may the Lord have mercy on me. I imagined that my corpse was stirring, that it uncovered itself and looked at me with half-shut eyes as though to say, "What did you have against me, young man? Why did you drag me off, a dead woman, the mother of young children, and then fail to bring me to consecrated ground?"

The wind blew. It shrieked with a human voice, whistled right into my ears, confided a horrible secret to me. Terrible thoughts, frightful images followed one another in my mind and it seemed to me that we were all buried under the snow, all of us, the driver, the horse, the dead woman and I. We were all dead, all of us. Only the corpse — isn't it remarkable? — only the dead woman, the innkeeper's wife, was alive!

Suddenly I heard my driver clucking to his horse cheerfully, thanking God, and sighing and crossing himself in the dark. I sat up and looked around. In the distance I saw a gleam of light. The light glimmered, went out, and glimmered again. A house, I thought, and thanked God with all my heart. I turned to the driver. "We must have found the road," I said. "Are we close to town?"

"Uh-huh," said the driver in his usual brief manner, without anger, and I could have thrown my arms around his wide shoulders and kissed him, I was so happy to hear that pleasant brief "Uh-huh," which was more wonderful to me at that moment than the wisest discourse.

"What's your name?" I asked, surprised at myself for not having asked it before.

"Mikita," he answered, in one short word, as was his custom.

"Mikita," I repeated, and the name Mikita took on a strange charm. He answered, "Uh-huh."

I wished that he would tell me more. I wanted to hear him say something more, at least a few words. Mikita had suddenly become something dear to me, and his horse too, a charming animal! I began a conversation with him about his horse, told him what a fine horse he had. A very fine horse!

To which Mikita answered, "Uh-huh."

"And your sleigh, Mikita, is a fine sleigh too!"

Again he answered, "Uh-huh."

Beyond that he would not say a word.

"Don't you like to talk, Mikita, old fellow?" I asked.

"Uh-huh," he said. And I burst out laughing. I was as happy as though I had found a treasure, or made a wonderful discovery. In a word, I was lucky. I was more than lucky. Do you know what I wanted to do? I wanted to raise my voice and sing. That's a fact. I have always had that habit. When I am feeling good I burst out singing. My wife, bless her, knows this trait of mine, and asks, "What happened now, Noah? How much have you earned today to make you so happy?" To a woman, with her woman's brains, it is possible for a man to be happy only when he has made some money. Why does it happen that women are so much more greedy than men? Who earns the money, we or they? But there! I'm afraid I've gone off on the road to Boiberik again.

Well, with God's help we came to town. It was still very early, long before daybreak. The town was sound asleep. Not a glimmer of light showed anywhere. We barely distinguished a house with a large gate and a besom over the gate, the sign of a guesthouse or inn. We stopped, climbed down, Mikita and I, and began to pound at the gate with our fists. We pounded and pounded till at last we saw a light in the window. Then we heard someone shuffle up to the gate, and a voice called out, "Who's there?"

"Open, Uncle," I cried, "and you'll earn eternal life."

"Eternal life? Who are you?" came the voice from behind the gate, and the lock began to turn.

"Open the door," I said. "We've brought a corpse with us."

"A what?"

"A corpse."

"What do you mean, a corpse?"

"By a corpse I mean a dead person. A dead woman that we've brought from out in the country."

Inside the gate a silence fell. We heard only the lock being turned again and then the feet shuffling off. The lights went out and we were left standing in the snow. I was so angry that I told the driver to help me, and together we pounded at the window with our fists. And we pounded so heartily that the light went on again and the voice was heard once more, "What do you want? Will you stop bothering me!"

"In God's name," I begged as if pleading with a highwayman for my life, "have pity on me. We have a corpse with us, I tell you."

"What corpse?"

"The innkeeper's wife."

"What innkeeper are you talking about?"

"I've forgotten his name, but hers is Chava Michel, daughter of Chana Raphael, I mean Chana Raphael, daughter of Chava Michel, Chana Chava Chana, I mean . . ."

"Go away, you *shlimazl,* or I'll pour a bucket of water over you!"

And with this, the innkeeper shuffled off again and once more the light went out. There was nothing we could do. It was only an hour or so later, when day was beginning to break, that the gate opened a crack and a dark head streaked with white popped out and said to me, "Was it you that banged at the window?"

"Of course! Who do you think?"

"What did you want?"

"I've brought a corpse."

"A corpse? Then take it to the shammes of the Burial Society."

"Where does your shammes live? What's his name?"

"Yechiel's his name, and he lives at the foot of the hill right near the Baths."

"And where are your baths?"

"You don't know where the baths are? You must be a stranger here! Where are you from, young man?"

"Where am I from? From Rademishli. That's where I was born. But right now I'm coming from Zvohil. And I'm bringing a corpse from a village close by. The innkeeper's wife. She died of consumption."

"That's too bad. But what's that got to do with you?"

"Nothing at all. I was driving by and he begged me, the innkeeper, that is. He lives all alone out there in the country with all those small children. There was nowhere to bury her, so when he asked me to earn eternal life, I thought to myself: why not?"

"That doesn't make sense," he said to me. "You'd better see the officers of the Burial Society first."

"And who are your officers? Where do they live?"

"You don't know the officers of our Burial Society? Well, first there's Reb Shepsel, who lives over there beyond the marketplace. Then there is Reb Eleazer-Moishe, who lives right in the middle of the marketplace. And then there is Reb Yossi, he's an officer too, who lives near the old synagogue. But the one you'd better see first is Reb Shepsel. He's the one who runs everything. A hard man, I'm warning you. You won't persuade him so easily."

"Thank you very much," I said. "May you live to tell people better news than you've told me. And when can I see these men?"

"When do you suppose? In the morning after services."

"Thanks again. But what shall I do until then? At least let me in so I can warm myself. What is this town anyway, another Sodom?"

At this the innkeeper locked the doors again, and once more it was as silent as a tomb. What could we do now? Here we were in the middle of the road with our sleigh, and Mikita fuming, grumbling, scratching his neck, spitting and roaring out his three-dimensional curses. "May that foul innkeeper roast in hell through all eternity, and every other innkeeper with him!" For himself he didn't care. Let the evil spirits take him. But his horse, what did they have against his poor little horse, to torture it, let it starve and freeze like that? An innocent animal being sacrificed. What had it ever done?

I felt disgraced before my driver. What could he be thinking of us? A

Jew treating another Jew like this. We who were supposed to be the wise and merciful ones and they, the common, unlearned peasants. Thus I blamed the whole tribe for the discourtesy of one man, as is always our custom.

Well, we waited for daylight to come and the town to begin to show signs of life. And finally it did. Somewhere we heard the grating of a door, the sigh of a bucket. From a few chimneys smoke curled up, and in the distance roosters crowed louder and stronger. Soon the doors all opened and God's creatures appeared, in the image of cows, calves, goats, and also men, women and young girls, wrapped up in shawls, bundled from head to foot like mummies. In short the whole town had come to life as if it were a human being. It awoke, washed, pulled on its clothes, and set out to work: the men to the synagogue to pray and study and say *T'hilim;* the women to the ovens, the calves, and the goats; and I to inquire about the officers of the Burial Society, Reb Shepsel, Reb Eleazer-Moishe, Reb Yossi.

Wherever I asked they put me through a cross-examination. Which Shepsel? Which Eleazer-Moishe, which Yossi? There were, they said, several Shepsels, Eleazers, and Yossis in town. And when I told them that I wanted the officers of the Burial Society, they looked frightened and tried to find out why a young man should want the officers of the Burial Society so early in the morning. I didn't let them feel me out long, but opened my heart to them and told them the whole secret of the burden I had taken upon myself. You should have seen what happened then. Do you suppose they rushed to relieve me of my misfortune? God forbid! They ran out, all right, every one of them, but it was only to see if there really was a corpse or if I had invented the whole story. They formed a ring about us, a ring that kept shifting because of the cold, some people leaving and others taking their place, looking into the sleigh, shaking their heads, shrugging their shoulders, and asking over and over who the corpse was, and where it came from, who I was, where I had got it, and gave me no help whatever.

With the greatest of difficulty I managed to find out where Reb Shepsel lived. I found him with his face turned to the wall, wrapped in his *tallis* and *tfiln,* praying so ardently, with such a melodious voice and so much feeling that the walls actually sang. He cracked his knuckles,

rocked back and forth, made strange movements with his body. I
enjoyed it tremendously, because in the first place I love to listen to such
spirited praying, and besides, it gave me a chance to warm my frozen
bones. When Reb Shepsel finally turned his face to me his eyes were still
full of tears and he looked like a man of God, his soul as far removed
from earth as his big fat body was from heaven. But since he was still in
the midst of his prayers and did not want to interrupt them with secular
discourse, he spoke to me in the holy tongue, that is, in a language that
consisted of gestures of the hands, winks of the eye, shrugs and motions
of the head and even the nose, with a few Hebrew words thrown in. If
you wish, I can relate the conversation to you word by word, and no
doubt you will understand which words were his and which were mine.

"*Sholom aleichem,* Reb Shepsel."

"*Aleichem sholom. I-yo. Nu-o.*"

"Thank you. I have been sitting all night."

"*Nu-o? Ma?*"

"I have a request to make of you, Reb Shepsel. You will earn eternal
life."

"Eternal life? Good! In what way?"

"I have brought you a corpse."

"Corpse! What corpse?"

"Not far from here there is a country inn. The owner is a poor man
whose wife just died of consumption, and she left him with several
small children, may God have compassion on them. If I had not taken
pity on them, I don't know what the poor innkeeper would have done,
alone out there in the middle of the field with the corpse."

"God have mercy on them. Well . . . and did he give you anything for
the Burial Society?"

"Where is he going to get the money for that? He's a poor man. Poor
as can be, and with a houseful of children. You will earn eternal life, Reb
Shepsel."

"Eternal life. Good. Very good! Jews. Poor people . . . ah, yes."

And here he broke in with a series of strange sounds accompanied by
so many gestures, winks, blinks, shrugs, and motions of the head that I
could not begin to understand what he was driving at.

And seeing that I could not follow him, he turned his face to the wall in disgust and once more began to pray, but not with the same ardor as before. His voice was lower, but he rocked back and forth faster than ever, till he came to the end, threw off his *tallis* and *tfiln* and fell on me with such fury that you would have thought I had outwitted him in some transaction and ruined him completely.

"Look," he said to me, "our town is such a poor one, with so many paupers of our own for whom shrouds must be provided when they die, and here you come from some strange place with a corpse. They come here from everywhere. Everybody comes here!"

I defended myself as well as I could. I said I was an innocent man trying to do only what was proper with respect to the dead. Suppose a dead body had been found in the street and had to be buried, laid to his eternal rest. "You are," I said, "an honest man, a pious one. You can earn eternal life with this deed."

At this he became even angrier and began to lash out at me, not with blows, but with words.

"Is that so?" he cried. "You are a man who craves eternal life? Then take a walk around our town and see to it that our own people stop dying of hunger and freezing of cold. Then you will earn eternal life. Ah-hah! A young man who deals in eternal life! Go take your merchandise to the ne'er-do-wells. Maybe they will be interested. We have our own duties to perform, our own poor to bury. And if we suddenly began to yearn for this eternal life you talk about we could find our own way to earn it!"

With these words Reb Shepsel showed me out and slammed the door behind me. And I swear to you on my word of honor that from that morning on I have despised all those overly pious people who pray out loud and beat their breasts and bow low and make crazy motions. I have hated those holy ones who talk with God all the time, who pretend to serve Him, and do whatever they want, all in His name! True, you might say that these modern irreligious people nowadays are no better and may even be worse than the old-timers with their false piety. But they're not so revolting. At least they don't pretend to be on speaking terms with God. But there! I'm on the way to Boiberik again.

Well, the president, Reb Shepsel, had driven me off. So what should I do next? Go to the other trustees, of course. But at this point a miracle occurred. I saved myself the trouble of going to them, because they came to me instead. They met me face to face at the door and said:

"Are you the young man we're looking for?"

"And what young man are you looking for?"

"The one who brought a body here. Is that you?"

"Yes, I'm the one. What do you want me for?"

"Come back with us to Reb Shepsel and we'll talk it over."

"Talk it over?" I asked. "What is there to talk over? You take the body from me, let me go on my way — and you'll earn eternal life."

"You don't like the way we do things? Is anyone keeping you here?" they asked. "Go take your body anywhere you want, even to Rademishli, and we'll be grateful to you."

"Thanks for the advice," I told them.

"You're welcome," said they.

So we went back into Reb Shepsel's house and the three trustees began to talk. They argued and quarrelled, called each other names. The other two said Reb Shepsel was stubborn, a hard man to deal with; and Reb Shepsel yelled back at them, shouted, ranted, quoted the law: the town's own poor came first. At this the other two fell on him.

"Is that so? Then you want the young man to take the body back with him?"

"God forbid," I said. "What do you want, I should take the body back? I barely came here alive, almost got lost on the way. My driver wanted to throw me out of the sleigh in the open field somewhere. I beg you. Have pity on me. Take the corpse off my hands. You'll earn eternal life."

"Eternal life is a fine enough thing," answered one of them, a tall thin man with bony fingers, the one called Eleazer-Moishe. "We'll take the body away from you and bury it, but it will cost you something."

"What do you mean?" I asked. "Here I undertook a responsibility like this, at the risk of my life, almost got lost on the way, and you want money!"

"But you're getting eternal life, aren't you?" said Reb Shepsel with such an ugly leer that I wanted to go after him as he deserved. But I managed to control myself. After all, I was still at their mercy.

"Let's get to work," said the one called Reb Yossi, a small man with a short scraggly beard. "I suppose you know, young man, that you have another problem on your hands. You have no papers, no papers at all."

"What papers?" I asked.

"How do we know whose body it is? Maybe it's not what you said it was," said the tall man with the bony fingers, the one called Eleazer-Moishe.

I stood looking from one to the other, and the tall one with the bony fingers, the one called Eleazer-Moishe, shook his head and pointed at me with his long fingers and said:

"Yes, yes. Maybe you murdered some woman yourself. Maybe it's your own wife that you brought here and made up this story about a country inn, the innkeeper's wife, consumption, small children, eternal life."

I must have looked frightened to death at these words, for the one they called Reb Yossi began to comfort me, telling me that they themselves had nothing against me. They understood very well that I was not a robber or a murderer, but still I was a stranger, and a dead body was not a sack of potatoes. We were dealing with a dead person, a corpse. They had, he explained, a rabbi and a police inspector in their town. A report had to be made out.

"Yes, of course. A report. A report," added the tall one, the one called Eleazer-Moishe, pointing with his finger and looking down at me accusingly as though I had committed some crime. I couldn't say another word. I felt a sweat break out on my forehead and I was ready to faint. I was well aware of the miserable plight I had fallen into. It was a disgrace, a sorrow, and a heartache in one. But, I thought to myself, what was the use of starting the whole discussion over again with them? So I took out my purse and said to the three trustees of the Burial Society:

"Listen, my friends, here is the whole story. I see what I have fallen into. It was an evil spirit that made me stop at that country inn to warm myself just when the innkeeper's wife had to go ahead and die, and I had to listen to the poor wretch left with all the children begging me, promising eternal life. And now I have to pay for it. Here is my purse. You'll find about seventy-odd rubles in it. Take it and do what you think best. Just leave me enough to get me to Rademishli, and take the body away from me and let me go on my way."

I must have spoken with great feeling, for the three trustees looked at each other and would not touch my purse. They told me that their town was not Sodom; they were not robbers. True, the town was a poor one, with more paupers than rich people, but to fall on a strange man and order him to hand over his money, that they would not think of. Whatever I wanted to give of my own free will was all right. To do it without charging at all was impossible. It was a poor town, and there were all the expenses, pallbearers, a shroud, drinks, the cost of the burial lot. But it was not necessary for me to throw my money away. If I started to do that, there would be no end to it.

Well, what more can I tell you? If the innkeeper had had two hundred thousand rubles, his wife could not have had a finer funeral. The whole town came to look at the young man who had brought the corpse. They told each other that it was the body of his mother-in-law, a rich woman. (I don't know where they got the mother-in-law story.) At any rate they came to welcome the young man who had brought the rich mother-in-law and was throwing out money right and left. They actually pointed their fingers at me. And as for beggars, they were like the sands of the ocean. In all my life I have never seen so many beggars in one place, not even in front of the synagogue on Yom Kippur eve. They pulled at the skirts of my coat, they almost tore me to pieces. How often do they see a young man who throws away money like that? I was lucky that the trustees came to my rescue and kept me from giving away all I had. Especially the tall one with the bony fingers, Eleazer-Moishe, did not step away from me for a moment. He kept pointing at me with his finger and saying, "Young man, do not hand out all your money." But the more he spoke the closer the beggars gathered around me, tearing at my flesh. "It's nothing," yelled the beggars. "It's nothing. When you bury such a rich mother-in-law you can afford to spend a few extra groschen. She must have left him enough money. May we have as much!"

"Young man!" yelled one beggar, pulling at my coat, "young man, give the two of us half a ruble! At least forty kopeks. We were born like this, one lame, the other blind. Give us at least a gulden, a gulden for two maimed ones. Surely we deserve a gulden!"

"Don't pay attention to him!" shouted another, pushing the first one aside. "Do you call them cripples? My wife is a real cripple. She can't use her arms or legs, she can't move a limb, and our children are sick too!

Give me anything at all and I'll say kaddish for your mother-in-law all year — may she rest in paradise!"

Now I can laugh about it. Then it was far from a laughing matter, for the crowd of beggars grew and multiplied about me. In half an hour they flooded the marketplace and it was impossible to proceed with the coffin. The attendants had to use sticks to disperse the mob, and a fight broke out. By that time some peasants began to gather about us too, with their wives and countless children, and at last the news reached the town authorities. The police inspector appeared on horseback with a whip in his hand and with one harsh look about him and a few sharp lashes of the whip sent the mob flying in all directions. He himself dismounted and came up to the coffin to investigate. He started by questioning me, asked who I was, where I had come from, and where I was going. I was paralyzed with fear. I don't know why, but whenever I see an officer of the law I go numb with fear, though I have no real reason to worry. In all my life I have never as much as touched a fly on the wall and I know quite well that a policeman is an ordinary human being, flesh and blood like the rest of us. In fact, I know a Jew who is so friendly with a police officer that they visit each other frequently and when there is a holiday the officer eats fish at my friend's house, and when my friend visits the officer he's treated to hard-boiled eggs. He can't praise the officer highly enough. And yet every time I see a policeman I want to run. It must be something I inherited, because, as you know, I come from a region where pogroms came one after another in the days of Vassilchikov, and I'm descended from the victims of those pogroms. If I wanted to, I could tell you stories enough about those days — but there, I must be well past Boiberik this time.

As I said, the officer began to cross-examine me. He wanted to know who I was, and what I was, and where I was going. How could I tell him the whole story — that I live with my father-in-law in Zvohil and I'm going to Rademishli to get a passport? But the trustees, long may they live, saved me the trouble. Before I could even begin, one of them, the one with the thin beard, called the officer aside and began to talk with him, while the tall one with the bony fingers quickly and in guarded language taught me how to answer the officer.

"Be careful what you say," he whispered. "Tell him the whole truth.

You live not far from town and this is your mother-in-law and you brought her here to be buried. Tell him your name and your mother-in-law's too. Your real names, you understand, straight out of the *Haggadah*. And give him the burial fee — don't forget."

And saying this he winked at me and continued, "In the meantime, your driver looks tired and thirsty. We'll take him across the street and give him a chance to rest."

Then the inspector took me into a large building and began to make out some papers. I have no idea at all what nonsense I told him. I said anything and everything that came to my mind and he wrote it all down.

"Your name?"

"Moishe."

"Your father's."

"Itzko."

"Your age?"

"Nineteen."

"Married?"

"Married."

"Children?"

"Of course."

"Your trade?"

"Merchant."

"Who is the dead person?"

"My mother-in-law."

"Her name?"

"Yenta."

"Her father's?"

"Gershon."

"Her age?"

"Forty."

"Cause of death?"

"Fright."

"Fright?"

"Yes, fright."

"What do you mean — fright?" he asked, laying down his pen and lighting a cigarette, looking me over from head to foot. Suddenly my tongue stuck to the roof of my mouth. I thought to myself, if I am inventing a story, I might as well do a good job. So I told him how my mother-in-law had been sitting all alone knitting some socks. She had forgotten that her young son, a boy named Ephraim, was in the room with her. A thirteen-year-old boy, very stupid, something of a clown. He was making shadow figures on the wall and he put his hands up high behind his mother's back, and making a goat's shadow on the wall, opened his mouth and bleated, "Ba-a-a-a." Struck with fright, she fell from her chair and died on the spot.

While I was telling him this story he kept looking at me strangely, not taking his eyes off me. He heard me out till the end, spat on the floor, wiped his red mustaches, and led me out again to the coffin. He removed the black cover, looked at the dead woman's face and shook his head. He looked from the corpse to me, and from me to the corpse, and then said to the trustees, "Well, you can go ahead and bury the woman. As for this young man, I'll have to keep him here until I satisfy myself that she was really his mother-in-law and that she died of fright."

You can imagine how I felt when I heard this. I turned aside — I couldn't help it — and burst out crying like a small child. "Look here, what are you crying for?" asked the little man they called Reb Yossi, and comforted me, cheered me up as best he could. I was innocent, wasn't I? Then what did I have to be afraid of?

"If you don't eat garlic, they'll never smell it on your breath," put in Reb Shepsel with such a smirk and I wanted to give his fat cheeks a couple of good hard slaps.

God in heaven, what good did it ever do me to make up this big lie and drag my mother-in-law into it? All I needed now was to have her find out that I had buried her alive and spread the news that she had died of fright.

"Don't be afraid," Reb Eleazer broke in, prodding me with his bony fingers. "God will take care of you. The officer is not such a bad fellow. Just give him the burial fee I told you about. He'll understand. He knows that everything you told him is true."

I cannot tell you any more. I don't even want to remember what happened to me after that. You understand, of course, that they took the few gulden I had left, put me in jail, and I had to stand trial. But that was child's play compared to what happened when the news reached my father- and mother-in-law that their son-in-law was in prison for having brought a dead woman from somewhere.

Naturally they came at once, identified themselves as my parents-in-law, and then the excitement really began! On one side the police went after me. "A fine fellow you are! Now, if your mother-in-law Yenta, daughter of Gershon, is alive, then who was the dead woman you brought?" On the other side, my mother-in-law, may she live long! "There is only one thing I want to ask you," she kept saying to me. "What did you have against me, to take me and bury me alive?"

Naturally at the trial it turned out that I was innocent, free from all guilt. Of course that cost some money too. Witnesses had to be brought in, the innkeeper and his children, and finally I was set free. But what I went through afterward, especially from my mother-in-law, that I don't wish my worst enemy to have to go through!

And from that time on, when anybody mentions eternal life, I run away as fast as I can.

SHIMON AN-SKI

✧ 1863–1920 ✧

YIVO Institute for Jewish Research

The life journey of the man known as Shimon An-ski, also known as Ansky, was outsized and dramatic, even in the framework of his cataclysmic time. He was at once theorist and artist, collector and creator; a man who reclaimed his past with the same intensity that had previously fueled his escape from it. At his death, he left behind a towering fictional work of artistic integration that interwove folk themes, religious rigor, aching sensuality, and existential yearning. His play, *The Dybbuk, or Between Two Worlds,* continues to cast its spell on successive generations.

Shloyme-Zanvl Rappoport was born in Vitebsk, Russia, in 1863, a city at the intersection of ecstatic, emotional Hasidism and enlightened, intellectual Jewish learning. Although he received a traditional religious education, as a teenager he learned Russian and became a convert to Russian radicalism. Because he feared that hidebound Jews would never rouse themselves to take advantage of the modern world, he joined the intellectuals who cast their lot with the Russian peasants. He changed his name to An-ski and spent three years living and working with Russian miners.

An-ski's Russian writings in got him into and out of trouble: A period in the literary world of St. Petersburg was followed by a stint in a czarist jail. In 1892 he left for the relative safety of Western Europe, but did not abandon his revolutionary work. In Paris, he found a job as secretary to a Russian radical theorist.

In 1901, An-ski underwent another conversion. Reading the modernist works of Yitzhak Peretz, he was inspired to return to writing in Yiddish after a two-decade-long hiatus. One of his first pieces was "The Oath," the anthem of the Bund, the international Jewish revolutionary party. An-ski also wrote Yiddish stories and translated some of his Russian writings into Yiddish.

In 1905, when the political climate in Russia heated up, An-ski returned home. But this time, instead of identifying with the Russian peasants, he embraced his Jewish past. At a banquet in his honor he said, "My life was broken, severed, ruptured. Many years of my life passed on this frontier, on the border between two worlds. Therefore, I beg you, on this twenty-fifth year of summing up my literary work, to eliminate sixteen years."

His earlier interest in the Russian "folk" now became an obsession with preserving and recording Jewish folkways, which, in the maelstrom of early-twentieth-century Russia, were beginning to disappear. From 1912 to 1914 he directed the extraordinary Jewish Ethnographic Expedition, which photographed people and places, and gathered thousands of stories, songs, tales, superstitions, beliefs, and artifacts.

The expedition was halted by the outbreak of World War I. An-ski returned to his fieldwork — but this time with a tragic difference. The Russians, who had captured the province of Galicia from the Austro-

Hungarian Empire, joined forces with the worst of the locals to target the Jewish population. At the same time, in Russia, the czar ordered hundreds of thousands of Jews into internal exile. The rupture between An-ski's Russian and Jewish selves deepened.

Although An-ski used his political contacts to mediate between conflicting factions, his deepest sympathies played themselves out as he traveled through the devastated regions. He kept up his ethnographic documentation and collection, but his real purpose was to organize relief committees and bring money and supplies to starving Jews. He kept a diary of his travels, later published as *The Destruction of Galicia*.

An-ski also created his best-known work, *The Dybbuk*, a deeply felt and finely wrought play that used the imagery and vocabulary of Jewish folklore and myth to express the ruptures and connections he knew in his bones. The play was to have been produced by the world-famous Moscow Art Theatre, under the direction of Stanislavsky, but the rush of politics intervened. The Bolsheviks came to power and An-ski had to flee, losing the original Yiddish and Russian manuscripts of his play. Later, he reconstructed the Yiddish from a stilted Hebrew translation.

In poor health, suffering from diabetes and heart problems, An-ski settled for a time in Vilna, a city grabbed by first one army then another. He threw himself into the Jewish literary, ethnographic, and political scene, setting up new organizations and parties while, in the chaos following World War I and the Russian Revolution, Jews continued to be killed.

Seeking some safety, he moved to Warsaw, but illness finally caught up with him. An-ski died there in 1920. In 1925, a grateful people erected a funerary monument to three men: Jacob Dinezon (a colleague of Yitzhak Peretz), An-ski, and Peretz himself.

Mendl Turk

TRANSLATED BY GOLDA WERMAN

I

In the summer and fall of 1877, at the height of the Russo-Turkish War, I was tutoring in one of the outlying Lithuanian towns where I lived a very lonely existence. One day, on my way home for lunch, I saw a sight that made me stop in my tracks. A young man whom I didn't know, wearing a skullcap but no jacket, had pushed his head through the open window of my room and, with both hands on my table for support, was reading the Russian newspaper that I had left there. When I approached him, he raised his head in alarm, quickly pulled his trembling upper body out of the window, and remained standing, confused and very embarrassed.

"Oh, please don't get the wrong idea," he stammered with a guilty half-smile on his lips. "I didn't touch a thing in your house, God forbid. I was just passing by when I noticed the newspaper on your table and a headline caught my eye. . . . I couldn't restrain myself from reading it."

I calmed him down and handed him the paper.

"Thank you! Thank you very much!" he said to me, warmly but still not entirely at ease. "Something caught my interest, something important."

"What was it that was so important?"

"What do you think? What is it that newspapers write about these days? Only war and politics."

"You're interested in politics?"

He gave me a penetrating look and then lowered his eyes; a little incoherent at first, he soon spoke up clearly, "What do you mean am I interested in politics? And who isn't interested in politics? In normal times, I agree, it's not worth spending time on. But it's different in wartime. Now politics is all-important!"

The young man roused my curiosity, so I invited him into my room.

"I would come with the greatest pleasure, but I have no time now," he answered me. "The boys are about to return from supper."

Now I realized who he was. My window overlooked a courtyard that resounded all day with the clamor of children's voices from the heder, which was located in an old house. I often saw emaciated little boys, dressed in rags, scampering across the yard like frightened mice — but I had never seen their teacher. I don't know why, but I imagined him to be an old man with an angry face. The teacher who stood in front of me was a young man of twenty-eight with delicate features and a short black beard. The deep, thoughtful look of his large, black eyes gave his face an unusually serious expression. His velvet skullcap, the long, curled earlocks, and his short beard framed his face beautifully.

He thought for a while, and then he said, "But if you're not busy in the evening I'd be happy to come then. It's been a long time since I've had the chance to speak to someone like you. Tell me, do you read the newspaper each day?"

"Yes, every day."

The teacher looked at me enviously.

"Oh, I can understand that," he said with a sigh. "That kind of reading makes sense; it has meaning."

"And you, what do you read?"

"What do I read? I catch things in the wind; I don't read. I get the newspaper *Halevanon* maybe twice a month;* the rest of the time I have to depend on the 'Telegrams' which are pasted on the walls in the market — and on what people tell me, always complete with their own opinions, of course, which are never based on facts."

I invited him to come that evening.

---

* Halevanon was a Hebrew newspaper published intermittently from 1863 to 1886 and based in Jerusalem, Paris, Mainz, and then London.

2

The teacher came as soon as heder was over. This time he wore a long frock coat and a velvet cap.

"Good evening," he said, remaining standing in the middle of the room without attempting to shake my hand. I motioned to him to sit down and as he did he carefully surveyed the room and saw at a glance that none of the books were traditional Jewish sacred texts.

"Are they all goyish books?" he asked, amazed.

"Most of them are Russian or German."

"Really?" he began hesitatingly. "What are they about? Law and grammar?"

The question didn't surprise me at all; I explained to my guest that grammars and legal texts were not the only books written in Russian; there were all kinds — stories, poems, science, and philosophy — in Russian and in other languages, too.

"You don't say! Philosophy? Are there really Russian books on philosophy?" he asked, astounded, and looked at the bookcase more attentively this time.

But a moment later he had regained his composure and turned to me with a deprecating smile. "Well, any passages of deep wisdom or of penetrating philosophic inquiry in these volumes must come from the Talmud or from *Rambam*. Politics is different," he continued, changing his tone of voice. "Politics is a special science, dealing with all the countries in the world; it has its own rules. Take Bismarck, for example. What a mind! A brilliant mind! Bikensfeld* is an even greater genius — his thinking is deeper, more penetrating. But that's to be expected — he's a Jew."

For a while he sat in silence, looking thoughtfully at the glass of tea which I had placed before him without his noticing.

"Listen," he said suddenly and emphatically, moving the glass of tea away as if he needed a clear space in front of him. "I want to discuss the war with you, to discuss it properly."

He pushed himself farther back in his chair, leaned over the table, and

---

* Lord Beaconsfield, i.e., Benjamin Disraeli.

began slowly and deliberately, "Everything in the world has its foundation, its substance, and its essence. In order to understand anything properly one must uncover its essence. Obviously, this war has its essence, too, its crux, around which everything revolves. Now please tell me what the war is all about, what is its substance, its essence — I'm listening with rapt attention."

But seeing that I was about to answer, he quickly raised both hands in my direction, gesturing me not to talk yet.

"Wait, just wait a minute, please!" he begged. "I said the 'essence,' but we must define our terms. We must be clear about what that essence is. What is the basic cause of the present war? How did it start and what propels it on? What are the assumptions of those who are responsible for seeing it continue? And now we come to the real point: pick up a newspaper, any paper at all, and read it. You'll soon discover that the same word — 'Slav' — is repeated over and over again. This view claims that the Russians are the righteous redeemers who are sacrificing their lives and shedding their blood to free their brothers, the Slavs, from the Turkish yoke. This is all very good, very fine! You couldn't ask for better. But then there is also the other side, presenting the more daring point of view: the Russians, say the proponents of this side, care as much for the Slavs as they do for yesterday's snow. So what is the fighting all about? It's very simple; the Russians want to capture Turkey's two seas, the Bosphorus and the Dardanelles. The Slavs only serve as their excuse. And that's not all; there's a third side which states that the war has nothing to do with either Russia *or* Turkey. England is the culprit. According to this view, she leads them both by the nose, inciting one side against the other, urging them to tear each other apart like fighting cocks. And then, when both sides are exhausted, England will step in and finish them off. Now I ask you, which view is correct? Obviously, each person must keep a clear head on his shoulders and decide for himself. But in order to find the correct path it is essential to look at the world objectively and to try to understand it. And this brings me to my request."

"Which is?"

"Very simple: give me the whole political story of everything that took place between the Russians and the Turks from the very beginning."

"From the beginning" was no simple matter, especially since my guest didn't even know that Russia and Turkey had been at war before. Nonetheless, I gave him a brief survey of the history and politics of the region, trying to draw a clear picture of the kind of country Turkey was and how her interests clashed with those of Russia. My guest was fascinated, leaning forward as he listened and looking up at me from time to time with a serious expression. When I finished, he remained in the same position, apparently still deeply absorbed in what I had told him.

"I must tell you that you've made me see things I never knew existed before," he stated in a quiet voice, but with genuine enthusiasm. "Now the world is open before me and I can see a road, a path — new ideas come to me, new hypotheses."

And then he lapsed into complete silence. He dipped a cube of sugar into his cooled tea, recited a blessing and began to drink. When he finished, he thanked me and picked up the discussion from where he had left off.

"I gather from your analysis that you also tend toward the view that the Russians care about the Slavs, the Bulgarians, and the Serbians. To tell the truth, I can't see it that way. To me it's sheer madness to think of Mother Russia as being altruistic."

Seeing that I was about to answer him, he quickly added, "But let's assume for argument's sake that you're right — it isn't the essence of the matter. I gather from your discussion that you believe that Russia is unconquerable. This is precisely the point that I don't understand. Do you really think that Russia will be victorious?"

"I am certain of it."

"Now hear me out," said the teacher with self-assurance. "It goes without saying that you know much, much more about the facts of the war and its politics than I do. And you may call me a fool and say that I'm arrogant, but I assure you that the Turks will win! To me it's as clear as day. Wait a week, just one week, and you'll see for yourself that I'm right."

And as if he were afraid that I might try to prove him wrong, he quickly buttoned his coat, said good-bye and left. At the door, he kept droning under his breath, scornfully, "Beh! Mother Russia will overcome! And whom? The Turks!"

3

In the morning as I was drinking my tea, the landlord, an elderly Jew, stopped by. He was one of those unfortunate men who were completely under their wives' thumbs. Very quiet and depressed, he was like a stranger in his own home, where his much younger, energetic third wife ruled the roost. There were no children. Whenever his wife left the house, she locked up all the cupboards and took the keys with her, afraid that the maid would steal; often she would forget to leave her husband the few cubes of sugar he needed for his tea, or the two kopecks for his snuff, without which he felt like a "goose going to the slaughter." She was barely civil to him and would sometimes scold him, as if he were one of the servants. The only time she showed him any respect was on the Sabbath and on the holidays when she needed him to recite the blessing over the wine or to usher out the Sabbath for her.

All day long the old man either wandered around the house or "sat" in the study house. At first he was afraid to look at me and would quickly get out of my way whenever we happened to meet. But he gradually got used to seeing me around and even began to visit me in my room to drink an occasional glass of tea or borrow a few kopecks for snuff. He was always diplomatic about hiding the purpose of these visits; before asking for the loan he would invent some question or other regarding the rent, a matter of only theoretical interest to him, since his wife handled all the money matters.

This time, too, he came under a pretext: he said he was looking for the copper ladle. I knew very well that the ladle was lying in its accustomed place near the well and that he had come only so that I would offer him a glass of tea. However, since a face-saving measure of this sort was essential, I shrugged my shoulders and told him that I had no idea where the ladle was, but would he do me the honor of joining me in a glass of tea?

"Eh? What?" the old man asked, as if he hadn't heard what I said.

"I asked if you wouldn't, just this once, have a glass of tea with me in my room?"

"Tea?" The old man looked at me as if this invitation came as a great surprise to him, even though I was sitting right next to the samovar. "No, thank you, not for me. I just had some," he declared emphatically.

That was the first part of the ritual. Now it was my task to urge him, to plead with him.

"I can never get you to drink a glass of tea," I said in a tone of annoyance. "What's wrong? Are you afraid that my house isn't kosher?"

"How can you say such a thing? Of course you're a God-fearing man," he shot back, flushed. "What do you mean not kosher? How can you even think such a thing? I simply don't want tea because I've just had some. But if it's so important to you, pour me a glass; I'll force myself to drink."

And, just as prescribed by the ritual, the old man was soon sitting at the table.

"Tell me, Reb Ber," I asked him, "what kind of person is the young man who teaches in the courtyard?"

"Who? Mendl Turk?" My guest put down his glass. "What do you mean by 'what kind of person'? A human being, a young man, a religious person, a Hasid, a scholar, a very learned and promising scholar, if you must know."

"What was that you called him — Turk? What kind of family name is that?"

"It's not a family name at all," said the old man, smiling. "They nicknamed him Turk in the synagogue, for some reason, so that's what I call him."

"Why did they give him that nickname?"

"Why? That's a good question. They gave it to him, that's all. You read the paper, so you know that we're at war with the Turks. And since Mendl sides with the Turks, they call him Turk. If he'd sided with the Russians, they would have called him Russky. It's as simple as that."

The old man looked at me with a satisfied expression and returned to his tea. When I poured him a second glass, he pushed it a bit to the side and continued the conversation. "Don't talk to me about Mendl! He's lost his head, along with everyone else in town! All they do is talk and talk. Actually, they don't talk — they scream, they argue, they fight, they pull down the walls. It's a regular war. And what is the fight about? About the Turks and the Russians."

"Tell me — where do these heated discussions and arguments take place?" I asked.

The old man looked at me, unbelieving. "What do you mean, where? Where do you think they argue? In the synagogue, of course. Where else? Oh, I forgot. You're a modern person and don't go to the synagogue on Sabbath. If you did, you'd see for yourself what amazing things go on there! Everyone, and I mean each and every one, young and old alike, is so hot under the collar about this that as soon as the 'Turks' and the 'Russians' get together they begin to fight; it's a real war, it's Gog and Magog."*

The old man spoke with such passion about the battle between the Jewish Turks and the Jewish Russians that I was curious to know which side he was on.

"And you, Reb Ber, where do you stand — with the Turks or with the Russians?"

"I?" he asked in a startled voice. "Ha, ha! Do you really think that I'd let myself get involved in all this? Do I look like a fool to you? No, I only listen while they talk — it goes in one ear and out the other."

"But, Reb Ber, you haven't told me everything. Tell the truth," I insisted, knowing that he really wanted to express his opinion but was too timid.

The old man suddenly became very serious, very grave indeed, and, leaning toward me, he began to whisper, as if he were sharing a secret with me, "Ishmael is a cutthroat, but he's better than Esau! Listen to me! If Ishmael should win, then the Messiah will have to come."

"Good God, Reb Ber," I interrupted. "What does Ishmael's victory have to do with the Messiah?"

"Don't press me," he blurted out. "I've heard them talking — Jews talk. Do I know what they're saying? People talk, that's all. I don't mean you or me."

Then he began to babble something incomprehensible. I didn't interrupt him, and little by little he calmed down.

"Last evening Mendl Turk visited me," I told the old man.

"Mendl? At your house?" — as if asking what a Hasidic teacher could possibly want with me. But then he had a sudden insight.

---

* Described in Ezekiel 38, the visionary battle of Gog and Magog fed the Jewish apocalyptic imagination for millennia.

"I've got it! I understand," he said resuming his secretive tone and twisting his long, dry, outstretched finger in the air. "You know what I think? It wasn't you he wanted; he wanted your newspaper. Yes, of course! Believe me, I know him well," he shouted, with rising excitement. "Isn't he a clever one! He doesn't miss a trick, our Mendl Turk!"

"You're right, that's exactly why he came," I said, confirming his hypothesis.

"You see, I'm no fool! It's obvious. Why else would Mendl visit you? To find out what's in the papers! So he must gather his politics the same way, in bits and pieces — like a chicken, peck, peck, peck, grain by grain until the crop is full and the egg is ready to be laid," he said, sharing a bit of incorrect embryological know-how with me.

"I shouldn't be telling you this," he continued confidentially, "but I have the feeling that since he became interested in politics he doesn't study Torah as fervently as before. He used to spend his nights in the study house and now — now he spends his time looking for newspapers to read. Yes, yes, that's how it is," he said, all excited, even giving me a little push as if to say that he wasn't about to accept any excuses for him. Since I had no intention of defending Mendl against his terrible suspicion, the old man calmed down and took a third glass of tea.

When he finished drinking, he thanked me and rose to go. Suddenly, a big, twinkling smile spread over his face, and with childish innocence and a pitiful look in his eyes, he blurted out, "Eh, eh, I have something to confess: I really wanted a glass of tea. My wife went shopping and forgot to leave me the sugar. . . ."

What a diplomat my old friend is! He's almost a Bismarck, even a Bikensfeld.

4

On the next Sabbath I went to the big synagogue in time for afternoon prayers so that I could see for myself the war of Gog and Magog as played out by the Jewish "Turks" and "Russians." It was dusk. All the contours were blurred, and the shadows of evening playing on the high walls of the synagogue created an eerie picture. The sight of several hundred men waving back and forth as they silently recited the eighteen benedictions made me think of a forest of trees stirring in the wind. And the spell of their muted, mystical chanting brought back memories from my own distant childhood.

I recalled the old synagogue of my youth in the shtetl where I was born and that special time on Sabbath between the afternoon and evening prayers. The old men would walk slowly back and forth in the little synagogue, their hands behind their backs, dreamily humming a tune while they waited for darkness so they could recite the evening prayers. When they got tired of walking, they sat on the benches and, still in a state of reverie, would tell each other stories. Someone would begin with a Hasidic legend, another would relate some interesting event in his life — and everything became bewitched and full of mystery in that shadowy twilight hour of early evening. The men listened, spellbound, and remained in their seats long after the stories were finished, so as not to interrupt the magical stillness.

At that hour the world of everyday cares was forgotten — everyone was pensive, lost in his own musing. Someone invariably began to sing a well-known melody, "Bim, bam, bom," and soon everyone would chime in, each adding his own dreamy tune. Then someone would suddenly jump up, as if awakened from a sleep and say pleadingly, "Zerach, begin!"

And Zerach always complied. From his seat, he would quietly begin to hum the traditional Rosh Hashonah and Yom Kippur melodies, and as one congregant after another joined in, the singing became louder and louder. The echoes of the infinitely sad High Holiday melodies would ring through the little old synagogue for a long time.

The singing continued even after the sky was filled with stars and the synagogue was dark. No one wanted to begin the evening prayers which usher out the Sabbath; no one was in a hurry to go back to the prosaic cares of the everyday world.

It was a golden hour for the children, too, for they were touched by the same special mood that overtook the grown-ups. Some youngsters would stay close to their fathers to listen to the tales the men told. Others formed little circles at various points in the synagogue and told each other ghost stories. The livelier ones found the darkness a good cover for their pranks and games of hide-and-seek; some even threw "bombs" made of twisted towels at the beadle or the congregants. No matter! At this magical hour childish tricks like these went unpunished. "They're only children; let them have fun" was the sentiment. The kind-hearted congregant would further express his warm feelings toward the youngsters by taking a mischievous little boy on his knees, stroking his head as tenderly as if he were his own son and singing all the while. He didn't even look to see who his captive was. The startled child would be silenced by this unexpected benevolence from a stranger. His heart would beat with joy, and he would smile contentedly, grateful for the gentle hand on his head.

I have never forgotten these hours of amity and love.

But in the large synagogue it was not like that. The storms of war had penetrated here and had displaced the dreamy quiet of the Sabbath dusk.

5

When the afternoon prayers were over, the members of the congregation left their seats and began a lively discussion. Everyone talked at once until a loud "Sha! Be quiet!" gradually calmed them down. In the middle of the synagogue a large circle formed around two or three men who were arguing; the others, curious to hear what was being discussed, cupped their hands over their ears while they shoved one another to get closer.

An elderly man of medium height with a broad build, intelligent gray eyes, and a tobacco-stained mustache stood in the center of the circle and spoke with quiet confidence. He gestured with his hand while holding a package of snuff between two fingers.

"Well, well, well — why are you so excited? So we didn't capture Plevne. So what? Show me a war in which there are only victories, where one victory follows on the heels of the other! If we didn't take Plevne this week, we'll get it next week."

"You, Mikhoel, say that the Russians will take Plevne" came the excited shout of a tall man with a blond beard and a red neck. "Are you mad enough to give us a guarantee? How do you figure the Russians will capture Plevne? Did you forget that they've already put half the army behind Plevne? . . ."

"Hold on there," interrupted a thin young man, who stretched his long neck out in the direction of the circle. "Why not put the question another way? You ask how the Russians will capture Plevne. What I ask is, how will the Turks restrain them? You're not taking into consideration what it costs the Turks every time Russians attack them."

"Tha-at is the poi-oint," responded a young man with a goatee, in a Talmudic singsong. "No bullets will reach Plevne. You can shoot where you want, even to the sky, it's all the same. And from Plevne . . ."

"You with the beard, shut up! You've got a lot of chutzpah to enter this argument, you dimwit! I'll give you such a beating that you'll forget you ever heard of Plevne," screamed an older Jew in anger. (He was the young man's father.)

The goateed fellow quickly disappeared.

"Can you beat that? Even he has something to say about Plevne! Another expert heard from," the father exclaimed, unable to calm himself down.

"And you, wise guy, what do you know about Plevne?" burst out the man with the blond beard. "Plevne is impenetrable. It is located in the hollow space inside a huge cliff; this cliff is three *versts* tall and has straight walls. How do you think it can be breached? How can such a fortress be captured?"

"Of course it will be taken," retorted a fat man with a wide satin sash around his protruding stomach and a face that had wealth written all over it. He pushed his way into the circle and thundered, "You fool! You're talking nonsense — all these stories about cliffs and fortresses. I wouldn't give three kopecks for your Plevne. More people, more talk. Plevne, Shmevne!"

"The kugel at Chaim Isser's must have been really special today to make him so aggressive," chimed in an old Jew with a long gray beard, bright eyes, and an ironic smile. "What does he need politics for? With a shout, and a kick of his boot, he topples nine in one blow."

"And you, where do you stand? Do you also believe that Plevne won't be captured?" asked Chaim Isser in a loud but less belligerent voice.

"My opinion is that to talk about the war you have to know what it says in the paper. Take a lesson from Mendl. Who is better informed about politics than Mendl? And what's he doing? Sitting on the side and reciting Psalms," he ended in a mildly ironic tone.

Mendl! I remembered him now and looked for him. He was sitting in the back of the synagogue huddled over a Book of Psalms, which he was reading with amazing speed. At first I thought that he was indifferent to what was going on in the synagogue. But on closer view, I realized that from his quiet corner he could hear and see everything, like a hunter.

Mikhoel, the man with the mustache who had spoken up at the beginning, was standing in the middle of the circle and talking loudly in a tone of bitter reproof.

"It's just as the Bible says: 'Eyes they have, but they cannot see; ears they have, but they cannot hear.'* So why won't you see? Why won't you realize that the Turks are finished? You're always arguing 'Plevne.' Don't you understand that Plevne will be captured in the end, if not by arms then by starvation? Just open your eyes — in the four or five months since the Russians crossed the Don they've captured several fortresses, taken tens of thousands of Turks captive, and crossed halfway into Turkey. Doesn't that impress you? What kind of signs and wonders do you need? A month ago you were screaming 'Suleiman Pasha, the great hero Suleiman Pasha'! Then it turned out that the hero was not Suleiman Pasha at all — it was Hurko.† And now you shout 'Plevne,' 'Osman Pasha.' Tell me, what will you shout about when the Russians take Plevne?"

"Then there'll be no need to shout. Now I'm screaming so that everyone will know what a liar you are!" thundered the man with the blond beard. Then he quickly went over to where Mendl was sitting and said to him reprovingly, "Mendl, honestly, it's not right! You're making a fool of yourself sitting on the side and reciting Psalms like an old lady! Just listen to him. He has the nerve to peddle lies in a holy place!"

---

* Psalm 115: 5–6, also recited in the Hallel service on festivals.

† "Hurko" is General I. V. Gurko (as his name is spelled in Russian), who commanded the Russian cavalry during the Russo-Turkish War and was instrumental in the capture of Shipka and Plevne.

"Mendl, Mendl, enough of your Psalms. Come, join us," came the cries from all sides.

It was obvious that Mendl had no great desire to get involved in the debate, but he put away his Psalms nonetheless and got up to join them, first motioning to a boy to come over to him.

"Velvl, run to the marketplace and see if a new notice has been posted."

The boy ran out and Mendl walked slowly over to the circle, turned to Mikhoel and said, smiling, "I hear that you turn the world around, that you uproot mountains and demolish countries. You ground the poor Turks to dust in no time and spread their ashes over all the seven seas."

"And you, Miracle Worker, have you come to gather the dust and to mold a golem out of it?" Mikhoel retorted.

Then, in a more serious tone, he asked, "Do you honestly believe that the Turks aren't finished?"

"For heaven's sake, where did you get that idea?" interrupted Mendl, angry. "You argue that Plevne is besieged. But a person has to be blind not to see that it's not Plevne but the Russian army that's under siege. Do you all hear that?" He was shouting at the crowd, which had formed a circle around them both and was listening to every word. "Do you want to hear how the war is really going? If you do, I'll make it all as clear as day. The whole Russian army and all its generals are now in Turkey between the Don and Plevne. Osman Pasha is waiting in Plevne with a division of one hundred thousand soldiers and is making it impossible for the Russians to advance. At the left is Suleiman Pasha . . ."

"Who was beaten by Hurko," said someone.

"Shsh, be quiet!" said Mikhoel.

"As I was saying, Suleiman Pasha has a strong army. To the right is Mohammed Ali with an even larger army. Now listen — and use your brains. The Russian army is besieged on three sides; they can't go forward and they don't want to retreat. The summer is over and the rains will soon begin. They're tired, hungry, and far from home. How do you think it will end?"

He looked at the audience thoughtfully and soon continued confidently, "One of two things will happen. Either a fresh Turkish division will encircle the Russians, capture the Don, and take the entire army and its generals captive, or Osman Pasha will join Suleiman Pasha and Mohammed Ali and strike the Russian army from all three sides and drive it out of Turkey."

Mendl's convincing argument and the clear picture he drew of the possibilities greatly impressed the audience, which now had some sarcastic comments to make against Mikhoel. He listened calmly and attentively, never taking his eyes off Mendl.

"Have you finished?" he asked.

"Finished," the other answered curtly.

"It's a pity, a real pity, that you're done so soon," said Mikhoel, with a look of disappointment on his face.

He took the snuffbox from the pulpit, tapped it with two fingers, opened it, and took a large whiff. Then he closed the case and put it back, slowly and deliberately.

"Yes, it really is a pity that you finished so quickly. You could have gone much further. You drove the Russians out of Turkey — that alone is worth something. But why did you stop there? Why didn't you also bring the Turks into Russia and have them capture a few cities such as St. Petersburg or Moscow? It wouldn't have been difficult to do that — here in the synagogue," he ended, laughing.

"The Turks took a vow never to tread on Russian soil," one of the synagogue wits called out.

"My friend," replied Mendl calmly, but looking at Mikhoel sternly, "you know very well that the Turks are primitive and cruel. If they were merciful people, they would be freeing nations from the yokes of their oppressors. Don't worry, there'd be plenty of candidates — Poland, would be one, for example. You think the Poles suffer less from their oppressors than the Bulgarians? But what's to be done with Ishmael, the wild man, who feels no mercy for anyone?"

"Do you mean to say you don't believe the Russians will free the Bulgarians from the Turks?" asked Chaim Isser.

"What do you mean, I don't believe?" asked Mendl, with a look of surprise on his face. "What do you think I am — an apostate, God forbid? How can you even suggest that I don't believe that the Russians only mean to free the nation? Who in the entire world is better cast in the role of a liberator than Russia-the-thief?"

The last was met with a resounding laughter.

"Well said!"

"On the mark!"

"Russia the Messiah!"

"Sha, I've heard these wisecracks," Mikhoel called out irritably. "Then tell me one thing — why did Russia start the war?"

"If you're really interested, I'll tell you," answered Mendl. "The Russians have always been enemies of the Turks. This is not the first war they've fought, and in the course of many battles through the years the Russians have captured a lot of Turkish territory. Russia's ultimate aim is Constantinople. In short, Russia wants to free Turkey and annex the greater part to herself."

Mendl was repeating everything almost word for word from my lesson on the military history of Russia and Turkey.

Mikhoel listened impatiently to what Mendl had to say. Finally, unable to restrain himself any longer, he screamed out, "Fool! Ass! You talk such nonsense that I get sick listening to it."

Then he turned to the audience and said, "Listen, Jews! Russia covers an area of ten thousand *versts,* which is one-sixth of the world's surface; its riches are greater than those of any other nation. Now, do you think that the Russians would spill rivers of blood just for a little corner of the Turkish desert?"

"Reb Gershon," said Mendl, turning suddenly to an obviously wealthy, older member of the congregation, "they say that you're worth thirty thousand rubles. Is that correct?"

Reb Gershon was a bit confused by this unexpected question about such a delicate issue, but at the same time he was pleased to have his reputation as a rich man made public. It goes without saying that Mendl didn't ask the question simply to satisfy his curiosity; he was leading up to something in his argument with Mikhoel. He slowly stroked his beard and continued with a coy smile on his face, "Thirty thousand rubles of your own, you say? Now let's figure that I have — it doesn't matter what I have. You don't stop doing business, do you? You continue going to your store every day, and you do other business, too. I hear that you're involved in a big venture to build meat markets right now. So, clearly, you don't think you have enough money — you want more."

"Oh, and do I ever want more!" chuckled Gershon good-naturedly.

"Do you hear what he said, Mikhoel? He said, 'I don't have enough; I want more.' Do you know the meaning of 'more'? 'More' means 'everything.' You talk about a sixth of the world, but why not the whole world? Haven't there been seven kingdoms in the world since the time of Nimrod? And not one of them — not Nimrod, not Sennacherib, not Nebuchadnezzar, not Alexander of Macedon were satisfied with their share. Believe me, the Russians aren't satisfied with their sixth of the world either. And it's not the Turkish deserts they're after; they want the Turkish seas — the Bosphorus and the Dardanelles."

"What you're saying is that the entire war is being fought only for plunder and that the Turks are pure and innocent," shouted a tall, thin man with an ascetic face and eyes alive with anger. "What's the real story? Are you fooling yourself, or do you take us all for idiots? Don't we know what those cruel Turks, the murderers — may their names be blotted out — are doing to the Bulgarians? They destroy whole cities, burn villages, murder people by the thousands — it makes your hair stand on end and your blood turn to ice to hear about their brutality. And you take their side and turn them all into innocent sheep. You deserve to be torn limb from limb!"

"Only a thief and a murderer could take the side of the Turks," repeated an intense young man. And jumping on a bench he began an emotional speech, which could be heard throughout the synagogue. "Listen, friends! As you see me stand here, as it is Sabbath today throughout the world, I swear to you that when the call is made for new recruits I'll be the first to enlist! I'll leave my wife and children and go to war. And if I'm killed, it will be a martyr's death; I will die for God's honor."

The overwrought speech aroused everyone. It was as if a dam had burst. There was a loud outcry in the synagogue. Everyone was screaming. The "Russians" attacked the "Turks" with the worst kinds of recriminations and invectives. The "Turks" came back at the "Russians" with accusations of their own. Mendl tried to take the floor, but they wouldn't let him.

Night had fallen; the synagogue was dark. The pale moonlight, which shone through the dusty windows, lent a melancholy glow to the strange scene of all these people arguing in the synagogue. The beadle, a small dark Jew, went from one congregant to the other, pleading with them over and over again to go to their seats. "It's time for evening prayers!"

But no one paid any attention to him. Who could think of the evening service at a time like this? And then, suddenly, the door flew open and in flew Velvl from the marketplace, where he had been reading the new notices for Mendl.

"There's a notice, a notice," he screamed breathlessly.

In an instant the synagogue was totally silent; everyone turned to the boy.

"Oh . . . a slaughter . . . it lasted three whole days . . . oh, Hurko!" was all Velvl could get out.

"Come, come — tell us. Did they capture Plevne?" asked Mikhoel impatiently.

"No . . . oh . . . they didn't take Plevne. They captured Hubniak and some other city. Two thousand Russian soldiers were killed . . . that's what was written, two thousand. And the Turks lost about ten times that number. They didn't say how many."

Everyone was shaken by the news. Mendl grew pale and nervous as he listened wide-eyed to Velvl's news. And then, suddenly, he stood up, looked at the congregation with intense loathing, and shouted: "Murderers! Innocent blood is on your heads!" Then he quickly ran out of the synagogue.

A tense silence reigned for several minutes. Then, as if they were personally to blame, the "Russians" and the "Turks" separated, their heads lowered in shame. One person mumbled to himself, "I can't understand why he's the only one who's right. Who knows who's to blame?"

As if in response, the restrained melody of the weekday evening service was heard from the pulpit, with the words: "And He, merciful one, will forgive our sins and keep us from destruction. . . ."

The "three-day battle," which Velvl reported on from the notice on the marketplace wall, ended with the Russians occupying Gorni-Dubniak and Telish. This meant that there was a total blockage around Plevne and that it was cut off from the rest of the Turkish army. Now no one but the "Jewish Turks" doubted that Osman Pasha would surrender. The newspapers assured us that Plevne had no provisions and that the beleaguered army would soon capitulate. Everyone was impatient for Plevne to fall; the long-awaited peace, or at least the cease-fire, depended on it.

Only it didn't happen quite so fast. Days, weeks, the entire month of October passed, and Plevne still did not surrender. Osman Pasha repulsed the mightiest units of the Russian army, and it became clear that the outcome for which we all waited was not as sure as we originally had thought. Pessimistic voices were beginning to be heard; Plevne, they said, was an unconquerable fortress and Osman Pasha was a mighty leader in war.

6

After that first encounter Mendl continued to drop by in my room from time to time. However, his visits were always brief and to the point. I didn't side with the Turks and I had no great passion for politics, so he never engaged me in political discussions. He came either to see if the paper reported on some new and important development or to ask me to explain a political issue.

A few days after the Russians had captured the fortress of Kars (November 6) Mendl dropped in and wished me a lukewarm "good evening." With an almost unfriendly expression, he walked over to the table where I was sitting and said with strained politeness, "They tell me that you're in thick with the local nobility. Could you possibly get me a Turkish newspaper?"

"A Turkish newspaper?" I asked, surprised. "What for? Why would you need a Turkish paper?"

"I need . . ."

"Take off your coat and sit down."

"Thanks, but I have no time," he replied, barely concealing his impatience. "What about a Turkish newspaper?"

"I don't know what to tell you. I can't think of anyone around here who would get a Turkish paper."

"What do you mean? Aren't there people among the local nobility who are interested in politics?"

"And if there are, why would they read the Turkish papers?" I asked, still puzzled.

"To find out what's happening on the other side," he shouted excitedly.

"Can't you see how impossible it is to get a Turkish newspaper around here? Just for argument's sake, let's say that we did manage to find one — who would be able to read it? Who knows Turkish?"

"What do you mean 'who knows Turkish?' " he asked, quite non-plussed. "I thought that all aristocrats know Turkish. I was sure that you knew Turkish, too. When they told me that you know both German and French, I took it for granted that you knew Turkish as well. No!" — he suddenly shouted with a new wave of energy — "say what you will, without a Turkish newspaper we can never know the truth."

"The truth about what?"

"About Kars! 'Kars is captured.' Do you think that the Russians took Kars so easily? There was probably some kind of double cross. Someone who shouldn't have been involved is responsible for this. The English? But what I don't understand is how Osman Pasha could have permitted it to happen!"

"For God's sake, Reb Mendl, what are you saying? Where is Kars and where is Plevne? They are at either end of Turkey. And besides, how could Osman Pasha have helped when he himself is beleaguered in Plevne?"

"Beleaguered — bah!" Mendl repeated angrily. "What kind of stories are you telling me? How do we know that Osman Pasha isn't holding the Russian army beleaguered and won't let them move?"

I didn't answer him on this point. A few minutes later, however, I asked him a question of my own, "Tell me, Reb Mendl, why do you hate Russia so much?"

My question didn't surprise Mendl, but he didn't answer immediately. He sat a while and answered calmly. "The truth is, I see no reason why I should love Russia. I would give away the favors I have gotten from Mother Russia in a moment. But if you must know, I don't hate Russia."

"How can you say that you don't hate Russia when you want the Turks to be victorious?"

"That's a different matter and has nothing to do with love or hatred.

If I believed that the Russians were in the right in this war, I would defend them with all my might, just as I defend Turkey. This is a question of honesty and justice. Blood is being spilled — can you think of love and hatred in these circumstances?"

"But don't you feel some sort of sympathy, a bond with the people with whom you have lived since you were born?"

"How can you say that I live with them? With whom do I live? With the Russians? When do I have any contact with them? And when you get down to it, with whom could I have a bond? With the peasant who begins his day in the pigsty and ends it in the tavern? With the nobleman who thinks about nothing but a good dinner, stylish clothes, and — please don't be offended — a beautiful woman? How can we be friends with them? And on the other hand," he added with a smile, "I understand very well that they can't take me seriously either. What sort of a person do they see? — someone who doesn't eat pork, who is called Mendl instead of Ivan, who wears earlocks and a long frock coat. To them I must look like a wild man or some sort of fool."

He smiled bitterly and ended the conversation with a wave of his hand.

7

Plevne finally fell on November 28 and Osman Pasha and his entire army of forty thousand men surrendered. I learned these facts from the posters that were pasted on the buildings on the same morning and ran home immediately, anxious to see how Mendl would take the news. For some reason I felt sure that he had already seen the news.

But I was mistaken. Mendl knew nothing about it. I caught him in the middle of a lesson with two of his six pupils. They studied with their bodies as well as their minds, shaking to and fro and gesturing with their hands while they discussed an important and puzzling Talmudic problem in the customary singsong. The other four pupils, swaying over their open Gemara texts, were listening quietly. It seems that they were studying a difficult and complicated subject that they couldn't grasp. They were tired and frightened and their eyes looked defeated. Mendl was even more exhausted than they. His yellow, waxen face was covered with perspiration as he worked with all his might — with his hands, his voice, his eyes — to make the boys understand the difficult subject. But in vain. The boys were giddy from their efforts and their chanting, and simply weren't in a condition to study seriously. They repeated Mendl's words mechanically, shouting them in confused and pained voices.

I had visited Mendl several times before, so he wasn't taken aback at my presence. He stopped shouting immediately, breathed deeply, wiped the sweat from his face with his sleeve (he didn't wear his coat, as usual), and in a weak voice asked, "Is there any news?"

I didn't have the heart to shock the exhausted teacher, so I only nodded my head uncertainly. He took a deep breath and said bitterly, "They've taken my last bit of strength and they just don't understand; even if I killed myself they wouldn't understand!"

He quickly returned to the pupils and, swaying back and forth, he called out in the Gemara chant, "Now, once again. Our rabbis teach . . ."

I wasn't there ten minutes when Mikhoel, the "Russian" who had stalked out of the synagogue, also appeared. He was Mendl's fiercest political opponent, but he was also his closest friend. Both were teachers, both were Hasidim who followed the same rebbe, and politics aside, they were bound by common interests and spent a lot of time together. Mendl didn't see anything unusual in Mikhoel's visit, but I understood immediately why he was there. He winked at me, as if to tell me not to say anything.

He had a sad expression on his face and entered the room slowly and quietly; then he mumbled "good morning," sat down on one of the benches, got up quickly, walked to the table, and looked into an open Gemara.

"Aha, this is what you're up to," he said in a tone of sympathy, "a familiar piece of ground. It's a mire that I don't wish on anyone. Last year I spent a whole week slogging through this passage with my dumb charges before they got anything out of it!"

"It's not such a difficult subject, really," Mendl replied. "If they would only give themselves to the subject, they would surely understand.

But what can I do? They don't want to. I'm so frustrated with these blockheads."

"Now you exaggerate. It is a difficult item. I've seen many older, learned Jews sweat over this passage. It's a kind of Plevne — it's hard to take hold of," Mikhoel finished with a good-natured laugh.

Mendl also smiled. "Still, we'll conquer it in less time than it will take the Russians to conquer Plevne," he said confidently.

"Oh, my friend — there you're making a big mistake. Plevne has been captured."

"Oh sure — it goes without saying," quipped Mendl ironically.

"No, it's true — Plevne was captured yesterday," repeated Mikhoel, looking at Mendl very seriously now.

Mendl shivered, but he still couldn't believe what he heard.

"What do you mean? What are you babbling," he shouted, in a state of agitation.

Mikhoel took out the snuffbox, opened it slowly, took a long whiff, wiped his nose with his handkerchief, and turned to Mendl. "My good friend, I'm not babbling at all. I came purposely to give you the good news. Plevne has been captured, and, what's more, Osman Pasha and his entire army have surrendered. That's it in a nutshell."

Mendl was astounded by the news. He turned to me, looking for help.

"What . . . what is he saying?" he asked me.

I could only confirm what Mikhoel said.

"What can it mean?" said Mendl, even more astounded. "You know about it, too? Why didn't you say anything? How do you know? Did you read about it in the newspaper?"

"No, a notice was posted."

"Where? In the market?"

And Mendl jumped up from his seat, ready to run to the market to read the notice.

"Sh, sh. Don't fly," said Mikhoel, stopping him. "I spent a few kopecks to bring the good news straight to you, all for your pleasure." And handing Mendl a folded gray paper with the printed news, he walked over to a small shelf on the other side of the room where some old, torn books were kept and searched among them for a thin notebook. It was a densely filled manuscript, written by his rebbe in a narrow, curved script. He sat near the window and concentrated on the text, as if he had forgotten all about Mendl and Plevne.

"Study the passage on your own for a while and see if you can understand it," said Mendl to his pupils.

The pupils, who were delighted to have their lesson interrupted even for a little while, were very interested in the news which Mikhoel brought. While pretending to be looking into their Gemaras, they were actually straining to hear every word of our conversation and kept up a constant whispering among themselves. From the few words that I overheard and from the expressions on their faces I understood that the boys were also divided into "Russians" and "Turks," and now under the cover of their texts the "Russians" were celebrating their victory over the "Turks."

Mendl nervously unfolded the paper and was entirely engrossed in it. He read Russian slowly and with difficulty and had to concentrate on every phrase, not satisfied to understand the content alone but anxious to get to the deepest meaning of every word. Several times he gestured, as if he wanted to say something, but he always restrained himself and returned to the paper.

When he finished reading, he sat deep in thought, his head lowered and his brow wrinkled, as if he were trying to remember something. With every passing minute, his face became calmer. Suddenly he raised his head, looked at Mikhoel, at me, at the telegraphic notice with a bright, wide-eyed look, and gave a shudder, as if someone had just woken him from sleep. Then an entirely different expression appeared in his eyes — more earnest, sterner, almost ascetic. It was as if he had experienced a complete change in personality in the last few minutes, as if he had found the answer to a difficult problem and had been released from a nightmare.

Mikhoel sat engrossed in the kabbalistic manuscript for about half an hour. Figuring that enough time had passed for Mendl to read through the notice and think about it, he slowly closed the notebook and put it back in place, took a stool and sat next to him. Staring at him apprehensively, he spoke quietly but with a certain hardness, "Well, Mendl, what do you have to say about this?"

Mendl didn't answer immediately. He looked back at Mikhoel with an equally unshaken expression, and with just as much control in his voice he answered, "And you, Mikhoel, what do you think about it?"

Mikhoel was not prepared for such a cool reply. He was amazed at Mendl's stubborn control and cried out indignantly, "*Meshugener!* You have to be crazy to talk the way you do! Isn't it enough for you that Plevne was captured and that Osman Pasha has surrendered? What kind of signs and wonders do you need? Do you expect the heavens to come down to earth?"

Mendl wasn't upset by Mikhoel's shouting.

"Don't raise the roof," he answered, calmly. "One might think that it was you, in your wisdom and strength, and not Skobelev who has taken Plevne. What would you like me to say? Do you want me to admit that you were right and that I was wrong?"

"Yes, yes, that's what I want," answered Mikhoel.

"Then I'll tell you straight off that I will not admit it."

"You're crazy, a complete *meshugener,*" shouted Mikhoel again.

"If you'll just listen calmly, you'll see for yourself that I'm not crazy. Think back — what argument did I use all the time?"

"You claimed that . . ."

"Just a minute. I'll review my arguments myself," Mendl interrupted. "My first premise was that the Turks were in the right, not the Russians. So, does the Russian victory prove that they were right? Is the victor always right? Don't we know that just the opposite is often the case: 'The evil man flourishes while the just man begs for bread.' "

"But you were always shouting . . ." Mikhoel began.

Mendl cut him short again. "Let me talk. I know what I said. I always pointed out that the Turks were stronger than the Russians, and I still believe that. The fact that the Russians were victorious proves nothing. The strong side doesn't always triumph; often the weaker party wins. A gnat, the tiniest of flies, vanquished the great Titus. Delilah outmaneuvered the mighty Samson . . ."

"David and Goliath!" cried out one of the pupils — and then hid his face in shame. The other children laughed.

"Children, don't mix into matters that don't concern you! Do what I told you to do," Mendl said to them mildly, and turned back to Mikhoel:

"My only error was to state that the Turks were certain to win. There, I agree, I was mistaken."

"Aha, so you do admit . . ."

"Now just hold on; you made the same miscalculation," declared Mendl.

"I? Where did I miscalculate?" asked Mikhoel, taken by surprise.

"My mistake wasn't in predicting that the Turks would be victorious, but in trusting the news in the papers and in the notices. And there you were just as mistaken as I was. We both ran around in search of the latest news as if we were drugged. But the newspapers and notices could tell us only what had already taken place, not what was about to happen. The true cause and significance of events could not possibly be discovered in the papers. Because neither the newspapers, nor Bismarck nor Bikensfeld, with all their political theories, have the slightest idea of the causes from which events stem!"

And he glared at me with a challenging expression, as if I were a journalist or commentator who reported on political issues.

Mikhoel listened attentively, but when he wanted to offer his own point of view, Mendl just continued, "If we really wanted to penetrate into the essence of the war, into all the events and victories, we should have searched sources besides the newspapers and the notices — we should have looked into the Zohar and other sacred texts."

Suddenly he became quiet and lost in thought; his expression took on a lofty air.

This made Mikhoel uneasy, and he didn't know what to answer. He pulled the snuffbox out of his pocket, opened it quickly, and took a good long whiff of snuff; it calmed him somewhat and cleared his mind.

"Perhaps . . . you are right. But that's a different matter altogether," he stated, as if to himself. He sat quietly for a while, and then added: "Just recently a young man showed me an allusion in the form of a *notarikon** based on the first verse of the Bible, 'In the beginning God made.' It's a very deep matter."

"What is it?" asked Mendl, suddenly interested.

"If interpreted according to the method of notarikon, the verse 'In the

---

* *Notarikon* is an acrostic, used both as a mnemonic device and as a method of uncovering the hidden meanings of Scripture. Here An-ski is tapping Jewish folk responses to war and historical catastrophe.

beginning God made' reads *In the days of the Romanov Alexander the second, the Turks will be caught in great Russia's net.*"

"What was that? Say it again," demanded Mendl, curious.

Mikhoel repeated the statement, and Mendl wrote it down.

Both teachers were quiet for a time; then Mikhoel got up wearily and asked, "Are you coming to the 'early risers' meeting this evening?"

"Of course," Mendl answered. "We have to discuss raising money for the delegate here to collect money for the holy land. It would really be a disgrace if we couldn't raise a few rubles for him."

"An absolute disgrace," agreed Mikhoel, sighing, and with a nod to Mendl and me, he left the room.

Mendl's eyes followed him up to the door; then Mendl returned to the table and said almost cheerfully, "Well, dear children! Now we have to get back to our text. If you give it everything you have, I'm sure you will understand it." He brushed both hands softly, almost caressingly, over the old, crumpled pages of the Gemara, sighed deeply, and began to intone in his singsong: "Our rabbis teach . . ."

When I came home, I found my old landlord in a state of nerves. He was walking restlessly from one side of the room to the other, and when he saw me, he rushed over and said excitedly, "Is it really true?"

"What are you talking about?"

"That the Russians captured — the city of — what is it called again? I forgot."

"Plevne?"

"That's it, Plevne. Did they really take it?"

"Yes, they captured it."

"*Ai, ai, ai,*" he cried in despair. "And what will happen now?"

"Now they'll sign a peace treaty."

"Peace treaty," he blurted out, shaking, "and that's it?"

"That's it."

The old man stared at me for a while with a frightened expression on his face. When he had calmed down somewhat, he turned to the door but added sadly, "What do you think of my good wife? She went off to the store without leaving me money for snuff. I've been walking around all morning like a slaughtered goose."

I gave him two kopecks, and this soon made him forget all about the historic events which had so disturbed him.

My acquaintance with Mendl came to an abrupt end. He stopped visiting me, and when we met by chance, he avoided talking to me. Soon after that I moved to another room, and some months later I left town for good.

YIVO Institute for Jewish Research, © 1983 Nancy Crampton

As Isaac Bashevis Singer would have been the first to point out, as a writer he was very much a product of his community. So it came as a matter of special pride that his 1978 Nobel Prize was widely seen as a recognition of Yiddish and its literature.

Although Singer had been living in the United States since 1935 and his English was excellent, he continued, throughout his life, to write in Yiddish. "I deal with unique characters in unique circumstances," he wrote, "a group of people who are still a riddle to the world and often to themselves — the Jews of Eastern Europe, specifically the Yiddish-speaking Jews who perished in Poland and those who emigrated to the United States. The longer I live with them and write about them, the more I am baffled by the richness of their individuality and (since I am one of them) by my own whims and passions."

Singer's ability to immerse himself in those passions gave a broad audience access to his world, and to their own.

Singer was born in 1904 in the small town of Leoncin, in Poland. His father, a Hasidic rabbi for whom compromise was anathema, firmly planted himself against the incursions of secular modernity. Even when the family moved to Warsaw, when the boy was five, their life remained resolutely separate.

Singer wrote, "My father used to say that secular writers like Peretz were leading the Jews to heresy. . . . Even though Peretz wrote in a religious vein, my father called his writing 'sweetened poison.' "

Singer's older brother, Israel Joshua, swallowed the poison early. He abandoned Hasidic dress and religious practices, became a Yiddish writer, and quit the family home for Warsaw's freethinking artistic crowd. When young Isaac brought home-cooked food to his brother in his avant-garde digs, he described the scene: "They neither prayed nor studied from holy books nor made benedictions. They ate meat with milk, and broke other laws. The girls posed nude with no more shame than they would have had about undressing in their own bedrooms." The contrast could not have been more extreme.

Isaac continued to live the life of a Hasid, but began reading European literature in Yiddish translation. When he was thirteen, however, he left the modern world behind. For four years he lived with his maternal grandfather, also a Hasidic rabbi, in Bilgoray, another small town where, he said, "time seemed to flow backward."

But he did not resent his time away from the cosmopolitan capital. "I lived Jewish history," he said. "I found a spiritual treasure trove."

Once back in Warsaw, however, Singer soon left the family. He translated modern European literature, including Thomas Mann and Carl Hamsun, into Yiddish, and worked as a proofreader for Yiddish publications. He also ate, with a hearty appetite, at the artistic and political smorgasbord that was Poland between the two world wars. He was frank about his love affairs. His left-wing girlfriend gave birth to his son, then took the child to Israel.

In 1925, Singer began to publish Yiddish stories. Eight years later, he published *Satan in Goray,* a sophisticated novel with multiple points of view, set in seventeenth-century Poland. It had been a tumultuous time for Jews, with massacres, false messiahs, and dramatic conflicts of faith. The era had special resonance for Poland in the 1930s. As Singer later described it: "I had always believed in God, but I knew enough of Jewish history to doubt in His miracles." In 1935, he followed his older brother, who had earlier moved to New York.

The move was traumatic. Yiddish literature did not have the status in the United States that it had in Poland. And war soon destroyed the world that Singer had left behind. He did not write for seven years.

In the middle of the war, though, he began to write again, this time maintaining a constant stream for the rest of his life. He published almost all his works first as serials in *Der forvarts* (the Forward), New York's leading Yiddish newspaper. In time, as more of his works were translated into English and published in book form, he gained a wider following.

In old age, he became a fixture on the New York Jewish scene. He was a popular lecturer, and developed a coterie of young fans who saw him as a link to a lost world.

But that world was always presented through Singer's mystic, probing eyes. He wrote, "Genuine literature informs while it entertains. It manages to be both clear and profound. It has the magical power of merging causality with purpose, doubt with faith, the passions of the flesh with the yearnings of the soul. It is unique and general, national and universal, realistic and mystical."

Singer's work is also mordantly funny. When, at the time of his Nobel Prize, one of his interviewers asked him why he continued to write in Yiddish he said, "I believe in reincarnation. In a thousand years when people return to this earth they will ask, 'Are there any good books available in Yiddish?' and then I'll earn a lot of royalties."

Singer died in 1991 in New York.

Growing Old

TRANSLATED BY GOLDA WERMAN

I

While his wife was alive Gimpel Bedner was still something of a "mensch." True, it was years since he had worked as a water carrier and they lived only on what Sheyndel was able to earn selling milk. But Sheyndel managed; she bought milk from the peasants and sold it from large earthen crocks that she kept in the storeroom of their house, she made her own butter, and from time to time she even carried home a sack of corn on her shoulders.

Gimpel always lay on the iron bed with his pants on and barefoot. He was half paralyzed and one arm was twisted, so he couldn't work anymore.

He hardly ever left the house except for the High Holidays, when he dragged himself to the synagogue on crutches. Meanwhile Gimpel's daughters, children of his old age, grew up and left for the big city, where they worked as servants. Every summer they came home for a week. They were tall, good-looking girls who wore low-cut dresses and flesh-colored stockings. Everyone in town talked about them but the ugly rumors never reached Gimpel.

When he saw them coming through the door his grimy, blackened face would light up and as he struggled to close his perpetually unbuttoned pants, he would draw a deep sigh and blurt out breathlessly: "Oy — ay — a good year to you!" Every year they brought new clothes and clean linens for their father. Then the windows that had been closed all year would be opened, and the sweet smell of perfume would fill the house, and the piles of rags that always lay in heaps on the floor would disappear, and the ceiling would light up and make the little house bright and festive. Gimpel never stopped sighing with the pleasure of it all. Once, with fatherly pride, he said to his wife: "I can't understand where the girls got their good looks. I don't remember that you were so pretty — eh? Ooh, aah," he suddenly cried out as his leg began to throb with pain.

In those days he was still the head of the family. He had a little house, an inheritance from his grandfather, he had a wife, and he had children. When a housewife came to buy milk and butter and Sheyndel was not home, Gimpel would haggle with her:

"I can't reduce the price, believe me it costs me as much . . . I should live so long . . ."

The real problems began when Sheyndel fell in a peasant woman's house and died.

By the next day there wasn't even a piece of bread in the house, and no one to bring him any. Good friends forgot about him and the peasants didn't honor the deposits that Sheyndel had left with them for milk. Elke, the neighbor with the long, yellow teeth, came in for the first few days to cook some unpeeled potatoes for him. She always let out a series of loud, heartbreaking sighs, a signal that she was ready to deliver one of her firsthand reports about the latest tragic events in town. Moaning and rocking from side to side, she would wait until someone asked her why she was groaning — what happened?

This time she had bad news for Gimpel.

"They say that your daughters are doing shameful things in Lublin . . . yes, they know it for a fact . . . and they say that they are coming back. . . ."

That's how Gimpel learned that he had lost not only his wife but his children, too. He kept his eyes fixed on the dark floor and his stiff hands shook so uncontrollably that he could hardly lift the potatoes that he had peeled with his long dirty nails to his mouth.

"Nu, if that's the way it is," he cried, scratching his tangled beard, "that's how it is."

✧ ✧ ✧

II

His daughters returned and rented a little house at the edge of town. They put flowerpots in the windows and wore silk scarves and smelled of perfume. And they paraded through the street wearing red dresses and green hats. Fat housewives pointed their fingers and cursed them. Shopkeepers who knew Gimpel looked them straight in the eyes and reproached them for their sins: "You should be ashamed of yourselves for bringing such disgrace on your father in his old age."

Gimpel began to spend his days in the synagogue. Day in and day out he sat near the stove, mumbling passages from the Book of Psalms and smoking cigarettes made of leaves taken from the bathhouse brooms. He always kept his stiff, twisted hand open at his side. His whole body had become stiffer after his daughters came home. But his appetite remained good, just like a peasant's. If they brought carrots to the house of study, he ate them; if they passed around handfuls of cooked beans, he ate them, too.

Since Gimpel's daughters came to town the young men in the house of study found it difficult to concentrate. They would take their large tomes to the window and smile — their heads were full of sinful thoughts as they stared out with glazed eyes, their books all but forgotten.

"Greetings from your daughters, Reb Gimpel," they taunted. "They want to catch a student from the house of study on their fishing pole. Would you know why? I mean, haven't they told you?" And choking with laughter, they would pinch each other.

Once, tired of reciting Psalms, Gimpel joined the young students in their vulgar patter.

"You're right, as I live. Quick, a radish, give me a radish. I need a radish for my dry throat."

The older members of the congregation were not around so the students indulged him with radishes that they peeled and cut into slices. Gimpel bit into them with his strong, bovine teeth and nodded his head, like an animal chewing its cud. Then he rewarded the group by talking about his own daughters. "Never mind, they earn their money honestly."

Suddenly, feeling his lips twist into a distorted smile, he realized that he was losing control of his body. One of his eyes closed and he couldn't speak. He waited for the crooked smile to disappear, and it was clear from the expression on his face that he knew that he had made a public spectacle of himself. Finally he returned to his tobacco-stained book — he moistened his dry finger to turn the page and mumbled something from Psalms. The young students pinched each other until their arms were black and blue as they heard Gimpel mispronouncing the words and inverting the order of the verses.

"It's a pity that you didn't learn the bakery trade, Reb Gimpel," they said. "You already know how to knead and mix, just like a real baker."

III

In the winter the roof of Gimpel's little house collapsed and he began to spend his nights in the synagogue. At first no one said anything, but after a while the older congregants became annoyed. They held their noses up high and sniffed the air for bad odors, complaining bitterly to each other.

"What a disgusting stench," they whispered, pointing toward the stove. "It's suffocating."

They took out their snuffboxes and passed them around to see if the smell of the tobacco canceled out the bad odor. After long consideration they finally agreed that their initial estimate was correct.

"It's a profanation of God's name," they said. "One may not even pronounce a holy word under these conditions."

Chanina, a young porter with a full head of hair, a fleshy face, and a little blond beard, said that he had seen with his own eyes how the old man had dirtied the washbasin. What a commotion broke out in the house of study! They threw out the water and everyone removed his phylacteries. Mordecai Joseph, the crippled trustee of the ritual bath and a very influential person, stopped reading the sacred text on his book stand, pressed his deformed body forward on his heavy cane, and shouted at the top of his lungs.

"Gimpel and his daughters have sullied the whole town," he screamed. "We've put up with enough from him, enough! Get a horse and wagon and take him away! Take him there to the, you know, his whores — the apple doesn't fall far from the tree."

His green watery eyes glared with anger under his thick eyebrows and his long nose turned red. He attacked the beadle for permitting the abomination to occur and accused the wardens of being ignoramuses — they are not fit to be officers in the synagogue, he charged. Then he sent the children to fetch him various books and pointed his long white finger at a passage in the Shulkhan Arukh. "Distance yourself the space of four arm-lengths from excrement and urine and if a night pot filled with feces and urine is left in the room, praying there is not permitted.

"Do you understand or not? It could not be more clearly stated, and it comes straight from the Talmud. Here, see for yourselves!"

Taking out one holy book after another and sneezing from the snuff, he ranted about the filth and the fact that today's prayers were an abomination. The synagogue wardens quaked in fear when they heard the rules he cited.

"That's it, take him away now," they ordered. "Tell Hirsh Malkha to bring his horse right away so that we can get this business over with!"

An hour later Gimpel was lying in a bed with a red quilt and a pillow under his head. All over the walls of the little room were pictures of naked women, and there was an odor of pork cooking in the kitchen. Gimpel's daughters, wearing nothing but their bodices and scandalously short red slips, were sullenly humming a tune as they ironed. They heaped abuse on Hirsh Malkha, the coachman, for bringing their father and they talked about sending him away to the hospital in Lublin that very night. And they argued about money. Gimpel lay with his eyes closed, half asleep, and heaved a deep and bitter sigh from time to time.

"Oy — ayyaiyai!"

The younger daughter, overcome with pity for her father, tried to comfort him. "You'll have everything you need in the hospital, Tatte. We'll work and pay, just like everyone else."

And while she was talking to him a tall, pockmarked soldier with a shining sword hanging at his side came to the door. For a few moments he stood motionless, staring at Gimpel with a stupid, drunken expression on his face. The older daughter shot an angry glance in her father's direction. For a while she couldn't figure out what to do with him and she scratched her ear, trying to think of a solution. Then she quietly stepped over to his bed.

"Move a little closer to the wall, Tatte," she whispered in a firm and businesslike tone. "Do you hear me or not? There — lie just like that until I tell you to move. That's the way . . . that's it."

The Bus

TRANSLATED BY JOSEPH SINGER

Why I undertook that particular tour in 1956 is something I haven't figured out to this day — dragging around in a bus through Spain for twelve days with a group of tourists. We left from Geneva. I got on the bus around three in the afternoon and found the seats nearly all taken. The driver collected my ticket and point out a place next to a woman who was wearing a conspicuous black cross on her breast. Her hair was dyed red, her face was thickly rouged, the lids of her brown eyes were smeared with blue eyeshadow, and from beneath all this dye and paint emerged deep wrinkles. She had a hooked nose, lips red as a cinder, and yellowish teeth.

She began speaking to me in French, but I told her I didn't understand the language and she switched over to German. It struck me that her German wasn't that of a real German or even a Swiss. Her accent was similar to mine and she made the same mistakes. From time to time she interjected a word that sounded Yiddish. I soon found out that she was a refugee from the concentration camps. In 1946, she arrived at a DP camp near Landsberg and there by chance she struck up a friendship with a Swiss bank director from Zurich. He fell in love with her and proposed marriage but under the condition that she accept Protestantism. Her name at home had been Celina Pultusker. She was now Celina Weyerhofer.

Suddenly she began speaking to me in Polish, then went over into Yiddish. She said, "Since I don't believe in God anyway, what's the difference if it's Moses or Jesus? He wanted me to convert, so I converted a bit."

"So why do you wear a cross?"

"Not out of anything to do with religion. It was given to me by someone dying whom I'll never forget till I close my eyes."

"A man, eh?"

"What else — a woman?"

"Your husband has nothing against this?"

"I don't ask him. There he is."

Mrs. Weyerhofer pointed out a man sitting across the way. He looked younger than she, with a fair, smooth face, blue eyes, and a straight nose. To me he appeared the typical banker — sober, amiable, his trousers neatly pressed and pulled up to preserve the crease, shoes freshly polished. He was wearing a panama hat. His manner expressed order, discipline. Across his knee lay the *Neue Zürcher Zeitung,* and I noticed it was open to the financial section. From his breast pocket he took a piece of cloth with which he polished his glasses. That done, he glanced at his gold wristwatch.

I asked Mrs. Weyerhofer why they weren't sitting together.

"Because he hates me," she said in Polish.

Her answer surprised me, but not overly so. The man glanced at me sidelong, then averted his face. He began to converse with a lady sitting in the window seat beside him. He removed his hat, revealing a shining bald pate surrounded by a ruff of pale-blond hair. "What could it have been that this Swiss saw in the person next to me?" I asked myself, but such things one could not really question.

Mrs. Weyerhofer said, "So far as I can tell, you are the only Jew on the bus. My husband doesn't like Jews. He doesn't like Gentiles, either. He has a million prejudices. Whatever I say displeases him. If he had the power, he'd kill off most of mankind and leave only his dogs and the few bankers with whom he's chummy. I'm ready to give him a divorce but he's too stingy to pay alimony. As it is, he barely gives me enough to keep alive. Yet he's highly intelligent, one of the best-read people I've ever met. He speaks six languages perfectly, but, thank God, Polish isn't one of them."

She turned toward the window and I lost any urge to talk to her further. I had slept poorly the night before, and when I leaned back I dozed off, though my mind went on thinking wakeful thoughts. I had broken up with a woman I loved — or at least desired. I had just spent three weeks alone in a hotel in Zakopane.

I was awakened by the driver. We had come to the hotel where we would eat dinner and sleep. I couldn't orient myself to the point of deciding whether we were still in Switzerland or had reached France. I didn't catch the name of the city the driver had announced. I got the key to my room. Someone had already left my suitcase there. A bit later, I went down to the dining room. All the tables were full, and I didn't want to sit with strangers.

As I stood, a boy who appeared to be fourteen or fifteen came up to me. He reminded me of prewar Poland in his short pants and high woolen stockings, his jacket with the shirt collar outside. He was a handsome youth — black hair worn in a crewcut, bright dark eyes, and unusually pale skin. He clicked his heels in military fashion and asked, "Sir, you speak English?"

"Yes."

"You are an American?"

"An American citizen."

"Perhaps you'd like to join us? I speak English. My mother speaks a little, too."

"Would your mother agree?"

"Yes. We noticed you in the bus. You were reading an American newspaper. After I graduate from what you call high school, I want to study at an American university. You aren't by chance a professor?"

"No, but I have lectured at a university a couple of times."

"Oh, I took one look at you and I knew immediately. Please, here is our table."

He led me to where his mother was sitting. She appeared to be in her mid-thirties, plump, but with a pretty face. Her black hair was combed into two buns, one at each side of her face. She was expensively dressed and wore lots of jewelry. I said hello and she smiled and replied in French.

The son addressed her in English: "Mother, the gentleman is from the United States. A professor, just as I said he would be."

"I am no professor. I was invited by a college to serve as writer-in-residence."

"Please. Sit down."

I explained to the woman that I knew no French, and she began to speak to me in a mixture of English and German. She introduced herself as Annette Metalon. The boy's name was Mark. The waiters hadn't yet managed to serve all the tables, and while we waited I told the mother and son that I was a Jew, that I wrote in Yiddish, and that I came from Poland. I always do this as soon as possible to avoid misunderstandings later. If the person I am talking to is a snob, he knows that I'm not trying to represent myself as something I'm not.

"Sir, I am also a Jew. On my father's side. My mother is Christian."

"Yes, my late husband was a Sephardi," Mrs. Metalon said. Was Yiddish a language or a dialect? she asked me. How did it differ from Hebrew? Was it written in Latin letters or in Hebrew? Who spoke the language and did it have a future? I responded to everything briefly. After some hesitation, Mrs. Metalon told me that she was an Armenian and that she lived in Ankara but that Mark was attending school in London. Her husband came from Saloniki. He was an importer and exporter of Oriental rugs and had had some other businesses as well. I noticed a ring with a huge diamond on her finger, and magnificent pearls around her neck. Finally, the waiter came over and she ordered wine and a steak. When the waiter heard I was a vegetarian he grimaced and informed me that the kitchen wasn't set up for vegetarian meals. I told him I would eat whatever I could get — potatoes, vegetables, bread, cheese. Anything he could bring me.

As soon as he had gone, the questions started about my vegetarianism: Was it on account of my health? Out of principle? Did it have anything to do with being kosher? I was accustomed to justifying myself, not only to strangers but even to people who had known me for years. When I told Mrs. Metalon that I didn't belong to any synagogue, she asked the question for which I could never find the answer — what did my Jewishness consist of?

According to the way the waiter had reacted, I assumed that I'd leave the table hungry, but he brought me a plateful of cooked vegetables and a mushroom omelette as well as fruit and cheese. Mother and son both tasted my dishes, and Mark said, "Mother, I want to become a vegetarian."

"Not as long as you're living with me," Mrs. Metalon replied.

"I don't want to remain in England, and certainly not in Turkey. I've

decided to become an American," Mark said. "I like American literature, American sincerity, democracy, and the American business sense.
In England there are no opportunities for anyone who wasn't born
there. I want to marry an American girl. Sir, what kind of documents
are needed to get a visa to the United States? I have a Turkish passport,
not an English one. Would you, sir, send me an affidavit?"

"Yes, with pleasure."

"Mark, what's wrong with you? You meet a gentleman for the first
time and at once you make demands of him."

"What do I demand? An affidavit is only a piece of paper and a sig-
nature. I want to study at Harvard University or at the University of
Princeton. Sir, which of these two universities has the better business
school?"

"I really wouldn't know."

"Oh, he has already decided everything for himself," Mrs. Metalon
said. "A child of fourteen but with an old head. In that sense, he takes
after his father. He always planned down to the last detail and years in
advance. My husband was forty years older than I, but we had a happy
life together."She took out a lace-edged handkerchief and dabbed at an
invisible tear.

The bus routine required that each day passengers exchanged seats. It
gave everyone a chance to sit up front. Most couples stayed together, but
individuals kept changing their partners. On the third day, the driver
placed me next to the banker from Zurich, who was apparently determined not to sit with his wife.

He introduced himself to me: Dr. Rudolf Weyerhofer. The bus had
left Bordeaux, where we had spent the night, and was approaching the
Spanish border. At first neither of us spoke; then Dr. Weyerhofer began
to talk of Spain, France, the situation in Europe. He questioned me
about America, and when I told him that I was a staff member of a
Yiddish newspaper his talk turned to Jews and Judaism. Wasn't it odd
that a people should have retained its identity through two thousand
years of wandering across the countries of the world and after all that
time returned to the land and language of its ancestors? The only such
instance in the history of mankind. Dr. Weyerhofer told me he had read

Graetz's *History of the Jews* and even something of Dubnow's. He knew the works of Martin Buber and Klausner's *Jesus of Nazareth*. But for all that, the essence of the Jew was far from clear to him. He asked about the Talmud, the Zohar, the Hasidim, and I answered as best I could. I felt certain that shortly he would begin talking about his wife.

Mrs. Weyerhofer had already managed to irritate the other passengers. Both in Lyons and in Bordeaux the bus had been forced to wait for her — for a half hour in Lyons and for over an hour in Bordeaux. The delays played havoc with the travel schedule. She had gone off shopping and had returned loaded down with bundles. From the way she had described her husband to me as a miser who begrudged her a crust of bread, I couldn't understand where she got the money to buy so many things. Both times she apologized and said that her watch had stopped, but the Swiss women claimed that she had purposely turned back the hands of her gold wristwatch. By her behavior Celina Weyerhofer humiliated not only her husband, who accused her in public of lying, but also me, for it was obvious to everyone on the bus that she, like me, was a Jew from Poland.

I no longer recall how it came about but Dr. Weyerhofer began to unburden himself to me. He said, "My wife accuses me of anti-Semitism, but what kind of anti-Semite am I if I married a Jewish woman just out of concentration camp? I want you to know that this marriage has caused me enormous difficulties. At that time many people in financial circles were infected with the Nazi poison, and I lost important connections. I was seriously considering emigrating to your America or even to South Africa, since I had practically been excommunicated from the Christian business community. How is this called by your people . . . *cherem?* My blessed parents were still living then and they were both devout Christians. You could write a thick book about what I went through.

"Though my wife became converted, she did it in such a way that the whole thing became a farce. This woman makes enemies wherever she goes, but her worst enemy is her own mouth. She has a talent for antagonizing everyone she meets. She tried to establish a connection with the Jewish community in Zurich, but she said such shocking things and carried on so that the members would have nothing to do with her. She'd go to a rabbi and represent herself as an atheist; she'd launch a debate with him about religion and call him a hypocrite. While she accuses everyone of anti-Semitism, she herself says things about Jews you'd expect from a Goebbels. She plays the role of a rabid feminist and joins protests against the Swiss government for refusing to give women the vote, yet at the same time she castigates women in the most violent fashion.

"I noticed her talking to you when you were sitting together and I know she told you how mean I am with money. But the woman has a buying mania. She buys things that will never be used. I have a large apartment she's crowded with so much furniture, so many knickknacks and idiotic pictures that you can barely turn around. No maid will work for us. We eat in restaurants even though I hate not eating at home. I must have been mad to agree to go on this trip with her. But it looks as if we won't last out the twelve days. While I sit talking here with you, my mind is on forfeiting my money and leaving the bus before we even get to Spain. I know I shouldn't be confiding my personal problems like this, but since you are a writer maybe they can be of use to you. I tell myself that the camps and wanderings totally destroyed her nerves, but I've met other women who survived the whole Hitler hell, and they are calm, civilized, pleasant people."

"How is it that you didn't see this before?" I asked.

"Eh? A good question. I ask myself the same thing. The very fact that I'm telling you all this is a mystery to me, since we Swiss are reticent. Apparently ten years of living with this woman have altered my character. She is the one who allegedly converted, but I seem to have turned into almost a Polish Jew. I read all the Jewish news, particularly any dealing with the Jewish state. I often criticize the Jewish leaders, but not as a stranger — rather as an insider."

The bus stopped. We had come to the Spanish frontier. The driver went with our passports to the border station and lingered there a long time.

Dr. Weyerhofer began talking quietly, in almost a mumble, "I want to be truthful. One good trait she did have — she could attract a man. Sexually, she was amazingly strong. I don't believe myself that I am speaking of these things — in my circles, talk of sex is taboo. But why?

Man thinks of it from cradle to grave. She has a powerful imagination, a perverse fantasy. I've had experience with women and I know. She has said things to me that drove me to frenzy. She has more stories in her than Scheherazade. Our days were cursed, but the nights were wild. She wore me out until I could no longer do my work. Is this characteristic of Jewish women in Eastern Europe? The Swiss Jewish women aren't much more interesting than the Christian."

"You know, Doctor, it is impossible to generalize."

"I have the feeling that many Jewish women in Poland are of this type. I see it in their eyes. I made a business trip to the Jewish state and even met Ben-Gurion, along with other Israeli leaders. We did business with the Bank Leumi. I have a theory that the Jewish woman of today wants to make up for all the centuries in the ghetto. Besides, the Jews are a people of imagination, even though in modern literature they haven't yet created any great works. I've read Jakob Wassermann, Stefan Zweig, Peter Altenberg, and Arthur Schnitzler, but they disappointed me. I expected something better from Jews. Are there interesting writers in Yiddish or Hebrew?"

"Interesting writers are rare among all peoples."

"Here is our driver with the passports."

We crossed the border, and an hour later the bus stopped and we went to have lunch at a Spanish restaurant.

In the entrance, Mrs. Weyerhofer came up to me and said, "You sat with my husband this morning and I know that the whole time he talked about me. I can read lips like a deaf-mute. You should know that he's a pathological liar. Not one word of truth leaves his lips."

"It so happens he praised you."

Celina Weyerhofer tensed. "What did he say?"

"That you are unusually interesting as a woman."

"Is that what he said? It can't be. He has been impotent several years, and being next to him has made me frigid. Physically and spiritually he has made me sick."

"He praised your imagination."

"Nothing is left me except my imagination. He drained my blood like a vampire. He isn't sexually normal. He is a latent homosexual — not so latent — although when I tell him this he denies it vehemently. He only wants to be with men, and when we still shared a bedroom he spent whole nights questioning me about my relationships with other men. I had to invent affairs to satisfy him. Later, he threw these imaginary sins up to me and called me filthy names. He forced me to confess that I had relations with a Nazi, even though God knows I would sooner have let them skin me alive. Maybe we can find a table together?"

"I promised to eat with some woman and her son."

"The one I saw you with yesterday in the dining room? Her son is a beauty, but she is too fat and when she gets older she'll go to pieces. Did you notice how many diamonds she wears? A jewelry store — tasteless, disgusting. In Lyons and Bordeaux none of us had a bathroom, but she got one. Since she is so rich, why does she ride in a bus? They don't give her a plain room but a suite. Is she Jewish?"

"Her late husband was a Jew."

"A widow, eh? She's probably looking for a match. The diamonds are more than likely imitations. What is she, French?"

"Armenian."

"Foolish men kill themselves and leave such bitches huge estates. Where does she live?"

"In Turkey."

"Be careful. One glance was enough to tell me this is a spider. But men are blind."

I couldn't believe it, but I began to see that Mark was trying to arrange a match between his mother and myself. Strangely, the mother played as passive a role in the situation as some old-time maiden for whom the parents were trying to find a husband. I told myself that it was all my imagination. What would a rich widow, an Armenian living in Turkey, want with a Yiddish writer? What kind of future could she see in this? True, I was an American citizen, but it wouldn't have been difficult for Mrs. Metalon to obtain a visa to America without me. I concluded that her fourteen-year-old son had hypnotized his mother — that he dominated her as his father had probably done before him. I also toyed with the notion that her husband's soul had entered into Mark and that he, the dead Sephardi, wanted his wife to marry a fellow Jew. I tried to avoid eating with the pair, but each time Mark found me and said, "Sir, my mother is waiting for you."

His words implied a command. When it was my turn to order my vegetarian dishes, Mark took over and told the waiter or waitress exactly what to bring me. He knew Spanish because his father had had a partner with whom he had conversed in Ladino. I wasn't accustomed to drinking wine with my meals, but Mark ordered it without consulting me. When we came to a city, he always managed that his mother and I were left alone to shop for bargains and souvenirs. On these occasions he warned me sternly not to spend any money on his mother, and if I had already done so he demanded to know how much and told his mother to pay me back. When I objected, he arched his brows. "Sir, we don't need gifts. A Yiddish writer can't be rich." He opened his mother's pocketbook and counted out whatever the amount had been.

Mrs. Metalon smiled sheepishly at this and added, half in jest, half in earnest, that Mark treated her as if she were his daughter. But she had obviously accepted the relationship.

Is she so weak? I wondered. Or is there some scheme behind this?

The situation struck me as particularly strange because the mother and son were together only during vacations. The rest of the year she remained in Ankara while he studied in London. As far as I could determine, Mark was dependent on his mother; when he needed something he had to ask for money.

At first, the two of them sat in the bus together, but one day after lunch Mark told me that I was to sit with his mother. He himself sat down next to Celina Weyerhofer. He had arranged all this without the driver's permission, and I doubted if he had discussed it with his mother.

I had been sitting next to a woman from Holland, and this changing of seats provoked whispering among the passengers. From that day on, I became Mrs. Metalon's partner not only in the dining room but in the bus as well. People began to wink, make remarks, leer. Much of the time I looked out of the window. We drove through regions that reminded me of the desert and the land of Israel. Peasants rode on asses. We passed an area where gypsies lived in caves. Girls balanced water jugs on their heads. Grandmothers toted bundles of wood and herbs wrapped in linen sheets over their shoulders. We passed ancient olive trees and trees that resembled umbrellas. Sheep browsed among cracked clods of earth on the half-burned plain. A horse circled a well. The sky, pale blue, radiated a fiery heat. Something biblical hovered over the landscape. Passages of the Pentateuch flashed across my memory. It seemed to me that I was somewhere in the plains of Mamre, where presently would materialize Abraham's tent, and the angel would bring Sarah tidings that she would be blessed with a male child at the age of ninety. My head whirled with stories of Sodom, of the sacrifice of Isaac, of Ishmael and Hagar. The stacks of grain in the harvested fields brought Joseph's dreams to mind. One morning we passed a horse fair. The horses and the men stood still, congealed in silence like phantoms of a fair from a vanished time. It was hard to believe that in this very land, some fifteen years before, a civil war had raged and Stalinists had shot Trotskyites.

Barely a week had passed since our departure, but I felt that I had been wandering for months. From sitting so long in one position I was overcome with a lust that wasn't love or even sexual passion but something purely animalistic. It seemed that my partner shared the same feelings, for a special heat emanated from her. When she accidentally touched my hand, she burned me.

We sat for hours without a single word, but then we became gabby and said whatever came to our lips. We confided intimate things to one another. We yawned and went on talking half asleep. I asked her how it happened that she had married a man forty years older than herself.

She said, "I was an orphan. The Turks murdered my father, and my mother died soon after. We were rich but they stripped us of everything. I met him as an employee in his office. He had wild eyes. He took one look at me and I knew that he wanted me and was ready to marry me. He had an iron will. He also had the strength of a giant. If he hadn't smoked cigars from early morning till late at night, he would have lived to be a hundred. He could drink fifteen cups of bitter coffee a day. He exhausted me until I developed an aversion to love. When he died, I had the solace that I would be left in peace for a change. Now everything has begun to waken within me again."

"Were you a virgin when you married?" I asked in a half-dream.

"Yes, a virgin."

"Did you have lovers after his death?"

"Many men wanted me, but I was raised in such a way I couldn't live with a man without marriage. In my circle in Turkey a woman can't afford to be loose. Everyone there knows what everyone else is doing. A woman has to maintain her reputation."

"What do you need with Turkey?"

"Oh, I have a house there, servants, a business."

"Here in Spain you can do what you want," I said, and regretted my words instantly.

"But I have a chaperon here," she said. "Mark watches over me. I'll tell you something that will seem crazy to you. He guards me even when he is in London and I'm in Ankara. I often feel that he sees everything I do. I sense it isn't he but his father."

"You believe this?"

"It's a fact."

I glanced backward and saw Mark gazing at me sharply as if he were trying to hypnotize me.

When we stopped for the night at a hotel, we first had to line up for the toilets, then wait a long time for our dinner. In the rooms assigned to us, the ceilings were high, the walls thick, and there were old-fashioned washstands with basins and pitchers of water.

That night, we stopped late, which meant that dinner was not served until after ten. Once again, Mark ordered a bottle of wine. For some reason I let myself be persuaded to drink several glasses. Mark asked me if I had had a chance to bathe during the trip, and I told him that I washed every morning out of the washbasin with cold water just like the other passengers.

He glanced at his mother half questioningly, half imperatively.

After some hesitation, Mrs. Metalon said, "Come to our room. We have a bathroom."

"When?"

"Tonight. We leave at five in the morning."

"Sir, do it," Mark said. "A hot bath is healthy. In America everyone has a bathroom, be he porter or janitor. The Japanese bathe in wooden tubs, the whole family together. Come a half hour after dinner. It's not good to bathe immediately following the evening meal."

"I'll disturb both of you. You're obviously tired."

"No, sir. I never go to sleep until between one and two o'clock. I'm planning to take a walk through the city. I have to stretch my legs. From sitting all day in the bus they've become cramped and stiff. My mother goes to bed late, too."

"You're not afraid to walk alone at night in a strange city?" I asked.

"I'm not afraid of anybody. I took a course in wrestling and karate. I also take shooting lessons. It's not allowed boys my age, but I have a private teacher."

"Oh, he takes more courses than I have hairs on my head," Mrs. Metalon said. "He wants to know everything."

"In America, I'll study Yiddish," Mark announced. "I read somewhere that a million and a half people speak this language in America. I want to read you in the original. It's also good for business. America is a true democracy. There you must speak to the customer in his own language. I want my mother to come to America with me. In Turkey, no person of Armenian descent is sure of his life."

"My friends are all Turks," Mrs. Metalon protested.

"Once the pogroms start they'll stop being your friends. My mother tries to hide it from me but I know very well what they did to the Armenians in Turkey and to the Jews in Russia. I want to visit Israel. The Jews there don't bow their heads like those in Russia and Poland. They offer resistance. I want to learn Hebrew and to study at Jerusalem University."

We said good-bye and Mark wrote the number of their room on a small sheet he tore from a notebook. I went to my room for a nap. My legs wobbled as I climbed the stairs. I lay down on the bed in my clothes with the notion of resting a half hour. I closed my eyes and sank into a deep slumber. Someone woke me — it was Mark. To this day I don't know how he got into my room. Maybe I had forgotten to lock it or he had tipped the maid to let him in.

He said, "Sir, excuse me but you've slept a whole hour. You've apparently forgotten that you are coming to our room for your bath."

I assured Mark that I'd be at his door in ten minutes, and after some hesitation he left. Getting undressed and unpacking a bathrobe and slippers from my valise wasn't easy for me. I cursed the day I had decided to take this tour, but I hadn't the courage to tell Mark I wouldn't come. For all his delicacy and politeness Mark projected a kind of childish brutality.

I threw my spring coat over my bathrobe and on unsteady legs began climbing the two floors to their room. I was still half asleep, and for a moment I had the illusion that I was on board ship. When I got to the Metalons' floor, I could not find the slip of paper with the room number. I was sure that it was number 43, but the tiny lamp on the high ceiling was concealed behind a dull shade and emitted barely any light. In the dimness I couldn't see this number. It took a long time of groping before I found it and knocked on the door.

The door opened, and to my amazement I saw Celina Weyerhofer in a nightgown, her face thickly smeared with cream. Her hair looked wet and freshly dyed. I grew so confused that I could not speak. Finally I asked, "Is this 43?"

"Yes, this is 43. To whom were you going? Oh, I understand. It seems to me that your lady with the diamonds is somewhere on this floor. I saw her son. You've made a mistake."

"Madam I don't wish to detain you. I just want to tell you they invited me to take a bath there, that's all."

"A bath, eh? So let it be a bath. I haven't had a bath for over a week myself. What kind of tour is this that some passengers get privileges and others are discriminated against? The advertisement didn't mention anything about two classes of passengers. My dear Mr. — what is your name? — I warned you that that person would trap you, and I see this has happened sooner than I figured. Wait a minute — your bath won't run out. Since when do they call it a bath? We call it by a different name. Don't run. Because you've forgotten the number, you'll have to knock on strangers' doors and wake people. Everyone is dead tired. On this tour, before you can even lie down you have to get up again. My husband is a good sleeper. He lies down, opens some book, and two minutes later he's snoring like a lord. He carries his own alarm clock. I've stopped sleeping altogether. Literally. That's my sickness. I haven't slept for years. I told a doctor in Bern about this — he's actually a professor of medicine — and he called me a liar. The Swiss can be very coarse when they choose to be. He had studied something in a medical book or he had a theory, and because the facts didn't jibe with his theory this made me a liar. I've been watching you sitting with that woman. It looks as if you're telling her jokes from the way she keeps on laughing. My husband sat next to her one time before she monopolized you, and she told him things no decent woman would tell a stranger. I suspect she is a madam of a whorehouse in Turkey. Or something like that. No respectable woman wears so much jewelry. You can smell her perfume a mile away. I'm not even sure that this boy is her son. There seems to be some kind of unnatural relationship between them."

"Madam Weyerhofer, what are you saying?"

"I'm not just pulling things out of the air. God has cursed me with eyes that see. I say 'cursed' because this is for me a curse rather than a blessing. If you absolutely must take a bath, as you call it, do it and satisfy yourself, but be careful — such a person can easily infect you with God knows what."

Just at that moment the door across the hall opened and I saw Mrs. Metalon in a splendid nightgown and gold-colored slippers. Her hair was loose; it fell to her shoulders. She was made up, too. The women glared at each other furiously; then Mrs. Metalon said, "Where did you go? I'm in 48, not 43."

"Oh, I made a mistake. Truly, I'm completely mixed up. I'm terribly sorry —"

"Go take your bath!" Mrs. Weyerhofer said and gave me a light push. She muttered words in French I didn't understand but knew to be insulting. She slammed her own door shut.

I turned to Mrs. Metalon, who asked, "Why did you go to her, of all people? I waited and waited for you. There is no more hot water anyhow. And where has Mark vanished to? He went for a walk and hasn't come back. This night is a total loss to me. That woman — what's her name? Weyerhofer — is a troublemaker, and crazy besides. Her own husband admitted that she's emotionally disturbed."

"Madam, I've made a terrible mistake. Mark wrote down your room number for me, but while changing my clothes I lost the slip. It's all because I'm so tired —"

"Oh, will that red-haired bitch malign me before everyone on the bus now! She is a snake whose every word is venom."

"I truly don't know how to excuse myself. But —"

"Well, it's not your fault. It was Mark who cooked up this stew. The driver told me to keep it secret that we're getting a bathroom. He doesn't want to create jealousy among the passengers. Now he'll be mad at me and he'll be right. I can't continue this trip any longer. I'll get off with Mark in Madrid and take a train or plane back to the border or maybe even to Paris. Come in for a moment. I'm already compromised."

I went inside, and she took me to the bathroom to show me that the hot water was no longer running. The bathtub was made of tin. It was unusually high and long. On its outside hung a kind of pole with which to hold in and let out the water. The taps were copper. I excused myself again and Mrs. Metalon said, "You're an innocent victim. Mark is a genius, but like all geniuses he has his moods. He was a prodigy. At five he could do logarithms. He read the Bible in French and remembered all the names. He loves me and he is determined to have me meet someone. The truth is, he's seeking a father. Each time I join him during vacation he starts looking for a husband for me. He creates embarrassing complications. I don't want to marry — certainly not anyone Mark would pick out for me. But he is compulsive. He gets hysterical. I shouldn't tell you this, but I have a good reason to say it — when I do something that displeases him, he abuses me. Later he regrets it and beats his head against the wall. What can I do? I love him more than life itself. I worry about him day and night. I don't know exactly why you made such an impression on him. Maybe it's because you're a Jew, a writer, and from America. But I was born in Ankara and that's where my home is. What would I do in America? I've read a number of articles about America, and that's not the country for me. With us, servants are cheap and I have friends who advise me on financial matters. If I left Turkey, I would have to sell everything for a song. I tell you this only to point out there can never be anything between us. You would not want to live in Turkey any more than I want to live in New York. But I don't want to upset Mark and I therefore hope that for the duration of the trip you can act friendly toward me — sit with us at the table and all the rest. When the tour ends and you return home, let this be nothing more for you than an episode. He's due back soon. Tell him that you took the bath. You'll be able to have one in Madrid. We'll be spending almost two days there, and I'm told the hotel is modern. I'm sure you have someone in New York you love. Sit down awhile."

"I've just broken up with a woman."

"Broken up? Why? You didn't love her?"

"We loved each other but we couldn't stay together. This past year we argued constantly."

"Why? Why can't people live in peace? There was a great love between my husband and me, though I must admit I had to give in to him on everything. He bullied me so that I can't even say no to my own child. Oh, I'm worried. He never stayed away this long. He probably wants you to declare your love for me so that when he comes back everything will be settled between us. He is a child, a wild child. My greatest fear is that he might attempt suicide. He has threatened to." She uttered these last words in one breath.

"Why? Why?"

"For no reason. Because I dared disagree with him over some trifle. God Almighty, why am I telling you all this? Only because my heart is heavy. Say nothing about it, God forbid!"

The door opened and Mark came in. When he saw me sitting on the sofa, he asked, "Sir, did you take your bath?"

"Yes."

"It was nice, wasn't it? You look refreshed. What are you talking about with my mother?"

"Oh, this and that. I told her she's one of the prettiest women I've ever met," I said, astonished at my words.

"Yes, she is pretty, but she mustn't remain in Turkey. In the Orient, women age quickly. I once read that an actress of sixty played an eighteen-year-old girl on Broadway. Send us an affidavit and we'll come to you."

"Yes, I'll do that."

"You may kiss my mother good night."

I stood up and we kissed. My face grew moist and hot. Mark began to kiss me, too. I said good night and started down the stairs. Again it seemed to me that I was on board ship. The steps were running counter to my feet. I suddenly found myself in the lobby. In my confusion I had gone down an extra floor. It was almost dark here; the desk clerk dozed behind the desk. In a leather chair sat Mrs. Weyerhofer in a robe, legs crossed, veiled in shadow. She was smoking a cigarette.

When she saw me, she said, "Since I don't sleep anyway, I'd rather spend the night here. A bed is to sleep in or make love in, but when you can't sleep and have no one to love, a bed becomes a prison. What are you doing here? Can't you sleep, either?"

She drew the smoke in deeply and the glow of the cigarette temporarily lit up her eyes. They reflected both curiosity and malaise.

She said, "After that kind of bath, a man should be able to sleep soundly instead of wandering around like a lost soul."

Mark began telling everyone on the bus that his mother and I were engaged. He planned that when the bus came back to Geneva I should ask the American consul for visas for himself and his mother so that all three of us could fly to America together. Mrs. Metalon told him several times that this would be impossible — she had a business appointment in Ankara. I made up the lie that I had to go to Italy on literary business. But Mark argued that his mother and I could postpone our business affairs temporarily. He spoke to me as if I were already his stepfather. He enumerated his mother's financial assets. His father had arranged a trust for him, and he had left the remainder of his estate to his wife. According to Mark's calculations she was worth no less than two million dollars — maybe more. Mark wanted his mother to liquidate all her holdings in Turkey and transfer her money to America. He would go to America to study even before he graduated from high school. The interest on his mother's capital would allow us to live in luxury.

Mark had decided that we would settle in Washington. It was childish and silly, but this boy cast a fear over me. I knew that it would be hard to free myself from him. His mother had hinted that another disappointment could drive him to actually attempt suicide. She suggested, "Maybe you'd spend some time with me in Turkey? Turkey is an interesting country. You'd have material to write about for your newspaper. You could spend two or three weeks, then go back to America. Mark wouldn't want to come along. He will gradually realize that we're not meant for each other."

"What would I do in Turkey? No, that's impossible."

"If it's a matter of money, I'll be glad to cover the expenses. You can even stay with me."

"No, Mrs. Metalon, it's out of the question."

"Well, something is bound to happen. What shall I do with that boy? He's driving me crazy."

We had two days in Madrid, a day in Córdoba, and we were on our way to Seville, where we were scheduled to stop for two days. The tour program promised a visit to a nightclub there. Our route was supposed to take us through Málaga, Granada, and Valencia to Barcelona, and from there to Avignon, then back to Geneva.

In Córdoba, Mrs. Weyerhofer delayed the bus for nearly two hours. She vanished from the hotel before our departure and all searching failed to turn her up. On account of her, the passengers had already missed a bullfight. Dr. Weyerhofer pleaded with the driver to go on and leave his lunatic wife alone in Spain as she deserved, but the driver couldn't bring himself to abandon a woman in a strange country. When she finally showed up loaded down with bundles and packages, Dr. Weyerhofer slapped her twice. Her packages fell to the floor and a vase shattered. "Nazi!" she shrieked. "Homosexual! Sadist!" Dr. Weyerhofer said aloud so that everyone could hear, "Well, thank God, this is the end of my martyrdom." And he raised his hand to the sky like a pious Jew swearing a vow.

The uproar caused an additional three-quarters of an hour delay. When Mrs. Weyerhofer finally got into the bus, no one would sit next to her, and the driver, who had seen us speaking together a few times, asked me if I would, since there were no single seats. Mark tried to seat me next to his mother and take my place, but Mrs. Metalon shouted at him to stay with her, and he gave in.

For a long while Mrs. Weyerhofer stared out the window and ignored me as if I were the one responsible for her disgrace. Then she turned to me and said, "Give me your address. I want you to be my witness in court."

"What kind of witness? If it should come to it, the court would find for him, and — if you'll excuse me — rightly so."

"Eh? Oh, I understand. Now that you're preparing to marry the

Armenian heiress, you're already lining up on the side of the anti-Semites."

"Madam, your own conduct does more harm to Jews than all the anti-Semites."

"They're my enemies, mortal enemies. Your madam from Constantinople was glowing with joy when those devils humiliated me. I am again where I was — in a concentration camp. You're about to convert, I know, but I will turn back to the Jewish God. I am no longer his wife and he is no longer my husband. I'll leave him everything and flee with my life, as I did in 1945."

"Why do you keep the bus waiting in every city? This has nothing to do with Jewishness."

"It's a plot, I tell you. He organized the whole thing down to the last detail. I don't sleep the whole night, but comes morning, just as I'm catching a nap he turns back the clock. Your knocking on my door the other night — what was the name of the city? — when you were on your way to take a bath at that Turkish whore's, was also one of his tricks. It was a conspiracy to let him catch me with a lover. It's obvious. He wants to drive me out without a shirt on my back, and he has achieved his goal, the sly fox. I won't be allowed to remain in Switzerland, but who will accept me? Unless I can manage to make my way to Israel. Now I understand everything. You'll be the witness for *him,* not for me."

"I'll be a witness for no one. Don't talk nonsense."

"You obviously think I'm mad. That's his goal — to commit me to an asylum. For years he's been talking of this. He's already tried it. He keeps sending me to psychiatrists. He wanted to poison me, too. Three times he put poison in my food and three times my instinct — or maybe it was God — gave me a warning. By the way, I want you to know that this boy, Mark, who wants so desperately for you to sit next to that Turkish concubine, is not her son."

"Then who is he?"

"He is her lover, not her son. She sleeps with him."

"Were you there and saw it?"

"A chambermaid in Madrid told me. She made a mistake and opened the door to their room in the morning and found them in bed together.

There are such sick women. One wants a lapdog, and another a young boy. Really, you're crawling into slime."

"I'm not crawling anywhere."

"You're taking her to America?"

"I'm not taking anyone."

"Well, I'd better keep my mouth shut." Mrs. Weyerhofer turned away from me.

I leaned my head back against the seat and closed my eyes. I knew well that the woman was paranoid; just the same, her last words had given me a jolt. Who knows? What she told me might have been the truth. Sexual perversion is the answer to many mysteries. I was almost overcome with nausea. Yes, I thought, she is right. I'm crawling into a quagmire.

I had but one wish now — to get off this bus as quickly as possible. It occurred to me that for all my intimacy with Mrs. Metalon and Mark, so far I hadn't given them my address.

I dozed, and when I opened my eyes Mark informed me that we were in Seville. I had slept over three hours.

Despite our late start, we still had time for a fast meal. I had sat as usual with Mrs. Metalon and Mark. Mark had ordered a bottle of Malaga and I had drunk a good half of it. Vapors of intoxication flowed from my stomach to my brain.

The topic of conversation at the tables was Dr. and Mrs. Weyerhofer. All the women concluded that Dr. Weyerhofer was a saint to put up with such a horror.

Mrs. Metalon said, "I'd like to think that this is her end. Even a saint's patience has to burst sometime. He is a banker and a handsome man. He won't be alone for long."

"I wouldn't want him for a father," Mark said.

Mrs. Metalon smiled and winked at me. "Why not, my son?"

"Because I want to live and study in America, not in Switzerland. Switzerland is only good for mountain climbing and skiing."

"Don't worry, there's no danger of it."

As she spoke, Mrs. Metalon did something she had never done before — she pressed her knee against mine.

✧ ✧ ✧

Coaches waited in front of the hotel to take us to a cabaret. Candles flickered in their head lanterns, casting mysterious designs of light and shadow. I hadn't ridden in a horse-drawn carriage since leaving Warsaw. The whole evening was like a magic spell — the ride from the hotel to the cabaret with Mrs. Metalon and Mark, and later the performance. Inside the carriage, driving through the poorly lit Seville streets Mrs. Metalon held my hand. Mark sat facing us and his eyes gleamed like some night bird's. The air was balmy, dense with the scents of wine, olive oil, and gardenias, Mrs. Metalon kept on exclaiming, "What a splendid night! Look at the sky, so full of stars!"

I touched her breast, and she trembled and squeezed my knee. We were both drunk, not so much from wine as from fatigue. Again I felt the heat of her body.

When we got out of the coach Mark walked a few paces in front and Mrs. Metalon whispered, "I'd like to have another child."

"By whom?" I asked.

"Try to guess," she said.

I cannot know whether the actors and actresses and the music and the dancing were as masterly as I thought, but everything I saw and heard that evening enraptured me — the semi-Arabic music, the almost Hasidic way the dancers stamped their feet, their meaningful clicking of the castanets, their bizarre costumes. Melodies supposed to be erotic reminded me of liturgies sung on the night of Kol Nidre. Mark found an unoccupied seat close to the stage and left us alone. We began to kiss with the ardor of long-parted lovers. Between one kiss and the next, Mrs. Metalon (she had told me to call her Annette) insisted that I accompany her to Ankara. She was even ready to visit America. I had scored one of those victories I could never explain except by the fact that in the duel of love the victim is sometimes as eager to surrender as the attacker is to conquer. This woman had lived alone for a number of years. She was accustomed to the embraces of an elderly man. As I thought these things, I warned myself that Mark would not allow our relationship to remain an affair.

From time to time he glanced back at us searchingly. I didn't believe Mrs. Weyerhofer's slanderous tale of mother and son, but it was obvious that Mark was capable of killing anyone he considered to be dishonoring her. The woman's words about wanting another child portended danger. However strong my urge for her body, I knew that I had no spiritual ties with her, that after a while misunderstandings, boredom, and regrets would take over. Besides, I had always been afraid of Turks. As a child, I had heard in detail of Abdul-Hamid's savageries. Later, I read about the pogroms against the Armenians. There in faraway Ankara they could easily fabricate an accusation against me, take away my American passport, and throw me in prison, from which I would not emerge alive. How strange, but when I was a boy in cheder I dreamed of lying in a Turkish prison bound with heavy ropes, and for some reason I had never forgotten this dream.

On the way back from the nightclub, both mother and son asked if I had a bathtub in my room. I told them no, and at once they invited me to bathe in their suite. Mark added that he was going to take a stroll through town. The fact that we were scheduled to stay in Seville through the following night meant that we did not have to get up early the next morning.

Mrs. Metalon and Mark had been assigned a suite of three rooms. I promised to come by and Mrs. Metalon said, "Don't be too late. The hot water may cool soon." Her words seemed to carry a symbolic meaning, as if they were out of a parable.

I went to my room, which was just under the roof. It exuded a scorching heat. The sun had lain on it all day and I switched on the ceiling lamp and stood for a long time, stupefied from the heat and the day's experiences. I had a feeling that soon flames would come shooting from all sides and the room would flare up like a paper lantern. On a brass bed lay a huge pillow and a red blanket full of stains. I needed to stretch out, but the sheet seemed dirty. I imagined I could smell the sperm that who knows how many tourists had spilled here. My bathrobe and pajamas were packed away in my valise, and I hadn't the strength to open it. Well, and what good would it do to bathe if soon afterward I had to lie down in this dirty bed?

In the coach and in the cabaret everything within me had seethed with passion. Now that I had a chance to be alone with the woman, the passion evaporated. Instead, I grew angry against this rich Turkish widow and her pampered son. I made sure that Mark wouldn't wake me. I locked the door with the heavy key and bolted it besides. I put out the light and lay down in my clothes on the sprung mattress, determined to resist all temptation.

The hotel was situated in a noisy neighborhood. Young men shouted and girls laughed wantonly. From time to time, I detected a man's cry followed by a sigh. Was it outside? In another room? Had someone been murdered here? Tortured? Who knows, remnants of the Inquisition might still linger here. I felt bites and scratched. Sweat oozed from me but I made no effort to wipe it away. "This trip was sheer insanity," I told myself. "The whole situation is filled with menace."

I fell asleep and this time Mark did not come to wake me. By dawn it turned cold and I covered myself with the same blanket that a few hours earlier had filled me with such disgust. When I awoke, the sun was already burning. I washed myself in lukewarm water from the pitcher on the stand and wiped myself with a rusty towel. I seemed to have resolved everything in my sleep. Riding in the carriage through the city the night before, I had noticed branches of Cook's Tours and American Express. I had a return ticket to America, an American passport, and traveler's checks.

When I went down with my valise to the lobby, they told me that I had missed breakfast. The passengers had all gone off to visit churches, a Moorish palace, a museum. Thank God, I had avoided running into Mrs. Metalon and her son and having to justify myself to them. I left a tip for the bus driver with the hotel cashier and went straight to Cook's. I was afraid of complications, but they cashed my checks and sold me a train ticket to Geneva. I would lose some two hundred dollars to the bus company, but that was my fault, not theirs.

Everything went smoothly. A train was leaving soon for Biarritz. I had booked a bedroom in a Pullman car. I got on and began correcting a manuscript as if nothing had happened.

Toward evening, I felt hungry and the conductor showed me the way to the diner. All the second-class cars were empty. I glanced into the diner. There, at a table near the door, sat Celina Weyerhofer, struggling with a pullet.

We stared at each other in silence for a long while; then Mrs. Weyerhofer said, "If this is possible, then even the Messiah can come.

On the other hand, I knew that we'd meet again."

"What happened?" I asked.

"My good husband simply drove me away. God knows I've had it up to here with this trip." She pointed to her throat.

She proposed that I join her, and she served as my interpreter to order a vegetarian meal. She seemed more sane and subdued than I had seen her before. She even appeared younger in her black dress. She said, "You ran away, eh? You did right. You would have been caught in a trap you would never have freed yourself from. She suited you as much as Dr. Weyerhofer suited me."

"Why did you keep the bus waiting in every city?" I asked.

She pondered. "I don't know," she said at last. "I don't know myself. Demons were after me. They misled me with their tricks."

The waiter brought my vegetables. I chewed and looked out the window as night fell over the harvested fields. The sun set, small and glowing. It rolled down quickly, like a coal from some heavenly conflagration. A nocturnal gloom hovered above the landscape, an eternity that was weary of being eternal. Good God, my father and my grandfather were right to avoid looking at women! Every encounter between a man and a woman leads to sin, disappointment, humiliation. A dread fell upon me that Mark would try to find me and exact revenge.

As if Celina had read my mind, she said, "Don't worry. She'll soon comfort herself. What was the reason for your taking this trip? Just to see Spain?"

"I wanted to forget someone who wouldn't let herself be forgotten."

"Where is she? In Europe?"

"In America."

"You can't forget anything."

We sat until late, and Mrs. Weyerhofer unfolded to me her fatalistic theory: everything was determined or fixed — every deed, every word, every thought. She herself would die shortly and no doctor or conjurer could help her. She said, "Before you came in here I fantasized that I was arranging a suicide pact with someone. After a night of pleasure, he stuck a knife in my breast."

"Why a knife, of all things?" I asked. "That's not a Jewish fantasy. I couldn't do this even to Hitler."

"If the woman wants it, it can be an act of love."

The waiter came back and mumbled something.

Mrs. Weyerhofer explained, "We're the only ones in the dining car. They want to close up."

"I'm finished," I said. "Gastronomically and otherwise."

"Don't rush," she said. "Unlike the driver of our ill-starred bus, the forces that drive us mad have all the time in the world."

MORRIS ROSENFELD

✧ 1862–1923 ✧

YIVO Institute for Jewish Research

For Morris Rosenfeld, the poet of the sweat-shops, writing was a way to transform his humiliating circumstances into something of transcendent value. As part of the emerging Jewish labor movement he wrote poems that inspired his readers to see themselves as belonging to the new proletariat, and then to work for its improvement. He was extraor-dinarily influential and popular at a time when the worst excesses of modern capitalism went largely unchecked.

Rosenfeld's poetry may strike a modern reader as didactic and lacking in subtlety, but his work existed in very particular circumstances, more likely to be declaimed in a concert or meeting hall than to be read in the quiet of a study. Often set to music, his poems were recited and sung at demonstrations, meetings, and strikes. A clear example of art in the service of society, they really did help to change the world.

Rosenfeld was born in a small town in eastern Poland in 1862. When he was a child, his parents sent him to Warsaw to escape a contagion that swept through the area, and took the precaution of changing his name to *Alter,* elder, so the Angel of Death would pass over him. He returned to find that all six of his siblings had succumbed.

He fled an unhappy arranged marriage at seventeen and went to Amsterdam, where he learned diamond cutting. He returned home, married again, and moved with his family to London, where he spent three years working in sweatshops and watching powerlessly as his first three children died.

He moved to New York in 1886, where he worked as a tailor and presser. The poems he published soon after his arrival were welcomed by a public that was eager to hear a voice from its own world. Although Rosenfeld read Goethe, Heine, Poe, and Whitman, his own work was more literal. This member of the first generation of modern Yiddish poets took as his subject the brutal and impoverished life that he himself lived. At a time of emerging political consciousness, he was an inspiration to the emerging socialist movement. And, though he never strayed from his cohort of Eastern European Jewish immigrants, he was in close contact with American reformers, such as Jane Addams and Upton Sinclair.

In 1898 a volume of his poetry, *Songs from the Ghetto,* was translated into English. His works were also translated into many European languages.

But Rosenfeld did not take solace in his growing influence, or in the successes of various movements for social reform. He was a tormented, bitter man. His anger fueled his writing, but it also prevented him from making peace with his life. Sometimes he held staff jobs on Yiddish newspapers, but he either quit or got himself fired. He regularly managed to alienate people who wanted to help him. An attempt by his supporters to set him up with a cigar and candy store was short lived, and his dramatic recitations of his poetry did not earn him much money. Unable to make a living as a writer, he was forced again and again to return to the sweatshops.

One of his most popular poems, "Yingele" (My Little Boy), describes the sorrow of a man forced to work such long hours that he is never able to see his son. Joseph, the beloved child who inspired this work, died at fifteen from injuries sustained during an attack by a group of Polish youngsters.

Rosenfeld was bereft. He began to go blind, but recovered enough to undertake a European lecture tour that was extremely successful.

In his later years he broadened his subject matter, writing love and nature poems. He composed a Yiddish version of the Song of Songs. He wrote a paean to Walt Whitman. He became an enthusiastic American, penning patriotic odes to Lincoln and Washington. He also tried writing in English. Unfortunately, the quality of his later work was poor. A younger generation of Yiddish poets derided his verses, and he responded by writing furious poems attacking them. Although he lived to see many advances in working conditions and in the strength of the labor movement, he felt himself abandoned by his comrades and friends.

Still, the Jewish left wing continued to honor his contribution. For his fiftieth birthday his supporters organized a celebration at Carnegie Hall. He was also honored on his sixtieth, in 1922. By that time, however, he was ill, lonely, and broken. He died a few months later.

One New York Yiddish newspaper, *The Day,* wrote, "Death has snatched from our midst the first significant poet that Yiddish produced in America." But another, *The Jewish Worker,* described the sad reality of his death, calling him, "the worker's poet, but the workers, who sang his poems, did not come to his funeral . . . the singer of the ghetto — but the ghetto was merely an indifferent spectator at the funeral."

Rosenfeld had three surviving children. In the 1990s, one of his grandchildren, retired from an academic career, took on the project of putting together a book about the poet's life and work. Before he could do so, however, he first had to study Yiddish. A century after Rosenfeld had come to the United States, his progeny inhabited a very different world.

Bread and Tea

Bread and tea and bread and tea!
What a menu! Woe is me!
I ask You, God, is this a joke,
to fix it so I'm always broke?
Can't You spare a few sardines,
a slice of lox, a can of beans,
a little milk, a piece of cheese?
Just bread and tea and bread and tea?
What a menu, woe is me!

Is this a judgment You've decreed,
just to make me come and plead?
Haven't I sought You day and night,
praying that You ease my plight?
Yet here I am in a fifth-floor flat,
and You care less than does my cat!
Apparently, God, it must be true;
things are not so "extra" with You.
Are You, Yourself, in trouble too?

Translated by Max Rosenfeld

To My Beloved

How good to look at you again
my love, my joy, one bright dream!
You come now and you come in vain
to be with me at my machine.

There's steam and smoke and madness here —
there's no place for a guest to stand.
I can't so much as touch you, dear,
for I have rented out my hand.

Come to me later! Come at night,
for then my darling, I am free.
My spirit wakes, my heart is light,
the flame of love revived in me.

I'll sing as I have never sung
the moment that your face appears,
and every word upon your tongue
shall turn to music in my ears.

I'll greet you then in such a way
as I would now, if I could dare.
Then all my troubles of the day,
my inmost wounds, will be laid bare.

And you will have my kisses all,
and tears enough, you'll have those too.
Whatever good is in my soul
I'll offer as a gift to you.

But now, beloved, you must go,
love has no business in a shop.
I can't so much as touch you — no!
My life starts when the treadles stop.

Translated by Aaron Kramer

Autumn Leaves

Alone, I sit as summer falls,
with feelings strange, unknown.
My spirit calls un-answered calls —
a fear within has grown.
My share of troubles and of luck
must have somehow gone awry.
One of us has gotten sick —
Is it the world? Or I?

Time's persistent flow I find
Destroys the hours without surcease.
Yet none affords my aching mind
and heart a moment's peace.
Weep I must, I cannot speak.
What I lack I can't deny.
I know that one of us is sick —
Is it the world? Or I?

Translated by Edgar Goldenthal

YANKEV GLATSHTEYN

✧ 1896–1971 ✧

Yankev Glatshteyn, also known as Jacob Glatstein or Gladstone, helped Yiddish poetry come of age, advancing it from what one critic called "the rhyme department of the labor movement" to a mature, nuanced and personal response to the world.

Glatshteyn was born in Lublin, a Polish city with a sizeable Jewish population, in 1896. His family encouraged his literary efforts and, at the age of thirteen, he even visited Yitzhak Peretz in Warsaw to seek the great writer's blessing. When he was eighteen, just before the start of World War I, he emigrated to New York.

His adjustment was difficult. Cut off from family and community and working in sweatshops, he wrote little. By 1918 he had earned enough money and learned enough English to enroll in New York University Law School. But his mind did not run to legal briefs and, in the end, his commitment to Yiddish poetry won out.

In 1920 Glatshteyn and two other Yiddish poets published an anthology. In addition to showcasing the work of eight poets, it contained the manifesto of a new school. Their title, *In Zizh,* can be translated as "Instrospectivists" or "Inside the Self." These young modernists placed the artist squarely at the center of the literary endeavor, filtering experience through a poetic sensibility. They also championed the switch to free verse. As Glatshteyn later described it, "The free verse of the first Inzikhists, the pioneer Inzikhists, sought a new musicality, the discipline of human speech, the rise and fall of human speech, the distilled music of human conversation."

Glatshteyn's group expanded the acceptable subject matter and stylistic range of Yiddish poetry. No longer limited to subjects of political or Jewish origin, they saw themselves mining the same vein as T. S. Eliot, Ezra Pound, and Wallace Stevens. Yiddish poetry was ready to take its place on the world stage.

But history had a special role for Jewish poets. In 1934, Glatshteyn returned to Lublin for a visit. "I began to see tragedy on the march," he said, although no one imagined the extent of the impending destruction. The world he had come from was utterly destroyed.

In the post–World War II era Glatshteyn, the man who had first defined himself by looking inward, found himself becoming a spokesman for remaining Jews. His subject became questions of death and survival, both of a language and of a people.

Although primarily a poet, Glatshteyn worked in a wide range of genres, always in Yiddish. He wrote novels and criticism, edited journals, and, throughout, supported his family as a working journalist. "The writer does not have two pockets for his work — one for writing on current public affairs and the other for poetry," he said. "There must be one pocket. The writer, even if he is a poet, must be connected with reality, with battles in society, with ideologies."

As a Yiddish writer who lived in the United States for more than half a century, Glatshteyn's reality was a steady diminution of his audience, as both his community and his native language declined. He wrote: "Today prophecy has left us; only the poet remains. In our time, when so many millions have been slaughtered, when so many lost souls seek some improvement of their lot, when science stands bewildered, there remains for the poet only his poetry, only his art as a lantern in the dark corridors of life's labyrinth."

But Glatshteyn's lantern shed its light primarily on the dwindling community of Yiddish speakers. He never developed an English-language audience. The bilingual critic Irving Howe wrote, "Glatstein knew — he had every right to — that he was a distinguished poet who, if he wrote in any other language, would be famous, the recipient of prizes, and the subject of critical studies. It was hard for me to explain . . . the utter indifference of American literary circles to the presence of a vibrant Yiddish culture that could be found, literally and symbolically, a few blocks away."

In later life, Glatshteyn was honored in the Yiddish community. Beyond it, he was largely ignored. He died in New York in 1971.

Seventeen Moons

Tell me, my child, how many wells
are in your little village?
Seventeen in all. — But that's not so incredible.
What's really wonderful is this: That on a moonlit night
seventeen moons swim there.

In that giant sky, one stingy moon.
And our little village — a hop, skip, and a jump —
revels in
seventeen moons
swimming in
seventeen wells
all alike.

And who, my child, has counted the seventeen moons?
We have seventeen tall lads
dressed in blue uniforms with giant buttons,
guardians who guard
the wells on moonlit nights.
Each one cries,
"Here's a moon!"
Seventeen lads,
all blue clad,
seventeen cries:
"Here's a moon!"

A handful of people poke their heads
out of little houses.
They laugh and give thanks that their little village
owns seventeen bright moons
and seventeen wells
while in that giant sky
one stingy moon swims around.
And that's what's so incredible.
Really, so help me, incredible.

Translated by Richard J. Fein

From Nakhman of Bratslav to His Scribe

I

Come on, Nathan, let's not think today.
Did you ever see such a world —
so fair, so gorgeous?
I'll box your ears
if you squeeze out a single thought today.
Will it hurt you just to live?
Live with each limb
and breathe in the sun like a fly.
Let's go backwards —
empty our minds,
fritter away our thoughts.
Let's become holy peasants
with cows in holy pastures.
Let's eat kasha with milk,
puff on stinking pipes,
and tell tall tales about dwarfs;
let's sing songs —
di-dana-di, di-dana-di.
Pure songs — wordless —
di-dana-di.

I see a cloud's come over you.
I'll smack you in the kisser
if you start thinking.
Today you're going
to put your thinking cap under lock and key.
Today we're singing idiots
who can't even count to two.
So, seize it — now —
how wonderful it is —
one — Oneness.
One and only One —
All — Oneness.
And again and again — Oneness.

Look how simple it is.
How absolute — how lovely — how sad and lovely,
one — Oneness.

> Sing, little grass,
> buzz, little bee,
> nuzzle in the flower;
> cloudlet of rain,
> freshen the paths.
> Soak it up, earth.

Nathan, soon night will fall,
so let's sleep — without dreams and without thoughts —
just like the peasants.
Today, let's put away the ladder
and not reach heavenward;
let the angels
go down and up, up and down.
Let's snort and snore
and wake up to the east ablaze
with that song —
di-dana-di, di-dana-di.

I'll break your bones
if you don't get that tune.
If you lose any part of it — a word, or even a letter.
It's got to be as simple as this —
di-dana-di.

2

There are some people
who think a year and a day,
and the head is a holy thing with them,
but the whole body just dust to dust.
They pore over a book
and their eyes roll upward,
but their feet and their hands
are merely dust and ashes,

and over the belt
and under the belt
is *treyf* and still more *treyf*.
They master beautiful words,
they go on foot to holy places.
But when someone down and out comes begging,
their hands are tight-fisted,
their hearts shut even tighter.
Their head is divorced from their senses,
and their poor brain spins in its tracks,
the little bit of a man doomed
forever and forever.

So, I tell you, Nathan,
thinking is what notes are to singing,
while singing lives deep within you.
See, when the heart thinks purely,
the head follows, cleared of its fumes.
I hate that kind of rabbi —
that seeming savant —
who drips his gray matter
on the words of holy books.
So, take a candle and light up Genesis —
B'reyshis boro elohim —
"In the beginning God created."
B'reyshis, "In the beginning," created.
For crying out loud, Nathan, what's the point of thinking.
Let's go together — in rain and in snow,
in the sun and in the cold.
And let's sing — *B'reyshis* —
"In the beginning" created worlds.

3

I'm telling it to you exactly as it happened.
At daybreak, strolling in the middle of the forest,
I see the morning coming up lopsided,
the whole creation struck dumb, out of sorts.

The trees stick out their behinds to me.
The birds hear my "good morning," but not a peep or a flutter.
A hare gives me the eye like some evil shrew,
and the water in the little well says to me angrily,
"Nakhman, 'scuse me, but don't make any blessings over me today."
And the flowers give off some dark stench.
My mind is a muddle, a jumble of thoughts,
and everything I say becomes muffled and turns into silence.
You better put on your running shoes, I tell myself.
Nathan, what good is it when the world is out of sorts.

Then I realize that the world is like a man.
Everything that grows and everything that flies
and everything that crawls just wants to be.
So I make a little joke:
"What good is the world?
A delusion, an illusion,
a fleeting moment,
a fanciful nothing."
And I keep jabbing the whole creation
in the ribs.
An old tree started sobbing.
I was suddenly sorry for what I said.
But it was too late.
With some hidden strength
the whole forest stirred
into morning.
The trees now turned their faces to me.
The birds chirped.
The hare smiled.
The water in the little well asked from the bottom of its heart:
"Nakhman, make a blessing over me."
And the flowers began to bloom,
like the Garden of Eden.
A crow laughed like a child.
All of that anger disappeared.
I breathed in that barmy air

and everything laughed and everything lived.
Over everything there spread a joyful clamor:
"Who is a delusion?
Who doesn't exist?
We are here, here, here."

And so an angry world
rose into morning, beamed and shed light.
A shrieking started up,
a hullabaloo, a chirping of loud voices:

"We are hereherehere.
We are hereherehere."
So I planted myself
in the middle of the forest,
my voice echoing like a *shofar:*
"World, I swear to you by this morning's hour,
world, you are here."

Translated by Richard J. Fein

Like a Mouse Trap

Like a little trap,
a shabby synagogue on Long Island.
Only a handful show up for prayer.
No one knows
if even God
drops in there.

The rabbi
is Conservative.
From his synagogue study
he drops God a note,
care of the old address:
Come and hear my sermon about You *shabes,*
don't forget.

Only a handful show up for prayer,
plenty of room for God's glory.
No one knows if God
will sneak in for an hour.

Translated by Richard J. Fein

My Tent

Embrace me with choking devotion,
language mine, like a jealous wife;
confine me to my tent;
let the world never grasp what I meant,
even in the best translation.
Let them exclude me,
diminish me, disparage me.
I don't care if I'm not in their number.
Summon me, irrevocably,
to your destiny.
Let no one coax me from your arms.
Take my word. I don't want to be universal.
When I take my leave
I will become a pillar of cloud,
a gleam of light,
above our small sanctuary.

Translated by Richard J. Fein

YIVO Institute for Jewish Research

It is difficult to imagine a life story more dramatic than that of Abraham Sutzkever, the partisan poet. Throughout a long life lived at the center of a wrenching history, Sutzkever has produced poems of heart-stopping clarity. His task has been to integrate the lyric and the historic, the personal and the political.

Abraham Sutzkever was born in 1913 in Smorgon, a small city near Vilna, in what is now Lithuania. Vilna, called the Jerusalem of the North, had long been a vibrant center of Jewish learning and culture. At the beginning of World War I, the Russians expelled the Jews of Smorgon, and the Sutzkever family found a home in western Siberia, where the young child resonated to the luminous landscape of ice and snow. In 1920 his father died, and his mother, brother, and sister returned to Vilna, where they lived courtesy of checks sent from an uncle in the United States.

Sutzkever was a sickly, poetic boy who first received a traditional religious education and then attended a modern Jewish high school. In interwar Vilna, he found himself at the center of an intense and thriving secular Yiddish culture. He joined the Jewish scouts whose hikes included pointed references to the Yiddish names of flowers and trees. He read the European and American romantic poets, studied medieval Yiddish texts, and began publishing Yiddish poems rich in natural allusions.

But history had other plans for the sensitive poet. The Germans conquered Vilna in 1941, murdering one hundred thousand Jews and forcing the remainder, including Sutzkever, into a tiny ghetto. He credited his poetic sensibility — a vision of fluttering birds — with saving his life when he found himself facing a firing squad. His mother was killed, however, and, when his wife gave birth, the child, like all Jewish children born in the ghetto, was poisoned by the Germans.

Sutzkever was assigned to work in the *papir brigade,* making heartbreaking decisions about which of the hundreds of thousands of captured Jewish books, documents, and artifacts should be destroyed and which saved for the Nazis' planned postwar Museum of the Science of Jewry Without Jews. The brigade managed to smuggle out or hide thousands of precious books. Through everything, Sutzkever continued to write.

When it became clear that the ghetto would be liquidated, Sutzkever and his wife escaped through the sewers to join the partisans in the swamps and forests. While they were hiding, one of his poems reached Moscow, where the Soviets understood the value of Yiddish literature for the wartime morale of Russian Jews. They sent a special plane to rescue Sutzkever and his wife. In order to reach the airplane, though, the couple had to cross a minefield while German soldiers shot at them. Sutzkever stepped between the mines to the rhythm of a poem he recited to himself.

In Moscow, the Sutzkevers met Soviet Yiddish writers and were honored in the official press. They were then sent back to Vilna in time for its liberation by the Soviet army.

Sutzkever and his fellow survivors then unearthed the treasures they had hidden, only to realize that, because Soviet policy had shifted to an anti-Semitic, anti-Yiddish stance, they would have to save the treasures again. This time they were able to ship many of them to the United States.

In 1947, Sutzkever and his wife made their way to Israel, stopping in Warsaw to pay tribute at Peretz's grave. To the landscapes of snowy Siberia and wooded Lithuania, the poet now added the biblical mountains and deserts of Israel. In 1948 he began publishing a Yiddish literary quarterly, *Di goldene keyt* (The Golden Chain), named after a Peretz play. The publication continued for four decades.

Always writing in Yiddish, Sutzkever has continually reworked his life's experience. The refrain of one of his poems sums it up: "Inside me, rivers of blood are not a metaphor." Although his work has been translated into English, it is hardly known outside the Jewish world.

War

The same ashes will cover all of us:
The tulip — a wax candle flickering in the wind,
The swallow in its flight, sick of too many clouds,
The child who throws his ball into eternity —

And only one will remain, a poet —
A mad Shakespeare, who will sing a song, where might and wit is:
— My spirit Ariel, bring here the new fate,
And spit back the dead cities!

Translated by Barbara and Benjamin Harshav

Untitled, from *Poems from My Diary 1974–1985*

Who will remain, what will remain? A wind will stay behind.
The blindness will remain, the blindness of the blind.
A film of foam, perhaps, a vestige of the sea,
A flimsy cloud, perhaps, entangled in a tree.

Who will remain, what will remain? One syllable will stay,
To sprout the grass of Genesis as on a new First Day.
A fiddle-rose, perhaps, for its own sake will stand
And seven blades of grass perhaps will understand.

Of all the stars from way out north to here,
That one star will remain that fell into a tear.
A drop of wine remaining in a jar, a drop of dew.
Who will remain, God will remain, is that enough for you?

Translated by Barbara and Benjamin Harshav

Deer at the Red Sea

Stubborn, the sunset insisted on staying
In the Red Sea at night, when they first
Come to the palace of water — the innocent-pink,
Noble deer, to still their thirst.

They leave their silk shadows on the shore.
With violin faces, they lick the rings of gold
In the Red Sea. And there it happens,
Their betrothal with silence — lo and behold!

Finished — they flee. Pink spots.
Enliven the sand. But the sunset deer,
Moaning, remain in the water, and lick
The silence of those who will no more appear.

Translated by Barbara and Benjamin Harshav

To My Wife

I

Don't count the toll of wounds,
The suffering, the scar.
You have ignited once
A newborn baby star.

And at your feet, a spring
In our dark cave has curled,
And suddenly a baby's
Cooing has touched the world.

And like the purest spring
The word was then revealed,
But up above us no one
Must hear what must be sealed.

I knelt for you in thanks,
My spirit too did lift,
I brought you from above
Two blades of grass, a gift.

II

A child is not an other —
It's you alone and me.
It leads up on a ladder
Close to ourselves, you see.

But still before we thought
A name for him that's right,
The axes and the crowbars
Have plundered in the night.

The babe knew not a thing.
It dozed off in its rest,
A German came and ripped him
Away from mother's breast.

And what can take its place,
Dear, desolate and wild,
When from afar they glow,
The small bones of our child.

III

— And breathlessly we rush,
Through swamp and growth so wild,
You hold in hand a rifle —
A shadow of your child.

And every time the rifle
Spits out the chunk of lead,
In its dull glow we see
The child that we have bred.

As air fills up the world,
It fills our minds, a shield.
In pink of dawn, it rises,
Appears here in the field.

And over all our wounds,
Our suffering, our scar,
It did not disappear,
The newborn baby star.

NAROCZ FOREST, SEPTEMBER 30, 1943

Translated by Barbara and Benjamin Harshav

I Am Lying in This Coffin

I am lying in this coffin
as I would lie
in stiff wooden clothing.
This could be a small boat
on dangerous waves,
this could be a cradle.

And here,
where bodies have been taken
from time,
I call out to you, sister,
and you hear me calling
in your distance.

What is suddenly moving in this coffin —
an unexpected body?
You come.
I recognize the pupils of your eyes,
your breath,
your light.

So this is the rule:
here today,
somewhere else tomorrow,
and in this coffin now
as in stiff wooden clothing
my speech
still moves into song.

VILNA, AUGUST 30, 1941

Translated by Seymour Mayne

On the Death of Yanova Bartoszewicz Who Rescued Me

Had it not been for you who rescued me
never, never
would I have beheld Jerusalem.
My very snow-covered poems
would have cried out
like Zechariah's blood
to the stars who would have turned but a deaf ear
(Then too my poems were like Jews
set in the verdant panes of my city —
now they moulder
without benefit of gravestones.)

Had it not been for you who saved me
I would have had to sever my life
knotted with other lives
and my sleeping, comforting daughter
would never have asked her marvellous question:
"Daddy, how old was I really
before I was born?"

It is raining now.
I'm up to the neck in hills
hanging from me with hands
slipping like waterfalls
beseeching that I take them across chasms.
Look: here comes a cloud, a cellar within it,
and you, in a kerchief, like a meadow among the gallows,
bent over me, mound of wounds that I was.

Dear Yanova, though you have been rained out today in Jerusalem
a rainbow breaks through, glistens in your memory.

Translated by Seymour Mayne

When the Temple in Jerusalem was destroyed in the first century of the Christian Era and the Jewish people dispersed, their mourning was so deep that for centuries, it is said, they neither played instruments nor sang. The chanting of prayers was their only musical sound.

But no one can mourn forever, and by the Middle Ages Yiddish-speaking European Jews were singing again. In their synagogues, hundreds of prayers were set to secular music. In their homes, around the table on Sabbath and at festivals, they sang wordless tunes called *niggunim,* and songs called *zemires.* At joyous occasions, weddings, and circumcisions, they sang about their history, their faith, and the joys of living very much in this world.

By the time medieval Jews were speaking Yiddish, they could hear French troubadours and German minnesingers perform storytelling songs. Jews composed their own additions to this genre. The Yiddish singers, like their Christian counterparts, almost always remained anonymous.

The twentieth-century poet Yankev Glatshteyn described the "'bonvivants, actors, and revelers [who] created and performed their songs, lived their free but impoverished lives, hungered weeks on end, and occasionally got good and drunk." And he lamented the fact that we know so little about them. "Who is the talented wedding poet-entertainer Eliakum Zunzer and the still more talented Velvele Zbarzher?" he asked. "It is simply exasperating that these people attached no importance to themselves, but regarded themselves as missionaries, no more than blind instruments, servants of the people, its comforters and awakeners. . . .

"The mother at the cradle, the shoemaker at his awl, the longing girl at the window all sang that song and . . . did not care to know who wrote it."

The question of authorship grew more complicated in modern Yiddish folk music. For many twentieth-century works, anonymity and notoriety coexist. Because a community of professional musicians grew directly and rapidly out of the folk tradition, song segments and, indeed, entire compositions that were written for plays and movies have been adopted into the folk idiom or else identified incorrectly as folk songs. "Oyfn pripetshik" (At the Fireplace), a sentimental tune that paints a picture of children learning the alphabet that would comfort them later, when they shed the tears of exile, is widely described as being a folk song. Yet it was written in the early years of the twentieth century by a Warsaw attorney named Mark Warshawsky. Its publication was championed by no less than Sholom Aleichem.

By that time, Yiddish speakers were becoming more aware of their folk heritage. Although Shimon An-ski's Jewish Ethnographic Expedition is the best-known undertaking of its kind, it is not the only example of urban Jews venturing into the hinterlands to record folk songs. Similar efforts continued until the world that produced them was extinguished in World War II.

The best-known song to emerge from the Holocaust, "Zog nit keyn mol!" (We Are Here), was written by the young poet Hirsh Glik while he was fighting as a partisan in the forests near Vilna. Although he did not survive the war, his words are now sung around the world. Its conclusion seems a worthy way to end our whirlwind tour of Yiddish literature: "Our yearned-for hour will come, already it draws near. / There's a drumbeat to our step; and we are here!"

Potatoes

Sunday — taters
Monday — taters
Tuesday and Wednesday — taters
Thursday and Friday — taters.
Sabbath for a change a pudding of taters
Sunday once more — taters.

Bread with taters.
Meat with taters.
Lunchtime and suppertime — taters.
But; and on the other hand — taters.
Once in awhile pudding made of taters
Sunday — once more — taters.

Rose, Rose

Rose, rose, how far you are!
Forest, forest, how large you are!
If the rose were not so far
The forest would not be so large.

God's presence, God's presence, how far you are!
Golus,* Golus, how long you are!
If God's presence were not so far,
Then Golus would not be so long.

* *Golus,* which is translated as "exile," is felt as a condition
of both the person and the nation.

Now It's Time for Singing

Now it's time for singing, now it's time for singing
A little song, a little song.
All about bread; meat and fish; and all kinds of delicacies.

Tell me oh papa please; tell me oh papa please, what is bread then?
For the big fancy rich folks, bread is a fresh, crusty bulky roll.
But then for us, the poor folk, only paupers
Bread is nothing but a hard and dry bit of crust.

Tell me oh papa please; tell me oh papa please, what is meat then?
For the big fancy rich folks, meat is a duckling with crispy skin.
Oh but for us the poor folk, only paupers
Meat is a dry bit of stomach skin stuffed and spiced.

Tell me oh papa please; tell me oh papa please, what is fish then?
For the big fancy rich folks, fish is a tasty pike.
Oh but for us the poor folk, only paupers
Fish is a herring all shriveled up.

Tell me oh papa please; tell me oh papa please, what is dessert then?
For the big fancy rich folks, dessert is fruit compote.
Oh but for us the poor folk, only paupers
Dessert is only minced troubles, of course.

I Don't Want a Husband Yet

She:

I don't want a husband yet
That's something I can save.
Take a husband while you're young
You'll have an early grave.

He:

But you are so young and pretty
How would you know such things?

She:

Because I'm so young and pretty
I'll wait for a wedding ring

While I'm so young and pretty
I want to live careless; free.
I'll wait for a year or two
And maybe even three.

A Toast to Life

A toast to life, let's raise up, let's drink it down today,
As we feast on this happy holiday.
A toast to life, let's raise up for friendship and for friends,
May we always be lively and be gay.
A toast to life, let's raise up for old and young who are now here,
And also for the others, though missing, we hold very dear.
A toast to life, let's raise up, so fill the glass with wine,
For the sun, may it always shine.

A toast to life, let's raise up, it simply goes like this:
Only joy do I wish to each of you!
A toast to life let's raise up, may nothing go amiss,
For the parents and child their whole life through.
A toast to life, let's raise up, and may the sun shine merrily,
And may no days of darkness descend upon our family.
A toast to life, let's raise up, it's good to drink it down,
When we see our friends from all around.

A toast to life, let's raise up, to our beloved land,
May the heavens above hear our song.
A toast to life, let's raise up, I wish you once again,
With a smile on your lips your whole life long.
A toast to life, let's raise up, may gladness cheer you every day,
Your nearest and your dearest shall never ever go away.
A toast to life, let's raise up, for all that we hold dear,
May the world live in peace, and without fear.

by Bergotz and Pulver

On the Hill

On the hill, around the hill
Doves came and they went.
I have not had any happiness
And my youth is spent.

Harness up the coal-black horse
Make him gallop; run.
If I can overtake my youth
I might again be young.

I met those years, those long-gone years
On the bridge so wide
Years, years, turn around
Back to the other side.

No no, we won't go back
There is no place to go.
You should not have shamed us then
A long long time ago.

Tumbalalaika

A young man worries what he should do
Thinks and thinks the whole night through
Which one to take and whose heart to break
Which one to take and whose heart to break.

Come my pretty one, I want to know
What has no rain, and still it can grow?
Tell what can burn throughout all the years
Or what can yearn without any tears?

Silly boy, why wouldn't you know
A stone needs no rain, and yet it can grow.
True love can burn throughout all the years
True love it can yearn without any tears.

Sound, ba-la, sound, ba-la, sound balalaika.

Sound, ba-la, sound, ba-la, sound balalaika
Sound, balalaika, play balalaika
Play balalaika, happy and free.

We Are Here

Never say that you are on your final way
Though leaden skies may block the blue of any day.
Our yearned-for hour will come, already it draws near.
There's a drumbeat to our step; and we are here!

From land of palm trees to the distant lands of snow
We arrive with all our suffering and woe.
And when the ground is dampened when our blood flows out
It is on that spot our victory will sprout.

The morning sun will bathe us in its gilded light.
All our enemies will vanish with the night.
And even if that fickle sun should take too long
Still let every generation sing this song.

It's not a song about a bird that's flying free
For it's written with the blood of you and me.
'Midst collapsing walls that could no longer stand
We sang it with grenades clutched in our hand.

Never say that you are on your final way
Though leaden skies may block the blue of any day
Our yearned-for hour will come, already it draws near.
There's a drumbeat to our step; and we are here!

by Hirsh Glik

Glossary

A note about spelling:

I have retained the transliterations — the English spelling of
Yiddish words — of each different translator, even though
these renderings of the Yiddish do not always conform to
accepted standards or current usage. I hope that the reader
will be flexible. The subject of Yiddish spelling, while mad-
deningly frustrating, can tell us a good deal about the histo-
ries, affiliations, hopes, and dreams of the people who wrote
and spoke this unique language.

balalaika stringed instrument
cheder, also **heder** school
farfl cut noodles
Gamorah, also **Gemara** commentary on law
groschen coins of little worth
Guide to the Perplexed central work by Maimonedes
gulden coins
gvald violence
Haggadah service for Passover
Hasid pious person
High Holiday New Year
kaddish memorial prayer for the dead
khosid see Hasid
kopeks coins
Ladino language spoken by Sephardi Jews, based on Hebrew and Spanish
Litvak Lithuanian Jew; thought to be cunning
lokshn noodle
lox smoked salmon
melamed teacher

mensch decent human being
meshugener crazy person
Nakhman of Bratslav eighteenth-century Hasidic spiritual leader
Ne'ileh prayer at end of Yom Kippur
niggunim melodies
Pentateuch the five books of Moses
Rambam Moses Maimonedes, twelfth-century sage
Reb honorific term similar to "Mr."
rebbe Hasidic leader
Rosh Hashanah New Year
ruble Russian money
samovar teapot
Sephardi descendant of Jews who lived in Spain and Portugal
shabes Sabbath
shammes synagogue functionary
shlimazl unfortunate person
Sh'ma Yisrael beginning of central Jewish prayer affirming faith
shofar, also **shoyfer** ram's horn blown at New Year
Sholom aleichem peace be with you
shoykhet ritual slaughterer
shtetl small town
Shulkhan Aruch sixteenth-century code of law
shvayg silent
tallis prayer shawl
Talmud central body of teachings
Tammuz Jewish month in summer
tatte father
tfillin, also **tfiln** phylacteries
T'hilim prayer
tkhines Yiddish prayers for women
Torah first five books of the Bible
treyf unkosher
tum sound
verst unit of measurement of distance
yingele young boy
Yom Kippur Day of Atonement
zemires songs
Zohar work of Jewish mysticism

Additional Reading

Now that you have had a taste of Yiddish literature, you can find many more places to satisfy your appetite.

The standard work for Mendele Moykher-Sforim is *Tales of Mendele the Book Peddler,* edited by Dan Miron and Ken Frieden, translations by Ted Gorelick and Hillel Halkin (New York: Schocken Books, 1996). Please note that the author is listed as Abramovitsch, S. Y. (Mendele Moykher Sforim).

For Yitzhak Leib Peretz, try *The I. L. Peretz Reader,* edited by Ruth R. Wisse (New York: Schocken Books, 1991).

Sholom Aleichem's stories can be found in many different editions. One is *Favorite Tales of Sholom Aleichem,* translated by Julius and Frances Butwin (New York: Avenel Books, 1983).

Your next step on the An-ski trail might be to read or see his play, *The Dybbuk.* You can even rent a video of the 1937 film of the play, in Yiddish with English subtitles, from the National Center for Jewish Film (781-899-7044 or www.jewishfilm.org).

Singer's output was prodigious. In addition to many collections of his stories, his autobiographical trio, *A Little Boy in Search of God, A Young Man in Search of Love,* and *Lost in America* is fascinating reading.

Rosenfeld's poetry can be found in *The Penguin Book of Modern Yiddish Verse,* edited by Irving Howe, Ruth Wisse, and Khone Shmeruk (New York: Viking, 1987).

Glatshteyn's work can be found in the same anthology, as well as in *Selected Poems of Yankev Glatshteyn,* edited and translated by Richard J. Fein (Philadelphia: The Jewish Publication Society, 1987).

To read more of Sutzkever's poetry, try *A. Sutzkever: Selected Poetry and Prose,* translated by Barbara and Benjamin Harshav (Berkeley: University of California Press, 1991).

For folk songs, two classics are: *Mir Trogen a Gezang!* by Eleanor

Gorden Mlotek (New York: Workmen's Circle, 1987), and *Pearls of Yiddish Song,* by Eleanor Gorden Mlotek and Joseph Mlotek (New York: Workmen's Circle, 1988).

A good introduction to the shtetl world is *The Shtetl Book,* by Diane K. Roskies and David G. Roskies (Hoboken, N.J.: Ktav, 1975).

A new book that places Yiddish literature in a broader Jewish, cultural, and linguistic context is Ruth R. Wisse's *The Modern Jewish Canon* (New York: The Free Press, 2000).

If you're interested in language and cultural history, I can recommend my own book, *Yiddish: A Nation of Words* (South Royalton, Vt.: Steerforth Press, 2001).

The worldwide center for research on Yiddish language and culture is the Yidisher Visnshaftlekher Institut (YIVO, the Yiddish Scientific Institute), at 15 West Sixteenth Street, New York, NY 10011 (212-246-6080; www.yivoinstitute.org).

And, if you'd like to see a fascinating institution with a wonderful exhibit on the history of the Yiddish language and culture, as well as a helpful bookstore, visit the National Yiddish Research Center in the Harry and Jeanette Weinberg Building, Amherst, Massachusetts 01002-3375 (1-800-535-3595; yiddishbookcenter.org).

Bibliography

Aleichem, Sholom. *Favorite Tales of Sholom Aleichem*. Translated by Julius and Frances Butwin. New York: Avenel Books, 1983.

An-ski, S. *The Dybbuk and Other Writings*. Edited by David G. Roskies. Translations by Golda Werman. New York: Schocken Books, 1992.

Blood, Peter, and Annie Patterson. *Rise Up Singing*. Bethlehem, Penn.: Sing Out Corporation, 1992.

Glatshteyn, Yankev. *Selected Poems of Yankev Glatshteyn*. Translated by Richard J. Fein. Philadelphia: The Jewish Publication Society, 1987.

Goldenthal, Edgar J. *Poet of the Ghetto: Morris Rosenfeld*. Hoboken, N.J.: Ktav Publishing House, 1998.

Moykher-Sforim, Mendele. *The Selected Works of Mendele Moykher-Sforim*. Vol. 1 of *The Three Great Classic Writers of Modern Yiddish Literature*. Edited by Marvin Zuckerman, Gerald Stillman, and Marion Herbst. Malibu, Calif.: Joseph Simon/Pangloss Press, 1991.

Peretz, I. L. *Selected Works of I. L. Peretz*. Edited by Marvin Zuckerman and Marion Herbst. Malibu, Calif.: Joseph Simon/Pangloss Press, 1996.

Silverman, Jerry. *The Yiddish Song Book*. New York: Stein and Day, 1983.

Singer, Isaac Bashevis. *The Collected Stories of Isaac Bashevis Singer*. New York: Farrar, Straus, and Giroux, 1982.

Sutzkever, Abraham. *A. Sutzkever: Selected Poetry and Prose*. Translated by Barbara and Benjamin Harshav. Berkeley: University of California Press, 1991.

Sutzkever, Abraham. *Burnt Pearls*. Translated by Seymour Mayne. Oakville, Ont.: Mosaic Press, 1981.